MAID TO ORDER

MAID TO ORDER

MAID TO ORDER

Penny Birch

Published by Accent Press Ltd – 2010

ISBN 9781907016264

Printed and bound in the UK

Cover design by
Zipline Creative

Prologue

'PANTIES DOWN, PENNY.'

Aunt Elaine knew she had to tell me, not because there was the slightest chance of me being allowed to keep them up, but because it was an important part of my spanking to be told they had to come down. I closed my eyes, allowing myself to concentrate fully on my feelings of exposure and shame as she peeled my big, white cotton knickers slowly down over my rear cheeks to leave me bare-bottomed over her lap: bare-bottomed, the way a girl about to be spanked should be. She took them right down, far enough to ensure that the rear view of my pussy would be showing from behind, then raised her knee to make my cheeks spread and add the pinkish brown pucker of my bottom hole to my thoroughly rude rear display.

'Look in the mirror, Penny. You should see how you look from behind.'

'Yes, Auntie.'

She'd put the mirror there on purpose, so that I could see my rear view reflected in the much bigger one on the front of her wardrobe. My bottom seemed to fill the glass; a full, pale moon between my upturned skirt and the tangle of my lowered panties; my plump, furry pussy lips pouting from between my thighs; my anus puckered and brown in a nest of hair pulsing gently. I could see my face too: my hair dishevelled, my mouth a little open, my eyes

1

big with a reaction to what was about to be done to me. Still being in my work clothes only made it worse; the way my smart jacket and trim skirt had been turned up to get me bare added to my disgrace; while my open blouse and dangling boobs added a touch of the absurd. I was no longer a respectable university reader, but merely a naughty girl stripped to put her in her place and about to be given a well-deserved spanking by her aunt.

I started to sob, no longer able to hold my feelings in as her hand had settled on my bottom, giving my cheeks a little rub before applying the first smack. With that I gave in completely to my emotions, the tears streaming down my face even before my spanking had properly begun and continuing to come in a choking torrent as my bottom bounced and quivered under the slaps of her hand. Fully aware that I needed what she was giving me and how I would react to it, Aunt Elaine took no notice of my response. It had become a ritual; over her knee like this once every week, with the occasional reinforcement spanking or spontaneous punishment when she felt I needed to be dealt with, or more often, when I did.

It hurt, quite a lot, but all my stresses and cares were melting away with the pain. I need to be spanked, regularly, and by somebody who understands what it does to me. Aunt Elaine is close to perfect for the job: naturally strict and with an authority that goes back all the way to when she first did it to me, with me in my pretty pink bridesmaid's dress and my frillies pulled down at her daughter's wedding; my first proper spanking and one of the most important moments of my life. Twenty-two years later and I was in the same humiliating position, having my bottom smacked with no more consideration for my dignity than when I'd been a teenager. And I was in ecstasy.

She knew I was ready, but she didn't stop. It had taken her longer to accept that she enjoyed spanking me than it had for me to accept that I enjoyed being spanked. The first time it had been genuine discipline, then something that needed to be done for my sake, and finally a mutual pleasure. I let her spank away, while trying to resist the need to touch myself as she enjoyed my bottom, but breaking well before she was satisfied.

My hand went back as I cocked my legs apart, stretching my panties taught between my thighs. She slapped my fingers as they found my sex but she didn't stop me, returning her attention to my now heated bottom as I began to masturbate. It felt so natural, so easy, yet still deliciously dirty with my bottom spread to her hand as I played with myself in full view of her, and with my eyes locked to the unspeakably rude reflection of my rear view in the mirror.

The moon of my bottom was no longer pale but a rich red, with my cheeks bouncing to the slaps as she spanked me and my bumhole winking lewdly as my muscles began to contract. I cried out as it hit me: the whole awful, perfect situation coming together in a long moment of pure bliss, while the spanking continued until I finally went limp across her knees. A long sigh escaped my lips as I came down from my orgasm, and as soon as I could get control of my legs I was wriggling into position between her knees, ready to say thank you with a willing tongue. To my surprise she shook her head.

'Not this time, thank you, dear.'

'Oh …'

'It's not you, Penny, but I'm afraid I have some rather bad news. Kate has left Jeremy.'

'I … I'm sorry.'

It was all I could manage, and as much a question as

anything else. I could hardly take it in, and barely remembered to pull my knickers back up as she started to talk.

'I wanted to look after your bottom before I told you. He was having an affair, apparently, with his secretary. She put up with it for months after she found out, but she met a man she likes, in Florence. With Pippa at university and Jemima out of school, she's decided to stay in Europe, at least for the time being.'

'That's awful!'

'Yes, and he's moved the secretary in. She's called Danielle. And she has a daughter called Summer, so Jemima tells me.'

'So Jemima's living with Jeremy and this Danielle?'

Chapter One

'YOU ARE NOT MY mother!'

'I will be.'

'No you won't, not ever, not my real mother.'

'Maybe not, Jemima, but I will be your stepmother, and as long as you're in this house you'll do as you're told.'

'Not by you I won't, you bitch!'

'What did you call me?'

'A bitch, which is what you are, Danielle, a vicious, gold-digging bitch!'

She came forward, so suddenly and with such a nasty expression on her face that I thought she was going to hit me. My hands came up by instinct. Instead of slapping my face she caught hold of my jacket and jerked it sharply down my back.

'What … what are you doing, you mad cow!'

Her hand was twisted hard into the material of my jacket, trapping my arms behind my back and holding me firmly in place. Then she answered me.

'Something your real mother should have done years ago, you little brat.'

I knew what she meant and started to fight, but I couldn't move my arms properly and I was starting to panic, because the thought of her spanking me was unbearable.

'No! You bitch, you do not spank me! You do not! You do not!'

'Oh yes I do.'

The first smack landed on my bum and it had been done; my bottom smacked by the evil bitch who'd broken up my parents' marriage. I went wild, screaming and kicking and calling her every name I could think of, but my struggles only seemed to amuse her. She wasn't even doing it hard, and it didn't hurt at all, but that wasn't important and we both knew it. What was important was that I was having my bottom smacked, by her, and I could hear the tears in my own voice as I wriggled in her grip.

'You're enjoying this, aren't you, you bitch!'

She just laughed and kept at it, smacking the seat of my jeans. Her hand was cupped, to make the smacks louder and to hold my cheeks, making me wonder if she wasn't only exerting her authority but also getting a kick out of feeling my bum.

'Get off me, bitch!'

'I don't think so, Jemima. You've had this coming a long time, and anyway, I'm definitely not going to stop until you learn to address me respectfully.'

'Let me up! What if Summer came in?'

'What about it? She'd see you getting a spanking. Why shouldn't you be spanked in front of your sister?'

'She's not my sister! And ... and, you couldn't, Danielle, not in front of her ...'

She was still spanking me, harder now, but it wasn't the stinging slaps that were bringing me to the edge of panic; it was the thought of her daughter coming in from the garden and seeing me get it.

'Fuck off!' I screamed.

She just laughed, tightened her grip and carried on with my spanking; taking one cheek at a time, still with her hand cupped, but slowly, so that every smack rang out loud and clear. There was no anger in it any more, but there was something else.

'You're playing with my bum, you dirty bitch!'

Again she laughed, and when the next smack landed she didn't take her hand away, but began to caress my bottom.

'Fuck … off, Danielle!'

I kicked out as I spoke, catching her shin. Her breath came out in a sharp hiss as I made contact, but she only grew more determined, holding me by my coat and under my bum as she forced me towards the back of an armchair.

'Right, enough games, you little cat! Over you go.'

'No!'

It was too late, my body pushed down over the back of the chair to leave me completely helpless, with my bum stuck high and my legs kicking furiously as my spanking began once more. Now it was hard, and fast, delivered full across my cheeks with real fury and I could do nothing about it at all. My feet were off the ground, my legs kicking wildly in the air, my face in the cushions and my fists beating pathetically at the arms of the chair. I was making my bottom wiggle too, and as she continued to slap at the seat of my jeans she had begun to laugh again.

'You do look funny, Jemima.'

'Fuck off, you stupid old bag!'

Her grip grew tighter and the smacks slowed to a hard, even rhythm as she went on.

'Oh, and that's another thing. I am not old. I am thirty-six. I am, however, in charge and you will do as you're told, or next time I'll do it properly, with your pants pulled down. In fact, maybe I should pull them down right now.'

7

The spanking stopped, but she kept her grip. I began to panic again, unable to bear the thought of being done on the bare, and struggled frantically as her hands circled my waist, her fingers going to the button of my jeans.

'No, you can't! Not that, Danielle! Not bare! What about Summer!?'

'What about her? Do you think I care if she sees your bare bum?'

'No, Danielle, please! Please!'

I was begging, desperate not to be stripped. She'd got my button undone and it was all going to come down to display my bare bottom. And she'd spank me like that, maybe with Summer watching, and they'd see, they'd see I was wet. I screamed out and lurched as hard as I could, but she clung on, pressing my body down over the back of the sofa as she fought to get my jeans undone.

'Oh no you don't!' she hissed, and I'd began to sob in helpless frustration, still kicking my legs as my zip was quickly pulled down.

'Well, what's it to be?' she demanded. 'A bit of respect when you talk to me or a bare bottom in your own living room? Maybe I'll even call Summer in to watch as you seem to find the idea so humiliating?'

My answer was a choking noise and she'd begun to tug my jeans down.

'Well?'

'Fuck you, Danielle!'

Again she tugged, exposing the top of my panties. She laughed.

'Knickers with little yellow ducks? I thought you said you were grown up, Jemima?'

I gave in, too humiliated to fight any more.

'OK! OK! Anything to get you out of my hair! I promise not to call you a bitch.'

'That's better, but I still think you need to be punished, don't you?'

'No! That's not fair, Danielle, you said …'

She hadn't let go, or stopped pulling at my jeans, which had come right down, leaving the seat of my panties on show to her. Again she began to spank, and to alternate the smacks with little pinches to the flesh where my cheeks were sticking out of my knickers.

'What do you call me?' she asked.

'Danielle,' I managed.

'Better, but not really appropriate, not when I'm going to be your stepmother, and I do think an apology might be in order.'

The spanking had stopped, but her hand had closed on the seat of my knickers, pulling them together to spill my cheeks out at the sides and leave a little of my slit showing. One good tug and they'd be down, to leave me bare bottom with my pussy showing, my wet pussy. I broke.

'OK, I'm sorry, I'm sorry! I won't call you a bitch again, I promise! Just let me up, please!'

She kept her grip.

'I don't think so, Jemima, not yet. No, I don't think you should call me Danielle. Let me see, what would be best? Yes, why not? You can call me Mummy.'

'No!'

'Well if you're going to be stubborn …'

'No, please, I'm begging you … not my panties, Danielle, please!'

She'd pulled my knickers halfway down my bottom. A moment more and I was going to be showing, and I was sure she could smell me anyway, but that didn't stop me fighting even more furiously than before. I felt cool air on my bumhole and screamed a final, choking plea, but she'd

9

already stopped, not from any sense of decency, but at the sound of tyres crunching gravel outside. For a moment we both stayed frozen; me with one leg in the air and my bottom almost completely out of my panties, then she'd let go, laughing.

'I suppose it would be inappropriate to spank you in front of your father, especially bare bottom. Why, he might realise what a slut his sweet little daughter is, getting all wet when her stepmother spanks her.'

I was choking with shame as I struggled to get my knickers up before Dad came in. Her words made it worse by far, but that didn't stop me catching the worried tone in her voice, or seeing the expression on her face. She even adjusted the cushions while I buttoned myself up, and by the time the door finally swung open she was all sweetness and light. I waited until the perfect moment, as Dad turned to pull his keys from the lock, then mouthed a single word to Danielle.

'Bitch.'

If looks could kill I'd have been toast – hot, buttered and with extra marmalade – but it was too late for her to retaliate and I was pretty sure she wouldn't dare say anything too bad in front of him. She didn't, but kissed him and went to make him a coffee, now the perfect little girlfriend. I gave him a hug and ran up to my room, close to tears as I brooded over what she'd done to me. She really was an utter bitch, but there was nothing I could do about it when she knew so much about me. And she'd only had to say two words when she first turned up with Dad to make very sure I couldn't call her on her nasty habits – Morris Rathwell.

That could only mean she knew about his spanking parties, which I'd been attending once a month in order to earn myself some decent pocket money over the last couple of terms. It had meant pretending to be where I wasn't, while in reality I was having my bottom smacked by a group of dirty old men. Very generous dirty old men. How Danielle knew I had no idea, but she did and if Dad found out I'd really be in trouble. So would she too, because even knowing about something so dirty was going to ruin the whiter-than-white image she tried so hard to keep up for him. So while she could be pretty horrid to me she could only push so far, and she knew it.

She understood about spanking as well, and all the little humiliations that make it worse, especially when it comes to pulling down knickers. That, and knowing about Morris, had to mean she'd had it done, which was at least some consolation as I inspected my cheeks in the bathroom mirror. She given me plenty and I was quite red, but I'd taken a lot worse, and on the bare. Anyway, I like to be spanked, but not by her, and just the thought of what she'd done brought tears to my eyes. I gave myself a rub and tried to pretend I wasn't reacting the way I would have done if I'd been over a man's knee voluntarily.

It just wasn't possible. The sight of my red cheeks sticking out between my top and my pushed down panties was too much on its own, without the heat of my skin and feel of my flesh in my hands. I tried to concentrate on the power getting it from men gives me and how I'd felt as I stood to have my smacked bottom inspected at Morris's last party. His wife Melody had dealt with me, a tall, powerfully built black girl who'd stroked my hair to help me get over my shyness, and then held me firmly in place across her knee as she turned my school skirt up and took down my panties.

I could remember the men commenting on my figure, their voices amused or hoarse with lust. Coltish, one man had called my legs, as if I was a young horse being

11

paraded at a show. Another had replied that he'd never seen such a pert bottom on such long legs, then asked Melody to pull my knickers down a bit more so that he could see my cunt properly. That single, crude word had been like an electric shock. Melody had obliged, adjusting my panties and then cocking her knee up to make my cheeks spread so they all got a good look at my bumhole too.

She'd spanked me so hard, with my arm twisted up into the small of my back just in case I tried to escape. I'd screamed and squirmed and kicked my legs up and down so hard my shoes had come off, but it had mostly been for show. With Danielle it had been real, but she'd had me, just as securely, holding me in place while she smacked me on the seat of my jeans, and on my panties. As I shut my eyes and stuck my hand between my legs I was thinking of how she'd threatened to strip me properly and what she'd have seen. She'd known anyway, because she'd smelt me, and I was absolutely soaking. It had felt awful having my jeans taken down, worse than when it had been my panties with a dozen leering old gits getting off over my bare rear view. But I wished she'd done it properly, spanked me on my panties and then pulled them down too, taunting me as my bottom came bare, telling me what she could see, telling me how wet I was, calling Summer in to watch …

'No!'

I cried out loud, determined not to do it, and forced my mind on to something else, my own rude rear view. My hand was cupped on my pussy and my bottom stuck out to the mirror, my spanked cheeks open to show off the tiny pink star of my bumhole and my fingers where I was holding myself. I was so wet my juices were running down my thighs, with my flesh pink and glistening as I slipped two fingers in to spread my hole. That looked so rude, and I tried to imagine holding myself that way for a man while he got his cock ready to put in me, but it wasn't a man who'd got me that way. It was Danielle, the vicious, evil bitch who d held me down and spanked me, who'd taken down my jeans and would have had my knickers down too if Dad hadn't turned up. I'd have been spanked bare bottom and she'd have seen exactly how I was reacting, and if Summer had come in she'd have seen too, both of them laughing at me as my bum cheeks bounced and my juices splashed ...

There was nothing I could do about it; I was going to come over my punishment. I cried out again, a raw, broken sob at the thought of what had been done to me: spanked by my stepmother and on that awful *word* I came, while frigging myself off, utterly ashamed of myself even as I watched my own busy fingers snatching at my pussy with the juice squashing out and my bumhole squeezing as my muscles contracted in a long, hard orgasm.

My legs were shaking badly as I came, as much from emotion as the strength of my climax. The moment I'd finished I sat down on the loo, biting my lip with shame as I pulled out some loo paper. As I cleaned myself up I was acutely conscious of the feel of my hot, bare cheeks on the cold wood; it kept what had been done to me and what I'd done afterwards fixed firmly in my head. At least there were consolations, and I tried to concentrate on them. For one thing nobody need ever know that I'd masturbated, least of all Danielle, which would have been really unbearable. Better still, Summer hadn't come in from the garden. Despite the situation I liked her, and she looked up to me. Being spanked in front of her would have been the final straw.

Eventually I got up and went back to the mirror to make sure it wasn't obvious I'd been crying. I couldn't bear to be in the same room as Dad and Danielle when they were together, so I intended to sneak into the garden and find Summer, but I was called down before I even crossed the landing.

Dad's tone sounded doubtful, making me wonder if she might have told him about my spanking, and even made him agree to let her discipline me. As I walked down the stairs, I was desperately trying to think how to get out of it if she had. Even admitting to my visits to the Rathwells was no good, because if I mentioned Morris's name first, all she had to then do was deny everything.

Dad was smiling, but he looked as doubtful as he sounded. Danielle was smiling too, like a crocodile. I tried to sound casual.

'What's up?'

Dad begun to drum his fingers on the table. 'We were thinking about the rest of your year off.'

'New York?' I opened my mouth without engaging my brain. Had Danielle persuaded Dad to get rid of me by letting me take up Hudson Staebler's offer of summer work in the States? He gave a long sigh and my hopes sank once more.

'No, Jem, we've been through that already.'

'Europe then.'

'No, Jemima. Danielle has a much better idea.'

'What?'

'My uncle is the manager of a hotel on the south coast,' she said, and I knew I was in trouble just from the tone of her voice. 'I've got you a place as a maid.'

'A maid!'

'Yes, a maid,' she answered and quickly turned to Dad. 'It would do her a lot of good, Jeremy. Teach her

14

about real life for a start. You've been far too soft with her and I'm not being harsh. It's for her own good.'

'I'm sure you're right, darling,' he answered, but I could tell he had his doubts.

'Dad!'

'I do think it would be a good idea, Jemima, just for a few months, and then we can talk about Europe for next year, when you're a little older and you've had a term at university.'

'And there's also the expense to think about,' Danielle broke in. 'Your trip would cost your poor dad several thousand pounds, and everybody's having to tighten their belts at the moment. This way you'll be earning your own money and learning to stand on your own two feet.'

'But I don't want to be a maid! I don't need to work, and there must be dozen of girls who do, so it's really not fair.'

'Don't talk nonsense,' she interrupted. 'Really, Jemima, it's for your own good. You must learn to stand on your own two feet.'

My mouth came open to protest that I had been standing on my own two feet when I was in the States, but I could hardly admit to what I'd been up to, let alone what I would have been up to if Aunt Penny hadn't ruined it for me. As it was I had to bite my tongue while she went on about how privileged my childhood had been and how much I'd benefit from a taste of the real world, until I finally managed to get a word in edgeways. Even then my every protest was ignored as the summer I'd been looking forward to for so long was destroyed bit by bit. The fact that I'd got a good place at uni didn't matter, nor that Dad had plenty of money, nor that the whole thing was just completely unfair.

I even came close to telling Dad about the spanking

parties and hoping to catch Danielle out. He knew Morris, and had some idea of what he got up to, but was blissfully unaware of my involvement. There would be real trouble, but there was no way I could prove Danielle knew what went on, and I didn't even know what the connection was. It was just too risky. I was going, and that was that.

Chapter Two

HERE'S WHAT I DON'T understand. If I take a job, a really boring, tedious job that means being bossed around by a lot of stuck-up people and doing all the really crap work they can't be bothered with, and work a full week, and they only pay me one hundred and sixty-nine pounds and forty-four pence before deductions, which was what I was going to be getting at the Friston Executive, and I'm supposed to be proud of myself. Alternatively, I can work one evening a month, getting my bottom smacked in front of a load of dirty old men, and, OK, maybe tossing one or two of them off, for a cool five hundred pounds plus tips and no deductions, and I'm supposed to be ashamed of myself. Why?

The argument that always gets trotted out is that providing sexual services is degrading, but that's just bullshit. Seriously, what's more degrading; having to clean the toilets in a big hotel, or dancing about in my knickers while a load of men try to get me drunk on champagne? Mopping up after a party of drunken chavs or being put over another woman's knee, given a slow sexy spanking and being brought to orgasm under her fingers? You prefer mopping up? You can keep it, and if that makes you proud I feel sorry for you.

I certainly didn't feel proud of myself as we drove down to the south coast, and I did feel very sorry for myself. Danielle had wanted me to go by train and bus, on my own, but the very difficulty of getting to the place had meant that for once she didn't get her way. Then she'd suggested driving me herself, but Dad and Summer had both wanted to come and wouldn't be put off. For some reason that was making her nervous and snappy, and when we stopped for petrol and Dad got out of the car she told me to grow up and stop sulking. I felt I had every right to sulk, and told her so. She had completely ruined the end of my year off, and was obviously getting a kick out of making my life miserable, because if she just wanted me out of the way it would have been better to let me go to Europe.

She and I hardly spoke all the rest of the way, but it was only as we got close that I realised how completely she'd spoiled things. I'd looked up the Friston Executive on the net and it had seemed quite nice: a big, spacious three-star hotel in its own grounds and right on the beach. What I hadn't realised was that it didn't just have its own grounds, it had its own valley, in a dip between two huge, bare hills without another house in a mile and five miles to the nearest town. It was a quarter of a mile just from the road to the actual hotel, with gates to close off the drive and the entrance to the car park.

We parked by the beach, which turned out to be a strand of enormous flints at the bottom of a twenty-foot chalk cliff. Dad seemed to be impressed, stretching his arms out and taking a deep breath of air.

'Ah ... smell that! I love the sea. You are a lucky girl, Jem. Just think, all summer at the beach.

I peered over the edge. There was a stair, of sorts, but just looking at it gave me vertigo, while as far as I could tell the smell Dad seemed to be enjoying was a mixture of rotting seaweed and very dead fish. Summer was equally unimpressed, wrinkling her nose and throwing me a knowing look as Dad admired the scenery. Along the beach in both directions, the dirty white cliffs rose higher, with the same drab grey shingle stretching to the limit of vision, where headlands jutted out to East and West. It was all very sunny and calm, but the trees planted to shelter fields in the valley bottom were bent away from the wind, showing that it could be as bleak and miserable as I felt inside.

The only building I could see was the hotel: a central whitewashed block three stories tall between a sprawl of single-storey wooden terraces, joined together by walkways, which continued to a line of chalets half hidden among the trees by a field. There had to be fifty or sixty rooms, and I could see that cleaning them was going to be a nightmare, never mind what else I might be expected to do; waitressing perhaps, bar work, laundry, and all the tedious jobs I'd worked so hard until now to avoid.

Danielle had seemed reluctant to get out of the car, but finally did so, joining us at the edge of the cliff. 'Hadn't we better be on our way, Jeremy darling?'

'There's no rush,' he answered, glancing at his watch. 'I could do with a coffee, and don't you want to say hello to your uncle?'

'I don't think he's here today, and it's a long way home.' She sounded more nervous than ever, making me wonder what was going on, but Dad started towards the hotel and she had little choice but to follow. It was warm and she was showing off as usual, in a crop-top with little red shorts that left half her bum showing, sandals, and sunglasses pushed back on her head. Seeing her like that made me wonder if she got spanked, maybe by Morris himself, and if so, how I could find out for certain and turn the tables on her. No doubt she knew that was a risk, which seemed to be another good reason for shutting me away, only it wasn't.

It wasn't because I'd met the man who was now walking towards us, beaming cheerfully as he embraced Danielle and then Summer, shook hands with Dad and favoured me with a knowing smirk. Shorter than me by at least two inches, but maybe twice my weight, his pear-shaped body topped by a head like a Halloween pumpkin decorated with a thick beanfeaster moustache, he was unmistakable: Mr Hegedus. Who I'd last seen tugging at a thick brown-skinned penis while begging me to take my knickers down so that he could get off over my bare bum instead of the panty show I'd promised him.

'Ah, Danielle, but it's been too long since you last saw your old uncle Vilmos, and you too, Summer. And Mr Bassington-Smyth, it is an honour to meet you, sir. And this must be Jemima, who will be working for us? What a pretty girl. Wonderful, wonderful.'

He recognised me, he had to, even though I was the wrong way round, but he gave no sign of it whatsoever. Danielle did, throwing me a look compounded of panic and threat as Dad walked forward. I ignored her, but I was trying to work out what it might mean if Mr Hegedus was her uncle and I was quickly coming to some extremely interesting conclusions. He had to have told her about me, for one thing, which suggested a very odd conversation for an uncle to be having with his niece. It also suggested that he was the driving force behind my being offered the job, and if that was true I was back in the driving seat.

'We are delighted to train Jemima,' he was saying as he led the way inside, his Eastern European accent now faint as he did his best to play the respectable hotel manager.

It had been a very different tone of voice before, so thick with excitement that I'd barely been able to understand him, as he begged me to show off for him. He'd tipped well too. So desperate was he to get his schoolgirl strip and panty show, he'd hardly been able to count out the notes as he passed them over. I'd stuck them in my stocking top, so that he could see what he'd paid as I danced for him and had it right in his face as I peeled down my knickers with him wanking dementedly at his chubby little cock.

He was very friendly, offering us drinks and a tour of the hotel, while Danielle constantly and desperately tried to find excuses to leave. I was sure he knew exactly what was going on, because his moustache kept twitching into a half smile, but Dad played his unconscious part superbly, accepting everything as Danielle squirmed in discomfort, while she'd obviously been hoping they wouldn't meet. Not that she had anything to worry about, because the last thing he was going to do was tell his new maid's father what he had in mind for her, and that was very clear. I wasn't worried, because I knew I could handle him, but there was going to have to be some negotiation.

We got the grand tour, at least of the main building, and I was introduced to two of my fellow staff: Chris, the barman, and Stefan, the head waiter. Chris didn't look more than twenty. He was in a smart blue uniform, but still managed to seem casual with his mop of sandy-coloured hair and a companionable smile. Stefan was older and had cropped his hair to hide advancing baldness, giving him a sinister look, menacing even. I could easily imagine him as a spanker, but Chris looked strictly vanilla. I was sure I'd find out, if I wanted to, because I seemed to be the only girl around, leading me to ask Mr Hegedus a cautious question. 'There's somebody to do the cleaning and stuff, isn't there?'

'All that is on contract with a firm from Eastbourne. It's more efficient. You'll do a little, though, in between assisting myself and my staff.'

We were going to have to see about that, but I simply nodded. Danielle was looking at her watch again.

'We really should be getting back, Jeremy darling.'

'Well, yes, I suppose we had better make a start.'

He swallowed what remained of his coffee and kissed me.

'Be good, Jem. Or if you can't be good, be careful.'

It was one of those embarrassing things he'd been saying to me and Pippa since we turned teenagers, but he had no idea. I smiled and hugged him, feeling a little homesick as Danielle hurried him out to the car to leave me standing under the porch with Mr Hegedus. There was nobody else about and it seemed sensible to sort out where I stood as quickly as possible, so I swallowed my feelings and asked him a straight question.

'I suppose you expect to spank me?'

He was taken aback, but only for a second. 'Yes, yes, why not? Each day I will inspect your work. If it is not good enough, hot botty for baby, yes?'

He'd used the same infantile phrase at Morris's party. At the time I'd been just about to go over Melody's knee and he'd really brought home the situation I was in, making me blush. I found my cheeks colouring again, but rallied quickly.

'Oh no you don't. If you want me over your knee then I don't have to work, and that's that.'

'Not possible. I pay. You work. And maybe a little something extra if you are a good girl.'

'You're a dirty old pervert, do you know that?'

'Why a pervert? You are a beautiful girl. I am a man. I like to see beautiful girls bare naked.'

'You like to spank them,' I replied, not certain if he knew I liked it, but fairly sure he thought I'd only take it from him in return for something.

He merely shrugged, indifferent, and I went on. 'And if you expect to spank me it's going to be on my terms. I get a nice room, I come and go as I please and nobody gets to tell me what to do. For that you get to spank me once a week.'

'Impossible! You have a good room, yes, but you must work like all the others and for the right wage, which is not my business.'

'Oh? Whose business is it then?'

'The owner. Mr Rathwell.'

'Morris owns the hotel!?'

'Yes, and you must do your work. Any extra you want to earn, well then ...'

He patted my bottom, although his shifty expression made it very clear what he meant anyway, but I wasn't finished.

'OK, so Morris is the big boss and I guess I'll have to talk to him about my wages and stuff, but you and I can come to a little private arrangement, can't we? I don't mind helping with the bar and waitressing, but no toilets or scrubbing the floor or anything like that, OK? Promise me that and maybe, just maybe, I'll give you a panty show like I did before. You'd like that, wouldn't you?'

He was going red in the face and I thought I'd won, only for him to shake his head. 'Yes, I love your panty show, but you must work, or what will Mrs Hegedus think? She will think we are ...' He made a rude sign, sticking one finger though a circle made with the other hand, which was far further than I intended going, but that wasn't the problem.

'Mrs Hegedus? I didn't know you were married?'

'Oh yes. Here my wife cooks. Harriet kitten, come and meet Jemima, our new maid.'

He'd turned to look back into the hotel and I did the same, to find the biggest woman I had ever seen advancing on us. She had a face like a pudding, and it was set in a suspicious frown, as if she'd heard every word we'd said. My hands went to protect my bottom by instinct, and just to look at her made me feel weak. She was vast, taller than me and enormously fat, with her massive hips and thighs, her great, bulging belly and colossal breasts straining the white cook's coat in every direction. It wasn't all fat though; she had the shoulders of a wrestler and the arms to match. I gave her my sweetest smile. 'Pleased to meet you, Mrs Hegedus … er, Harriet.'

'Mrs Hegedus will do,' she answered. 'So you're the new maid? Good. You look the part.'

She sounded sarcastic. I couldn't think why, or what to say, but Mr Hegedus took over, his voice wheedling. 'Mr Rathwell chose her specially.'

Her answer was a sceptical grunt. 'Well you just mind where you put your hands, Vilmos Hegedus.'

He smiled and laughed, but only succeeded in looking and sounding guilty. 'I have eyes only for you, my kitten,' he assured her.

She gave another grunt. 'How many covers tonight, and what fish did you get?'

They began to discuss hotel matters and I waited politely while I struggled to make sense of what was going on. From what had been said it was Morris himself who'd suggested I be hired. He'd told Mr Hegedus, who in turn had told Danielle, and yet nothing had been said at the last party. Yet Morris was a businessman. He moved fast and was always looking for new opportunities, both to make money and indulge his penchant for humiliating girls, preferably both at the same time. I was caught up in something and I didn't mind all that much, but I did need to speak to him.

'... and there is only one lobster,' Mrs Hegedus finished, as if making a threat, and turned away.

I found my gaze following her in horrified fascination, hypnotised by the roll of her monstrous buttocks beneath her coat. Mr Hegedus gave me a sad look. 'You see, you must work, but still, maybe, now and then, it will be hot botty for baby all the same, yes?' He gave me a slow wink and his eyes flickered down to my hips before he went on. 'You are in chalet nine, up the hill. Morris ... Mr Rathwell says to put you there. Your uniforms are on the bed. Would you like a hand with your cases perhaps?'

I'd only brought two, both the wheelie sort, and I could tell what he was up to, hoping I'd let him watch me change. Judging by the expression in his eyes and the way his fat, pink tongue flicked out to moisten his lips, he might as well have just come right out with it.

'Yes, thank you,' I replied.

I wasn't really in the mood for giving him a show, but he was my boss and it would pay to be on the right side of him. Then again, I very definitely didn't want to be on the wrong side of his wife, who already seemed to have her suspicions. I decided to tease instead, and hope I could keep him under control that way, so I deliberately walked ahead, allowing him to admire the shape of my bum in my jeans as we crossed the reception area. There was a door on the far side that led towards the chalets, but it was opposite the one leading into the kitchen and as I pushed it open we were brought up short by a roar.

'She can do that on her own, Vilmos Hegedus! You

25

can take out the bins for me.'

He winced. 'Yes, my kitten.'

I took over the cases, hauled them through the door and away down a glass-roofed terrace set with cast iron tables overlooking the sea. The door at the end led to a corridor with rooms to one side and windows to the other, which led in turn to a walkway connecting the line of chalets. Mine was the furthest away of all; a fair way up the hill and sheltered beneath the last of the trees. It was rather nice, with a bathroom and even a tiny kitchen, while the bed was a big, soft king-size with a fluffy coverlet on which were laid out three uniforms.

Two were exactly the same smart dark blue maid's uniforms, knee-length with a white collar and white trim on the sleeves, rather boring really. The third was very different, and had obviously designed by a dirty old man; in black satin with a skirt so short it obviously wasn't going to cover my knickers and lacing down the front of the bodice, which was so low cut that what little I had would be in danger of spilling out. There were accessories too: stockings, suspenders, black high-heels, a layered underskirt and a hideous pair of froufrou panties, as big as gym knickers with a dozen layers of see-through lace at the back.

'Perverts.'

I'd spoken to myself, but I'd have said it to Morris's face. He'd have laughed. Mr Hegedus I wasn't so sure of, as he seemed to take himself rather more seriously and had immediately grown defensive when I'd called him a dirty old man. That was what he was though, and Morris, and all the other men who like girls done up in tarty uniforms and naughty lingerie and weird outfits. It's fun though, and at least with men like that I don't have to pretend I'm something I'm not.

26

Nobody had told me which uniform to put on, but when Mr Hegedus was talking to his wife they'd mentioned a wedding party that evening and I didn't imagine they'd want me strutting about with my knickers on show. There was no rush though, and as I stripped off for the shower I was growing increasingly tempted to try the naughty one on first.

Until I got under the water I hadn't realised how tired I was. It had been a long and stressful day, what with Dad and Danielle and the drive down to the coast. With my eyes closed and the hot water cascading down my body I was growing rapidly sleepy, making me wonder if I dared snatch a nap before reporting for duty. It was still mid afternoon, and nobody had said I had to be anywhere at any particular time, so once I was out of the shower I hung my uniform up in the cupboard and lay down on the bed with just a towel wrapped around me.

I felt drowsy and relaxed, a little naughty too, with thoughts of what Morris and Mr Hegedus might have in store for me running through my head. At the very least I was plainly expected to serve at meals in my kinky maid's outfit, and that meant the guests would have been carefully selected to appreciate what was on show. Maybe it would just be stag parties, but that wasn't really Morris's style. More likely it would be the sort of men who came to his private parties, discreet, older men with plenty of money and specialist tastes. I could probably expect to have my bum pulled out of my ridiculous froufrou knickers for spanking, a thought that sent a shiver of excitement and shame the length of my spine.

There's something about being warm and drowsy that always makes me want to masturbate. Being sleepy makes my defences come down too, so I can be really dirty with myself without feeling bad. I was tempted now,

27

just to throw the towel away and roll over, face down on the bed with my bottom pushed up so that I could explore myself from behind while I thought of being in the same, rude, vulnerable position for punishment. My hairbrush was in my case, and it was just right to apply a few firm swats to each cheek before sticking the handle up my pussy while I finished off, or even into my bumhole.

It was a deliciously dirty thought, and I bounced over on the bed, stretching for my case with my legs cocked wide and my toes dug into the coverlet to stop me overbalancing. I must have looked a fine sight, with my bum turned up and my pussy wide open, which was why the sound of a creak from the walkway outside had me snatching for my towel and trying to cover myself behind at the same time. Unfortunately I fell off the bed, landing on the floor with a thud just as a knock sounded at the door.

'Hang on, I'm not decent!'

'It's only me,' Mr Hegedus answered, his voice unmistakable.

That was what I'd been worried about, and although he'd seen everything already there's a big difference between having Melody show me off over the knee, and being caught masturbating by Mr Hegedus. There was something about him that made his attention particularly intrusive. I was blushing furiously as I dug my bathrobe out of my case and struggled into it, and he must have noticed me doing this when he opened the door.

'I'm sorry,' I explained. 'I was having a shower. Did you want me at the hotel?'

'Not yet, no. But is your uniform good? Does it fit?'

'I haven't tried it on yet. I expect you want me to wear a decent one this evening?'

'Oh, of course. Yes. The other is for special

occasions.'

'I'd guessed that. Um ... well, I'll be down later, OK, about six?'

He was angling to be invited in, but he'd caught me off guard, leaving me unsettled. I was fairly sure he'd peeped in at the window too, which made me feel he'd taken advantage. When he saw I wasn't letting him in he drew back, but hesitated, throwing a guilty glance back along the walkway before he spoke again, his voice now wheedling. 'Maybe baby needs a hot botty? I think she does, yes?'

I shut the door on him without bothering to answer. Another man I might have let in, and it wasn't because he was older or ugly. I've always preferred older men. A father figure I suppose you could say, and my need had grown stronger since Dad had taken up with Danielle. Mr Hegedus wouldn't do. He was too weak, and odd. The way he spoke to me when he wanted to get dirty was weird, and humiliating, as if I didn't know my own mind but could be tricked into thinking I deserved spanking. Part of me wanted to do it, to let him make me feel small and stupid while I lay over his knee, with him gloating over his victory and perving over my bum. I knew he wouldn't just spank me. He'd play with my cheeks, and if I stayed down he'd start taking liberties, maybe tickling my bumhole, maybe fingering me, maybe rubbing me off for the dirty thrill of having me come under his fat, pasty fingers ...

No. I was in control and I wasn't going to surrender to him. I was going to get him back for the way he'd made me feel. He was still outside, I was sure of it, so I shut the curtain of the window by the door, then the ones on the other side, where the window looked out among trees and over a field, leaving just a crack. That way he could peep

29

at me without risking being seen from the hotel, and I was sure he would.

It felt great. As I dropped my robe to go nude once more a shiver of pleasure ran through me, for being naughty, and because it felt a little dangerous too. I was teasing him, on purpose, and it was sure to get him horny. He'd be resentful as well as excited, and want to punish me and fuck me too, maybe bent down over my bed with his cock in me from behind while he slapped my cheeks and told me off for being a dirty little tease.

I was sure he didn't have the guts, but it was lovely to think about it while I made a big show of towelling myself down, deliberately paying a lot of attention to my tits and pussy, even holding my cheeks open to dab between and make sure he got a peep at my bumhole. He was out there for certain, his shadow visible through the curtain, but I feigned innocence, quite sure he'd be getting off thinking I didn't want him to see me, just as much as he'd be getting off over my body.

There was talc in my bag, and I made a point of bending down to get it out, with my bum stuck out at his window. A tall, thin mirror decorated the wall opposite my bed and I went to stand in front of it to put the talc on, doing under my arms and breasts, my neck and tummy, sticking my hips out to powder my pussy, and then extending my bottom to do between my cheeks. I could just imagine him, cock in his hand, full of guilt and dirty lust as he masturbated over the sight of me powdering my bottom slit.

Really, I was no better; enjoying the feel of my fingertip in the soft, powdery dimple of my bumhole, tickling to make my ring twitch and spreading my cheeks to inspect my rear view. I was soaking, my pussy lips pale and smooth, pinkish white where I'd powdered, but glistening and rosy in my slit, while the mouth of my bumhole showed as a tiny, moist star at the centre of my powdery ring.

I wanted my hairbrush up, and to walk about nude with it sticking out from between my cheeks, openly dirty. Then he'd have known what I was up to, or would he? Maybe he'd still think he was really spying on me and get an even bigger kick out of it because I was being a dirty little bitch, or maybe he'd just kick the door down, put me over his knee, pull the hairbrush out, spank me with it until I howled and then make me suck on the handle while he fucked me over the bed.

The thought was almost too much. My hand had gone to my pussy and I was cupping my mound with my bottom pushed out behind, thinking of how long it was since I'd been entered. All I had to do was open the door and I could get it; a fat, brown cock thrust up me for a good, hard fucking. He wasn't right though, not for that, fine to watch me, to spank me, to fiddle with me and make me feel dirty and small, but not to fuck me.

I had to come anyway; I could no longer hold back. My hands were shaking as I went back to my pretence of innocently getting changed, but when I opened the wardrobe and saw the rude maid's outfit hanging there I knew my orgasm wouldn't be the same unless I dressed up. It took all my will power to do it, holding off from my need as I made a show of putting the uniform on. My stockings came first, each leg raised to the bed as I rolled them on and clipped my suspenders into place; making a point of checking that the tension was just right so that I could pose with my pussy and bum still bare between the nylon and lace of my undies. The froufrou panties followed; huge things that came right up to my waist but left most of my cheeks spilling out behind. I pulled them up tight to give myself what my American friends called a camel toe, with the white cotton taut over my shaved mound and caught in a furrow between my lips.

'Camel toe cunt.'

My words sounded loud in the quiet of the chalet, and wonderfully dirty, bringing back memories of posing in little cut down jeans shorts to give the boys a thrill, or in nothing but tiny red bikini briefs pulled up tight between my cheeks while Penny spanked me. I looked just as sexy in my froufrous, and deliciously available, as if being in such a silly garment made it very clear that I could be pinched, and groped, and spanked.

If the front looked silly, the rear view was ridiculous, a great puff of frills sticking out over my bum, but see-through, so that my slit showed beneath, while the little lacy panel that covered the turn of my cheeks meant that when I bent over I was going to be showing pretty well everything. I was going to have to bend too, and I'd been taught to do it properly, from the hips with my back pulled in so my bottom sticks out, round and tempting with the bulge of my pussy peeping out from between my thighs.

I spent a while posing, but being topless spoilt the teasing effect so I hurried into the frilly underskirt, the dress and heels. With the laces done up at the front I actually had a little cleavage, which felt nice and looked the part, but I knew that wouldn't be what Mr Hegedus wanted to see. Bum and pussy were more his style.

He was going to get plenty. Pausing only to put my hair up in a ponytail, I began to pose again, pretending I was serving at table and admiring the way my froufrous showed under my skirt as I bent with my bottom pushed out to the mirror. It was deliciously rude, with just a hint of my bumhole visible through the lace panel and the cotton cupping my pussy already wet where it was caught between my cheeks.

'You dirty girl, Jemima. How what if they were pulled down, nice and slow.'

I was talking to myself, but for him, sure he'd be at bursting point if he hadn't come already. My hands had gone back to take hold of my froufrous as I spoke, but I still wanted to tease and simply adjusted them to leave a little more cheek showing at each leg hole. Instead of taking them down I turned, holding up the front of my dress to show off my camel toe in the mirror, and to him.

'That's best, and knickers down at the back as if I've just been spanked, and my hairbrush ...'

That was how I wanted to come. A quick rummage in my case and I had my hairbrush; the long, round handle just right for eager little holes. I no longer cared if he'd realised I knew he was there, but stuck my bottom out towards the window as I began to peel my panties down.

'Here you are, Mr Hegedus. Here's what you want to see, my bare bum, knickers down, just like I'd be if you were going to spank me. You want to spank me, don't you, Mr Hegedus? You want to spank me bare bottom over your knee, wriggling and kicking and ...'

I trailed off with a sigh. My bottom was bare and I could feel the cool air on my pussy lips. I could imagine his face, his eyes feasting on my naked bum and the wet pink hole between my thighs as I stuck it right out, showing him everything. A few firm smacks of the hairbrush got my cheeks rosy and left them tingling as I pushed the handle in, up my pussy, gasping as I filled myself. Now I was ready, perfectly ready.

'Watch this, Mr Hegedus.'

Again I went to the mirror, but sideways on, so that I could see my bare bottom sticking out under the frills, with my froufrous in a tangle around my thighs, my suspender straps taught at the sides and the hairbrush sticking out from between my smacked cheeks. Up came the front to show off my camel toe to Mr Hegedus for just an instant before I gave in completely, grabbing my pussy and rubbing through the wet cotton as I jammed the hairbrush handle in and out of my hole from behind.

It happened almost immediately, the slow build-up of excitement bursting like a dam to leave me gasping and gulping in air, trying to spank myself and fuck myself at the same time, rubbing furiously at my sopping pussy through my panties and all the while imagining his fat brown cock spurting come as he brought himself off over my dirty behaviour, yearning for what I'd denied him but unable to stop himself.

My orgasm had only just begun to fade when a sudden, mischievous thought hit me. He might have heard what I'd said, or he might not, but either way he was sure to be riddled with guilt if I caught him peeping and had a go at him. The moment I could cope I jumped forward and snatched the curtain open, expecting to find him, staring and red in the face as he tossed off over my dirty little show.

He wasn't there, but when I opened the window and leant out to make sure he wasn't lurking nearby I realised he had been, and had been unable to hold back. On the flat concrete directly below my face was a little puddle of sticky white.

Chapter Three

MY FIRST WEEK AT the Friston Executive was more like being back at school than anything. I had to get up early, dress in my uniform and go through a routine that barely changed from day to day. The staff at the hotel weren't so very different from the staff at school either, expecting me to do as I was told and generally behave myself. It would have to have been an old-fashioned school though, because I had Mr Hegedus constantly threatening to spank me, even to cane me. Not that he got the chance, because his wife seemed to have a pretty good idea of what he was like and was not about to let it happen.

That made teasing him all the more fun, because I do like to be in charge, and to see the desperation in men's faces, especially when it's somebody who can tell me what to do. He hated it, but there was a whining, pleading tone to his threats and I was sure he didn't have the guts to just do me when his wife wasn't looking. It was much the same with Chris and with Stefan, who were in charge of me when I was helping with the bar or waitressing, but would both have liked to get me into bed. I could have let one of them, and might have done if I hadn't been sure that whoever I chose would get possessive. The last thing I wanted was a boyfriend, because I was sure not everything was as it seemed.

The guests couldn't have been more ordinary; business

people, couples and families taking a break, locals coming to the bar of an evening. None of them did anything worse than pass an innuendo, and I didn't even get my bottom pinched, which I'd assumed was something all maids would have to put up with. Yet there was my alternative uniform, and there was Morris. I rang him several times to ask if there was another party, and whether he was planning anything at the hotel, but he simply laughed and told me to be patient. In the end I decided that the uniform was just some pervy idea Mr Hegedus had dreamt up, and that while I'd probably end up in it at some point, it would be just for his personal amusement. I knew he'd get what he wanted too, because the thought of being made to dress up like a little tart and spanked by him was disgusting and delicious all at the same time.

That's the funny thing about spanking. The worse the situation the more I like it, so if I'm getting it from Pippa or Penny it's pure fun, and really only naughty because it's from another girl. If I get it in front of an audience I feel embarrassed and ashamed and foolish, but still love being the object of their desire and ultimately in control. When Danielle had done me and I'd thought Summer might see, I'd hated every second of it, but I'd been wet right from the start. With Mr Hegedus it would be the same, which was why I knew that if he proved to have the courage and just caught me at the right moment, I wouldn't be able to resist.

What he did to me was far worse than I'd expected.

Saturday morning was exceptionally busy because all the guests seemed to be leaving at once, and everybody expected me to be their personal skivvy and put their tasks first. By the time the contract cleaners left, I didn't know if I was coming or going, and it got worse. New guests started to arrive; a group of mainly foreign businessmen who wanted everything done instantly and to the highest possible standard, right down to finding an improvised kennel for the biggest, shaggiest dog I'd ever seen, which must have been something like a cross between a mastiff and a borzoi.

At lunch I was trying to help Chris and Stefan at the same time, also Mr and Mrs Hegedus. Inevitably I made a mistake, serving a bottle of red wine to a table of six who said they'd ordered white, and I was trying to apologise when Mr Hegedus appeared.

'Is something the matter, gentlemen?' he asked, bowing.

One of them answered immediately; a completely bald Russian with a face like a hatchet. He was the one with the gigantic dog, and I'd known he would be a nuisance from the moment I'd met him.

'Yes. We ordered Pinot Gris and this idiot girl has brought us Pinot Noir.'

'I'm really sorry,' I protested, 'but bottles are the same shape, and …'

'Incompetent!' he snapped.

'I shall deal with the matter immediately, Mr Morozov,' Mr Hegedus said, gave a second bow and pulled a chair out from a vacant table.

I should have known, but I never even saw it coming. Even when he grabbed my wrist I thought he was going to take me outside and tell me off, and it was only as I was pulled into position that I realised I was going to be spanked. It was so sudden that all I could manage was a scream of utter horror and then my uniform skirt had been whipped up and I was showing my panties, but not for long. One good tug and they were down, baring my bottom to the room in general, and to the table who'd complained in particular.

He cocked his knee up and I'd had my pussy spread, wide open to everybody as my spanking began, hard across both cheeks with my face an inch above the carpet and my legs waving in the air. I was screaming my head off, but he just didn't care, spanking so hard he was knocking the breath from my body, while it stung so badly I couldn't even try to get my thighs together.

They were laughing, all of them; not one giving so much as a sympathetic word as I had my bare bottom turned red in front of them with my bumhole and pussy on full show. That was what made me realise I'd been set up, because you can't just spank a young girl in public and expect to get away with it, not nowadays. By then it was too late anyway. I'd genuinely thought I was being done in front of a room full of ordinary people and I'd burst into tears, hot, shame filled tears that wouldn't stop.

Nor would Mr Hegedus. I suppose I had been teasing him for a week, but he was a real bastard about it, ignoring my tears and snivels and making sure my thighs and bottom cheeks were well open as he administered a really hard spanking. It hurt so much I couldn't even speak properly to protest, and he did my thighs as well as my bum, drawing fresh applause from my audience.

When he finally let me up I could barely stand, and I was sure I'd have fallen over if I'd tried to run, while he'd kept a firm grip on the skirt of my maid's uniform, holding it up at the back to show off my red bottom. I tried to pull my panties up, but he slapped my hand, then hauled up the front of my dress as well to show off my pussy, not that they hadn't already seen every detail.

'Hands on your head, Jemima.'

I obeyed, too broken to resist, the tears still running down my face as he tucked up my skirt and turned me slowly around, exhibiting my smacked bottom and bare pussy to the audience, leaving me with my back to the Russian as he spoke.

'I trust that was satisfactory, Mr Morozov?'

He put a hand to my bum, lifting my cheeks for the Russian's inspection. They were all clapping and I found myself smiling despite the state I was in, blushing too, for the exhibition I'd made of myself. Mr Morozov was now grinning as he answered Mr Hegedus, then me.

'That will do very well, for now at least. You are a good girl, Jemima. What a pretty bottom you have. Now, show me from the front.'

I turned, blushing hot as his gaze moved to where my pussy showed above my lowered knickers. His eyes were steel grey, and very hard, as was his voice; polite words spoken in a tone that allowed no refusal. I knew he could see I was excited, and he took ages inspecting me before finally looking up once more.

'You juice well,' he remarked. 'Morris said you were special.'

'Morris?' I asked, still too dazed to really take in what was happening.

'Morris himself,' a voice spoke from behind me and a large hand closed on my bottom.

I let him feel, too shocked to resist, while there was no denying the effect the sudden spanking was having on me. My thighs felt sticky and the shaking wouldn't stop, and yet I was burning with resentment for the way they'd treated me.

'Welcome to the Friston Executive, gentlemen,' Morris went on, still fondling. 'I hope you enjoyed our little show, which we put on just to assure you that this is the real thing. Nor is Jemima the only young lady who will be entertaining us this weekend, far from it. There will be eight girls in attendance, including my own lovely wife and Miss Amber Oakley should any of you gentlemen prefer to be on the receiving end now and again.'

Melody stepped in from the reception area, her dark skin and full curves displayed to perfection in a scarlet dress with short boots, gloves and a neat little pillbox hat to match. In her hand she held a school cane, the sight of which made my tummy go tight. It was only then I realised how complete my disgrace had been. It wasn't just the businessmen who'd watched my spanking, but the staff. Chris was behind Melody, Stefan and Mrs Hegedus in the door to the kitchen. Both the men were grinning, which brought fresh blood to my face at the thought of what they'd seen. She was harder to read, her expression neutral, maybe a touch disapproving, but definitely not sympathetic, and she'd just seen me spanked by her husband. My blushes grew hotter still at the thought of her indifference, even contempt, and I wondered if the only reason she even bother to keep him away from me was because she thought he might waste his money.

'...wish you all an enjoyable stay,' Morris was saying, 'but as Jemima will still be serving your lunch perhaps I should be kind and make her bottom better. Take off your panties, Jemima, and turn around.'

They had already fallen down to my ankles and I kicked them off without having to be told twice. Morris kept his hold on me anyway, turning me around by my waist and pushing me gently but firmly down over the back of a chair, making sure Mr Morozov got a prime view. I'd begun to sob again as he pressed down on the small of my back to make me stick out my bottom, once more showing off my pussy and bumhole to the audience.

'Hold still,' he ordered and I nodded weakly.

They were all staring, some openly, some less so, but

every single one of them with his gaze feasting on my bare red bottom as Morris took a tube of cream from his pocket and laid a thick, cool worm on each of my cheeks. I was struggling to stay still as he began to rub it in, tickling me, but soothing me too, so that I was struggling not to giggle at first, but was quickly having to resist the urge not to close my eyes in bliss. My feelings of resentment were still too hot and I was determined not to show them what had been done to me, for all that they knew anyway. Morris doesn't hire unwilling girls.

I only broke when he slid one creamy finger in-between my cheeks to tickle my bumhole, a little cry of shock that became a sigh as the pleasure got too much for me. He gave a quiet chuckle and began to tease my hole, setting me gasping and sobbing once more, but now with as much pleasure as shame. I wondered if he was going to bugger me, in front of all of them, and I knew I'd let him, but he let go, giving my creamy, glistening bottom a resounding slap as he spoke again.

'That's all for now, Jemima. But we don't want cream on your pretty uniform, do we, so I think you'd better stay as you are while you serve lunch.'

All I could manage was a nod, but the audience had begun to clap again for the way Morris had handled me. Once more I couldn't help but smile and even managed a little curtsey before making a dash for the loos with every pair of eyes in the restaurant following my shiny red bottom as I went. I had to go through reception to get there, adding to my embarrassment as more people were coming in, including two enormously fat men I'd met at Morris's last party, Mr Enos and Mr Protheroe. Both laughed as they saw me, adding a final stab of humiliation before I reached the safety of the Ladies.

My face was a mess, wet with tears and sticky with

snot all round my nose, while my hair looked like a bird's nest after being turned almost completely upside down for my spanking. All my stuff was in my room, but to get there meant walking past everybody again and even if I was going to have to serve lunch bare-bottom I wanted to be tidy. I'd just splashed water on my face when the door opened and Melody Rathwell came in. My tummy went tight as I saw the school cane in her hand, and my reaction must have shown on my face because she laughed.

'Don't worry, I'm not going to cane you, Jemima. Not yet anyway. Here, let me help.'

She had a bag with her, a big one in red leather to match her dress, and I let her take over. It was very easy, and soothing, because she always looked after me at the parties, making sure the men stayed in line and always ready with a kiss and a cuddle when I needed it. She knew exactly how to handle me too, wiping my nose and kissing away my tears before cuddling me close. I shivered as her hand cupped my bottom, knowing what she was going to do to me but too resentful to let myself go.

'No, Mel …'

'Hush, Jemima.'

Her voice was calm and so full of authority, making me feel I was wrong to resist. She'd cradled my head to her chest and started to stroke my hair too, and with that I just gave in, sticking out my bottom and letting her cup me from behind. Her thumb went in up my pussy and she'd begun to masturbate me, whispering softly into my ear as her fingers worked my sex. I melted into her, snuggling against her chest until she paused to lift one heavy black breast from her dress, offering me her nipple to suck. Only then did I hesitate, not sure if I could surrender so completely.

'Come on, Jemima,' she urged, her voice soft but firm.

'Mel, I …'

'Uh, uh, hush.'

She'd pulled my head in as she spoke, pressing her stiff, dark nipple to my lips. I just couldn't stop myself. My mouth came open and I was doing it, suckling her as she cradled me to her breast. Her hand found my pussy once more, entering me behind and rubbing at my clit.

'That's better, isn't it?'

I nodded on my mouthful of nipple, unable to deny how good it felt. She hadn't been the one to spank me, not this time, but I had been dealt with, hard, and then had my bottom creamed in front of maybe thirty people. It was what I deserved: a good, firm punishment to keep me in my place and then a nipple in my mouth to calm me down as I had my pussy frigged to ecstasy. I'd began to cry again, bitterly hard, and was gulping badly as I mouthed on her nipple. But it was good, so good, and with her fingers working my clit the sobs had quickly turned to gasps and I'd come under her hand.

She held on, my ecstasy fading to a sense of perfect, peaceful satisfaction as she let me suckle, still stroking my hair and whispering to me as I came slowly down. I was lost to the world, completely wrapped up in what she was doing to me and wondering vaguely if she'd put me on my knees to make me lick, so that the click of the door came as a shock. It was Mrs Hegedus, and I found myself blushing furiously as I met her astonished gaze. She'd seen what we were doing and I was immediately stammering apologies, but Mel wasn't bothered in the least, speaking with exactly the calm authority you might have expected from the owner's wife even as she dabbed my spittle from her breast.

'Is everybody here?'

'Just about everybody, Mrs Rathwell,' Mrs Hegedus replied and for the first time I heard respect in her voice. 'We've thirty-four guests already, so that leaves five.'

Mel had covered herself up and was digging in her bag as she went on.

'Good. Send somebody up to the gate then, and have them lock it when the last car's through.'

'Yes, Mrs Rathwell.'

Mrs Hegedus disappeared into a cubicle as Mel took my chin in her hand.

'Hold still.'

I obeyed, allowing her to clean my face up again and make me up, concentrating on her task until she was satisfied. She gave me just a touch of green eye shadow, lip gloss, then pulled my hair up into a high ponytail. 'That's better.'

'Thanks. But don't I look a bit plain, if we're having a party?'

'No. Most men prefer a natural look, as if you're a perfectly ordinary waitress who just happens to have been spanked rather than a girl who's into spanking who just happens to be a waitress.'

She was right, of course, and I stepped back a little to adjust my uniform, tucking the skirt right up at the back so that it was obvious my bottom was bare to humiliate me as part of my punishment, but leaving the front only half up so that a seated man could just see my pussy peeping out from beneath the hem. Melody gave me an approving nod.

'Good. You're learning. We have a lot of new clients this evening, including some very important men. I want you to be particularly nice to Karay … Mr Morozov, and if he's happy there'll be a little extra in your envelope at the end of the week. By the way, you know Amber Oakley, don't you?'

'Penny's ex-girlfriend? Yes.'

'Good. I'd like you to do me a favour later.'

'OK. What is it?'

'We're going to be playing a game this evening. Every time a girl gets spanked she has the right to choose who's next, and who does it. You'll be first, and I want you to choose Amber.'

'OK, but she's domme, isn't she?'

'Yes, normally. The truth is she loves to be spanked, but she needs an excuse to give in to it.'

From what I knew of Amber it didn't sound very likely, but I was happy to play along.

'Who should I choose for her, you?'

'No, a man, some real sleaze ball.'

'And she'll really like that?'

'Sure.'

I didn't believe her, but I wasn't going to argue.

'And think about it. She's bound to choose you next.'

'That's true.'

It was, giving me a lovely touch of apprehension as Mel slapped my bottom to send me towards the door. Obviously she just wanted Amber spanked, and I knew they were rivals. But the way the game worked, she couldn't do it herself without getting the same treatment first, which would have made it a bit pointless. As it was, Amber wouldn't know if I'd chosen her out of simple mischief, because I wanted it from her, or because I'd been put up to it. And even if she suspected she couldn't be certain Melody was responsible. She was sure to take her revenge on me, which was frightening and exciting at the same time, but not necessarily my best choice.

Chapter Four

NOW THAT I KNEW what was going on, I was in my element and I felt a lot better for my orgasm, my spanking too, which had left me with a lovely warm glow. Mr Hegedus had taken me completely by surprise, leaving me off balance and unsure of myself, but after Melody's special treatment I was feeling confident again, and full of mischief. It was great fun parading with my bottom and pussy bare, especially serving lunch and being able to bend so that everybody behind me got a prime view. I was only wishing there were a few more mirrors so that I could see how my bum looked as well as everybody else.

Several of the men I'd met at earlier parties were there, and also some of the girls, as well as others I didn't know. Melody's twin sister, Harmony, was sitting with Annabelle, their house slave, and at another table was Amber Oakley, with her girlfriend Kay. I was too busy to talk, but smiled for everybody, all the while wondering how to get the best out of the game. There were plenty of options, but by the time lunch was over I'd come up with one so good I couldn't keep the smile off my face. Mr Hegedus noticed, grinning through his moustache as he approached me.

'I'm glad you enjoy your work, Jemima, and may I say how very pretty you look. Now, run along and change into your other uniform. And you are to wear knickers, yes? Because if you don't have any on, how are we supposed to pull them down so baby gets a hot botty, yes?'

He laughed at his own humour and sent me on my way with a pinch. It wasn't the first, as the men had soon realised I could be touched and there probably wasn't a single one who hadn't given me a pat at the very least, while I'd been squeezed, slapped, pinched and even had my cheeks held open while I'd been serving. All the attention had left me hot and flustered; I was high on being their maid and what it meant to be used as a plaything, by so many men and so casually.

If Melody hadn't already brought me off I'd have treated myself to a sneaky frig in the shower, and as it was I enjoyed soaping myself and posing in the mirror as I dressed, all the while thinking about the way the men had handled me and what I had coming. I was also thinking about Melody and what she'd done to me; being so firm and yet so caring as she made me suckle and masturbated me. She'd seemed to know exactly how I felt, and exactly what to do about it, getting rid of all my bad feelings and replacing them with excitement and mischief. Perhaps rather too much mischief.

I couldn't resist making it worse, seeking her out for some advice on Amber's coming spanking the moment I came back to the main part of the hotel. She was talking to Mr Todmorden, who Pippa had worked for in her year off, but excused herself when I signalled to her.

'Is everything all right?' she asked.

'Fine. I was just wondering who to choose for Amber. What really gets to her?'

Melody gave a soft laugh, her eyes shining with pleasure as we cast our eyes over the men. Lunch had broken up, but many of them were still at their tables, drinking coffee or spirits, or loitering in the reception area. Of the thirty or so we could see more than twenty. I carried on as Melody pondered our choice.

'Protheroe always gropes us. Or there's Enos, who's gross but he doesn't spank very hard. Or maybe Mr Judd? He doesn't look much, but he's a real perve. Penny hates it when she gets it from him ... well, you know what I mean.'

I nodded my understanding and went back to scanning the men. Even by Morris's standards they were a right set of dirty old gits, and any one would have done the trick.

'How about having her passed around?' I suggested.

'It's got to be one on one,' Melody told me. 'Otherwise the game takes too long. Anyway, the thing about Amber is that once she's been given a good spanking she won't be able to stop herself. If she gets passed around at least she has the excuse of playing the game, but this way she loses her dignity completely.'

I couldn't help but laugh and she returned a wicked grin for my sense of humour.

'OK, let's look at it another way. You're domme, so who would you hate to get it from the most?'

'Amber, of course,' she answered without a moment of hesitation. 'And we can't have her spank herself, even though it would be quite funny. Go for Judd ... no, Protheroe. If he's on form he'll make her talk about it. You know, make her ask to have her knickers pulled down and that sort of thing. She hates that.'

'OK.'

I kissed her and moved on. The party proper wasn't due to start for a while, but everybody was plainly in the mood, including Amber. She'd taken Kay over her knee and was dishing out a hairbrush spanking, ostensibly for flirting with Harmony, but really just showing off. Nearly all the men were watching; most from a respectful distance, some trying to get close, while a little queue had begun to form at one side. Protheroe was quite close to me, looking flabbier than ever, his bald patch larger and his face redder. A bead of sweat had formed at one temple, probably more from watching Kay get it than the heat of the day. As he moved to get a better view of her bum he lifted his massive fleshy buttocks from the chair, grunting as he shifted and I saw that his trouser seat was caught between his cheeks; a grotesque detail I really could have done without. The thought of being spanked by him was deeply humiliating, even for me. For Amber, who was pretty much one hundred percent lesbian and a domme, it would be torture, especially if Melody was right and the treatment left her needing more.

Then again, she could be pretty cruel herself. She had Kay's dress up, showing off a pair of see-through panties framed in stockings and suspenders, with a lot of very pink bum cheek sticking out from either leg hole. Poor Kay was shaking badly and gasping at every smack of the hairbrush, which must have stung like anything. Amber wasn't finished either, pausing to rub Kay's bottom and then sliding a thumb down the back of her knickers. Kay gave a sharp intake of breath as she realised she was to be done bare; then her knickers had been pulled down and she was showing everything behind, her pussy half hidden by a puff of dark gold hair and her tiny brown bumhole peeping out from between her cheeks.

A murmur of approval ran through the room at Kay's exposure and several of the men crowded closer. Amber went back to work with the hairbrush, applying hard slaps to one cheek at a time and to a steady rhythm. Kay couldn't cope at all; gasping and pleading as she was spanked, with her legs kicking up and down and her tawny hair tossing wildly as she struggled. Amber kept her grip, apparently without effort, her expression stern but also amused, until Kay's bottom was a rich glowing red all over. Only then did she finally stop.

The men began to crowd round immediately, before Kay had even had a chance to pull her knickers up, no doubt asking if they could have a turn. My tummy was fluttering and I felt badly in need of a drink, so I went out to the bar, where Annabelle was helping Chris. He had to be the only man in the hotel who missed seeing Kay spanked, and I couldn't help but tease him.

'You missed a great show there, Chris. Amber Oakley spanked her girlfriend, on the bare.'

He shrugged.

'I'd rather watch you get it still in your panties.'

It wasn't the answer I'd been expecting and I couldn't think of a comeback, so came around behind the bar to get a beer from the fridge, deliberately bending to let him see my froufrous. He watched, not bothering to hide his attention.

'Now that,' he said, 'is worth watching. Long legs, that's the thing, and the panties still up.'

'Pervert.'

He just grinned and I walked away, deliberately wiggling my bottom and wondering if he was quite as straight as I'd first thought. A lot of men were coming out of the restaurant and one of them gave me an order before I could sneak away, leaving me serving behind the bar. I got stuck there, and it was quite a while before I managed to get away and see what was going on.

Morris, the perfect host as always, had managed to persuade Amber to join Melody in dishing out punishment to those men who preferred to take it, or liked both. It wasn't really my thing, because while there is a

50

certain satisfaction in watching them get what they love to dish out it just feels wrong. If men are going to spank me, or even enjoy watching me punished, I like them to keep their authority and I do like the humiliation of knowing that I'm the one who gets it and they don't. One who definitely didn't was Mr Todmorden, and I went to sit on his lap, allowing him to feel me through my panties as I sipped my beer.

'Is Hudson around?' he asked after a moment.

'New York,' I told him. 'I wanted to go and join him, but I got sent here instead.'

'Ah, ha,' he remarked and his fondling grew a little firmer.

I stuck my bottom out, enjoying the attention. He was fatter than Mr Protheroe, and just as dirty, but fatherly, which was something I badly needed at that moment. Just being cuddled by him had suddenly brought me close to tears, but I swallowed the lump in my throat, determined to enjoy what he was doing to my bum and ignore my fragile emotions.

'And no Pippa?' he asked.

'She's up at uni, and she's spending most of the summer in Australia,' I told him, although I was surprised he didn't know.

'That's a pity,' he went on. 'I do enjoy the little shows you give together. I suppose you always used to do that sort of thing?'

'Sometimes,' I admitted, thinking of how it felt to lie across Pippa's knee as she spanked me. 'Quite a lot, actually.'

'Your own sister, tut tut.'

He patted my bottom and I found myself blushing.

'Perhaps you even deserve a little spanking?' he suggested.

It was all I could do to nod, giving in to him. He eased me into position, not over his knee as I'd expectedly, but cuddled into him with my thighs cocked wide across his, my uniform skirt puffed up to show off my bottom and the seat of my froufrous spread to the room. My face was against his shoulder and I put my arms around him, clinging tight for comfort as his hands found my bottom. Suddenly I needed it desperately, not for the sex, but for the comfort of being held while I was punished.

'Spank me, Lucius,' I whispered. 'Spank me properly.'

'I intend to,' he assured me, 'but I think we'd better pop your panties down first, don't you?'

'Yes.'

He hadn't waited for me to agree, but had eased my froufrous down as he spoke, baring my open bottom to the room. I knew an awful lot of people were watching, and exactly what they could see, but I didn't care. All I wanted was my bottom smacked while I was cuddled, and as his big, powerful hands closed on my cheeks I gave in to my tears. He held me open for a moment, making very sure I knew my bumhole was stretched wide for inspection and then began to spank, a cheek at a time, cupping each and slapping upwards to make them bounce and jiggle.

I clung on tight, the tears streaming down my face, abandoned to my punishment. He knew how to handle me, maybe even knew what I was going through, letting me sob my heart out as he attended to my bottom, until at last the warmth in my cheeks had begun to grow again. I began to want to come, imagining my pussy on show to the entire room as I was casually masturbated to orgasm by the man who'd spanked me and held me. He had other ideas, pausing to kiss my forehead, still holding my hot bottom as he spoke.

'Would you like to continue in my room, perhaps over a bottle of something?'

'Yes, please.'

He gave me a last pat, then pulled up my panties. Only as I sat up on his lap did I realise that a crowd had gathered to watch my spanking; eight men, including Stefan. They could all see I'd been crying, and it was that and not the display I'd been making of my bottom which had me blushing as Lucius helped me to my feet. He took my hand, leading me through the semi-circle of men towards the door. Two of them clapped, another gave me a pinch and my blushes had grown hotter at the thought of them all knowing more or less what was about to happen to me once Lucius had got me in his room. I was ready for it too, maybe a harder spanking and then down on his cock to suck him off, or perhaps a fucking with me bottom up and his belly resting on my smacked cheeks, always a lovely rude position to be in. Unfortunately Morris headed us off as we entered reception.

'Not just yet, Lucius, if you wouldn't mind. Jemima has to choose the first official spanking of the day. After that you can do what you like with her.'

Lucius began to protest, but Morris had already taken him by the arm, to lead both of us back into the dining.

'I think we'd better make it now,' he said, glancing to where Melody was riding a man across the room and using her school cane like a riding crop to flick at his buttocks. 'Er, Mel darling, if you wouldn't mind?'

Melody glanced up, pulled hard on the man's tie, which she'd been using for reins, and stood up.

'You, stay,' she addressed the man. 'Sorry, Morris. I'm ready when you are.'

She'd adjusted her dress as she spoke and stood back a little, looking absolutely magnificent; her full, firm figure sheathed in scarlet silk, the strength in her face tempered by amusement, the cane in one hand. Her arms were folded across her chest, lifting her breasts a little and I remembered how it had felt to be made to suckle her, with one big, dark globe pressed to my mouth as she masturbated me. I smiled and she gave an answering grin as Morris began to speak.

'Ladies and gentlemen, as most of you know my parties always involve a little game. Tonight's game is very simple, but I think it will prove amusing. After each girl has been spanked she will have the right to choose who goes next, and who does the spanking. But to ensure that everybody gets a fair share nobody can be chosen twice for the spanker. Any girl may decline, but only if she is prepared to take six of the cane from my dear wife. Once she has been caned she is out of the game. We finish when everybody present has dished out a spanking or been eliminated, and the winner is the girl to be chosen most often. Who receives a bonus of five hundred pounds for the evening. Is that clear?'

It was clear to me, and might have sounded simple, but I could tell it had been carefully thought out and probably by Mel. Kay was whispering urgently into Amber's ear and I knew that if any man, but for one or two particular friends, was chosen to spank her she would decline. With thirty-nine men and just eight girls, or nine if Mrs Hegedus was included, which didn't seem likely, Kay was going to end up being caned by Melody. I could just imagine how Amber would feel about that, but it was nothing to what would happen to her, because when I chose her she'd have a straight choice, to go over Mr Protheroe's knee or to be caned, and either way it would be in front of Kay.

Morris had dealt with a couple of questions,

establishing that all girls were expected to go bare bottom; that no spanking could exceed five minutes in length and that men could take it if they preferred, but would still be eliminated.

'Is that everything?' he continued. 'Good. Our popular manager, Mr Hegedus, had to spank little Jemima at lunchtime, so that will count as our opening sally, which leaves Jemima with the chance to choose the next victim. Jemima.'

I stepped forward, curtsied and turned to Morris.

'Thank you, Mr Rathwell. OK, the first girl to be spanked will be …'

I paused, grinning as my eyes flicked across the seven young women I could choose between. Some looked keen, others worried, but only one knew that nobody would dare put her forward to have her bottom smacked, or so she thought.

'Melody Rathwell,' I announced.

There was an immediate susurration of noise; gasps, whispers, giggles. Melody made to speak, her eyes blazing as they met mine, but there was no doubt at all that I had the right to choose her. The next question was who should do it; perhaps Mr Protheroe, the fate she had intended for Amber. Or I could do it myself if I dared, but there was really only one choice.

'To be spanked,' I began. 'By … Miss Amber Oakley.'

Amber had been looking fairly fed up until I'd nominated Melody, then hopeful, and now her face lit up in delight. She stood up, smiling as she addressed me. 'Thank you, Jemima. And may I just say that you could not have made a more appropriate choice, because if there is one person in this room who really, really deserves a smacked bottom it is Mel. Come along, Melody, over my knee.'

Her voice was firm, full of authority, but also of sadistic glee. She stepped forward and pulled out a chair from under one of the tables, positioning it in an open space to ensure that everybody got a good view. Melody was struggling not to pout as she too came forward, and as she reached Amber she threw me another filthy glance and mouthed two words: *you wait*. I gave her a cheeky wave. Now I was really going to get it, not playfully, but properly, which was exactly what I wanted. Meanwhile, I could enjoy the show.

Amber had sat down on the chair, her knees extended, her body straight, her expression stern; creating an image of dominant womanhood, spoilt only slightly by the way her mouth kept flickering into an impish smile. She looked Melody up and down, then nodded in approval.

'You look very pretty, Melody,' she said. 'And I see you came ready for a spanking, which was sensible. You don't have anything on under that dress, do you?'

Tight-lipped with fury, Mel shook her head, then mumbled something about her panty line. Amber's eyebrows rose a fraction and her voice was loud and clear as she spoke. 'You were worried the men might see the outline of your panties in such a tight dress? I'm afraid they're going to see a lot more than that. Hands on your head, and let's have that dress up.'

Melody hesitated; made to say something but thought better of it. Her hands went to her head, very slowly. Amber nodded. 'Good girl. After all, Morris did say bare-bottom, didn't he? What did Morris say?'

'He ... he said all girls had to go bare-bottom.'

'Yes, he did, didn't he?'

As Amber spoke she had leant forward, to take hold of the hem of Melody's dress and tug it up. She was magnificent: her thighs long and muscular, her bottom full and heavy, the dark cheeks tucked well under and spreading from a tight waist that exaggerated how big she was.

'Very pretty,' Amber remarked as she reached out to stroke the curve of Melody's bottom and weigh one heavy cheek in her hand, 'firm too. You should be spanked more often, Mel. A lovely bottom like yours needs to be given plenty of air, and plenty of attention.'

She gave the cheek she'd been fondling a gentle pat, then sat back, now smiling openly. Melody did her best to look calm and composed, but one leg had begun to tremble slightly and I could just imagine what was going on in her head. Amber was taking her time and I wondered if she was trying to make Melody break and ask for it, but then she spoke again. 'In fact, you have a beautiful figure in every way, so it would be a shame not to give all these gentlemen the full benefit, wouldn't it? I don't suppose most of them have even seen your breasts, have they?'

I saw Melody swallow and shut her eyes for a moment as she realised what was about to be done to her, but she stayed as she was. Amber reached up for Melody's breasts, cupping one plump scarlet globe in each hand, giving a gentle squeeze, then abruptly tugging down the silk to spill them out – fat and black and heavy, the nipples stiff in erection. My tummy went tight as I remembered how strong she'd seemed as she fed me at the teat, but it was very different now; her naked breasts merely an added humiliation for a girl about to be spanked.

'Beautiful,' Amber remarked. 'A picture or two perhaps, Morris? Come on, if it was me you'd have the video camera out.'

Morris had hesitated, but then took out his camera,

earning himself a furious glare from his wife as she was made to wait, everything on show, and then photographed.

'And while she's being spanked,' Amber instructed. 'Face and bum, so you can make one of those diptychs where you get to see the girl's rear view side by side with her expression. Right then, over you go, darling.'

She patted her lap, now grinning like some mad she-devil as Melody lowered herself into position; bare bottom lifted at one end and heavy black breasts swinging free at the other. Amber took a firm grip on Melody's waist, then applied a sharp swat to the inside of each thigh. 'Come on, you always say a spanked girl shouldn't be allowed any modesty, let's have that fanny showing.'

Melody was biting her lip in fury, but allowed her thighs to be smacked apart, showing off the full, pouted rear lips of her sex. Her bottom was too plump to let us see her bumhole properly, but I was sure that was another indignity Amber would inflict before she was finished. Already she'd began to caress Melody's bottom, in no hurry whatsoever, only for Morris to speak up. 'Five minutes only, remember.'

'From when?' Amber demanded. 'From bare or from going over the knee?'

'Bare,' Morris responded. 'You have two minutes left.'

'You didn't say ...' Amber began, then changed her tack. 'OK, you sneaky old sod, have it your way. Hairbrush please, Kay.'

'Hey, no!' Melody squeaked, creating a ripple of laughter and excited comment to see her nerve break.

Kay had dipped into Amber's handbag, to pull out a long handled, wooden hairbrush, much like mine and something no spanking enthusiast should be without. Melody swore under her breath, her lips pursed hard in determination, struggling to remain cool as Amber held her with the brush lifted to strike, and then she broke.

'Get on with it, you bitch!'

'With pleasure,' Amber replied and brought the hairbrush down across Melody's cheeks.

I'd never witnessed such a thorough, no-nonsense spanking, except maybe the first time I got it from Pippa, and then all I'd been able to see was a small square of carpet. Now I had the perfect view: Melody's face full of shock and consternation as the hairbrush went up and down on her bottom, which was flaunted to the room, high and round and proud, only not so very proud after about fifty hard smacks had been applied and she gave in to the pain. I'd have been screaming with the first smack, and I was amazed how long she stood it, but when she gave in, it was as if all her pent up emotions had come out at once.

One moment she was silent and absolutely still across Amber's lap, her fingers and toes braced on the carpet, and the next she was squealing like a baby, begging for mercy and thumping her fists on the floor in an agony of frustration and pain, with her legs pumping wildly up and down and her bottom bucking high to the smacks so we all got a good view of the puckered black hole between her cheeks.

The audience had been watching in quiet appreciation, with only the occasional murmured remark on how she looked and the way the spanking was being done, but they now began to clap and cheer, egging Amber on to do it harder and laughing over Melody's plight. One old boy even had his cock out, with Harmony sitting on his lap, idly playing with it as she watched her sister beaten. We could all see that the spanking was getting to Melody in the right way too, because for all her protests, all her fury, her pussy was wet and open, glistening pink flesh showing between her full sex lips, which had been closed when she'd first been put over the knee. Finally Morris called out the two minutes. Amber gave Melody's bottom one last hard swat and it was over.

It was also Melody's turn to choose the next girl and my tummy had gone tight with apprehension at the thought of what I was surely going to get. As she climbed off Amber's knee she was shaking badly, and she took a moment to recover herself, but turned to me even as she adjusted her dress. 'Right, you little brat, Jemima, you're next, and in private!'

'In private?' I asked, surprised and suddenly more scared than needy. 'But Mel ... ouch! Mel!'

She got me by the ear, pinching hard between finger and thumb. 'In private,' she repeated. 'But don't worry, I'll bring her back, eventually.'

'Ow! Mel ... no. Morris, help!' I babbled as I was dragged across the room and towards the door.

Not one person moved to help me; most of them were laughing and the only protests raised because I wasn't going to be done in front of them. I didn't know why not either, except that it definitely wouldn't be to spare my modesty, and I was begging to be taken back all the way to her room. It was the Honeymoon Suite, in the middle of the first floor with a huge four-poster bed occupying most of the main room and a bay window looking out over a sparkling blue sea dotted with the coloured triangles of dinghies out from a local club.

I wasn't given time to admire the view, but thrown over her knee with the door still wide open to the passage, my skirts flipped up and my froufrous dropped before I'd so much as caught my breath. She laid in, spanking hard, but only by hand and I was already warm. It hurt, but I couldn't stop giggling, which only made her angry.

'So it's funny is it?' she snapped. 'Come in, Mr Morozov.'

As she spoke I twisted violently around, to find the Russian who'd earned me my first spanking in the open doorway, his harsh face twisted into a smirk of amusement. I struggled to rise, but Melody held me firmly in place as she went on.

'Oh no you don't, Jemima. Shut the door please, Mr Morozov, and pass me Morris's toy bag, if you would. The long black one by the dressing table.'

I went limp, surrendered to my fate as he did as she had asked. She thanked him, keep a firm grip on my waist as she rummaged in the bag, finally pulling out an American style spanking paddle. 'This ought to do the trick.'

I'd had one used on me before, by Hudson and others, and I'd began to sob as she patted it across me cheeks, but she just began to rub it on me, still talking.

'Right, Mr Morozov, as you're here, sit down next to me and pop your cock in her mouth. Jemima, you'd better suck, and suck well, because the spanking doesn't stop until he's come. Do it in her face please, Mr Morozov.'

He didn't hesitate for a moment. Melody took hold of my hair and pulled me sharply upright, allowing him to sit down on the bed, his hip pressed to hers, his crotch directly under my face. I couldn't have escaped if I'd wanted to, with her hand twisted tight in my hair as he lay back and unzipped, flopping out a long, pale cock and a good size pair of balls. Melody pushed my head into his lap, rubbing my face on his genitals until I managed to get my mouth open around him. He sighed as I began to suck, only for his cock to shoot out of my mouth as the paddle landed across my bum.

'Ow! Mel!'

'Suck him, you little bitch!'

My head was forced back down, Mr Morozov's cock fed into my mouth and another swat applied to my bum. I couldn't take it; the pain was far too bad to let me concentrate on cock sucking, but Melody had my head pushed down onto him and he was pumping into my mouth, his erection already growing. What I could or couldn't do no longer mattered; my bottom was beaten so hard I was utterly out of control right from the beginning, and my mouth just used to fuck into, with my body writhing and my spittle splashing out around his shaft with every agonising smack.

I couldn't even think straight, and they were really cruel about it; Melody laying into my bottom and Mr Morozov fucking my mouth; both of them enjoying my pain and my helpless wriggling. He gripped my hair, allowing her to take me around my waist, more helpless still as the beating grew harder and his cock stiffened to full erection. Soon his knob was pushing down my throat with every thrust, making me gag and blow snot bubbles from my nose as I struggled to breathe. And still the paddle smacked down on my bottom, over and over again, until I thought I would pass out, only for him to spunk, completely unexpectedly.

It went down my throat, then exploded from my nose as I started to retch, all over his balls and his trousers too. He called me a dirty slut, which seemed so unfair, jerked my head up and pushed my face into the mess, rubbing it well to smear me with spunk and snot before putting me back on his cock and holding me in place until I was forced to swallow what was left in my mouth. Finally he pulled me up by my hair and twisted my head around to show Melody the state of my face.

'I'm done,' he announced.

'Well I'm not,' Melody answered and carried on with my paddling, ignoring my yelps and wails of protest.

Mr Morozov was laughing at me as my beating continued, and congratulating Melody on taking a firm line. She didn't answer, concentrating on my bottom, which I'd begun to stick up as my arousal finally began to get through, only for her to suddenly stop and throw the paddle to one side. 'Sod this,' she snapped, 'she's too into it.'

She let go and stood up in one motion, tumbling me off her lap and onto the floor, where I landed with a bump and a squeak of alarm. Her hand closed in my hair and I was forced to scramble over onto my knees, or get dragged, as she made for the bathroom. My froufrous were around my knees, leaving me shuffling along as best I could with my blazing bottom on full show to Mr Morozov, who seemed to find the whole thing hilarious.

'Come and watch,' Melody invited him and as she pushed open the bathroom door, dragging me in behind her. 'This is what I do two-faced little bitches.'

I thought my head was going down the toilet, but she rolled me over onto by back, straddling me so that I could see her pussy and the turn of her full, dark cheeks up inside her dress. He'd followed, to stand in the doorway, calm and amused, his cock and balls still wet with my spittle and snot where they hung out of his trousers. I'd already realised I was going to have my face sat on, maybe worse, and was having trouble not sticking out my tongue in anticipation.

'Open your mouth, Jemima,' Melody ordered.

I obeyed, gaping wide as she tugged up her dress, once more exposing the full glory of her heavy black bottom, so full and womanly, perfect to go onto my face for a good lick. No longer able to resist my feelings, I stuck my tongue out and let my thighs come open, slipping my fingers between so that I could masturbate in front of Mr Morozov while I licked Melody's bottom.

'You're a natural-born slut, Jemima,' she told me as she moved forward to set her boots either side of my head. 'But let's see if you can get off over this.'

My fingers were already busy with my clit and I'd guessed she was going to put her bum in my face and not her pussy, so I stuck my tongue out further still. She smiled and began to squat down, lowering herself over my face with her cheeks opening to show off the tight black knot of her bumhole. I wanted to lick it, badly, tonguing her bottom while I frigged myself off, and with a man watching. It was perfect; the ideal punishment for what I'd done and it was going to be so much more exciting because I deserved it, just as I'd deserved my paddling and being made to suck on Mr Morozov's cock, and have my face soiled with spunk.

'Keep it wide, Jemima,' Melody order as she settled her weight onto me, trapping me helpless on the floor with her big, black bum right in my face.

I didn't need telling, craning up to dab at her anus, pushing my tongue into the moist pink star that showed at the very centre, my mouth just as wide as she could possibly have wanted it to be. Mr Morozov had come around so that he could see, his patrician face full of amused contempt as he watched me lick Melody's bumhole and rub at myself. I'd never felt so dirty, making a complete slut of myself, on purpose, and I was already near to orgasm, the muscles of my bottom and thighs tightening as I focussed on how she'd beaten me and then made me lick.

'Keep it wide, Jemima,' she repeated, and lifted up a

little to show me her pussy.

She was open and wet, the pink flesh showing clearly between her dark lips, her clit ready for my tongue. My back had already began to arch in orgasm, and I wanted to lick her bottom while I came so badly that I was babbling as I struggled to lift my face and get my tongue back in her bumhole.

'Please, Mel ... in my face ... sit on my face and I'll lick you ... make me, Mel, give me what I deserve!'

'This is what you deserve.'

I saw the set of her muscles change and realised what she was going to do, but I couldn't stop myself, rubbing furiously at my slippery cunt with my jaws gaping wide to take in what she wanted to give me. Her pussy erupted, a thick stream of pale golden pee, aimed full into my mouth. I let it happen, deliberately, my mouth quickly filling up, with her pee gurgling in my throat and splashing over my face as my body began to jerk in orgasm. Soon it was more than I could take, and had begun to slop over the sides of my lips, soiling my hair and my neck, and at the very peak of my orgasm she sat down, full in my face.

I couldn't help myself. My tongue went back up her bumhole, licking eagerly as I continued to rub, driving myself to orgasm after orgasm. She too had her fingers between her legs, rubbing her bottom in my face as she masturbated to the feel of my face between her cheeks and my tongue up her bottom hole. I had to swallow, I couldn't help it, and with that I came again, so hard it hurt and left me weak, but still licking until she too had come. Even then I didn't stop. I'd swallowed what she'd done in my mouth, leaving my belly full of her pee. And I had to come a third time just for that, never mind everything else she had done to me.

She understood, no longer vindictive, but content that I had been thoroughly punished as she squatted forward, allowing me to admire her beautiful bottom, so big and dark and powerful; with the tight little hole that I'd had my tongue up, now open and pink between her cheeks and her pussy wet. Again she let go, completely this time, in my mouth and all over my chest, her piddle splashing on my tits where they'd popped out of my maid's uniform during my spanking. I lay there, my mouth loaded to the brim, masturbating, my back arching in ecstasy one more time as she deliberately soiled me. And as I cried out her name she sat down in my face again, smothering me between her cheeks and staying as she was until my body had finally stopped jerking and my fingers had gone limp on my aching pussy.

It wasn't going to be such a bad summer after all.

Chapter Five

THE NEXT WEEK WAS completely routine, and it was just as well. By the end of the party my bottom had been one huge bruise and definitely unfit for further attention, although the dull ache served to keep me firmly in mind of what had been done to me. I would masturbate late at night, lying on my tummy with the sheets pulled down as I thought back to the party, and when I came there would always be one of three people at the front of my thoughts: Lucius Todmorden, Mr Morozov or Melody. Lucius had been nice, giving me a cuddle and a spanking at the same time, which was just what I'd needed. I'd gone to him later, in his room, and sucked his cock before bed so he'd cuddle me without groping too much, which had been the perfect end to the night. Mr Morozov had been the exact opposite; cold and callous, openly enjoying my pain and humiliation, but while he scared me, he excited me too. Then there was Melody and the way she'd punished me, which made me shudder just to think about it; and I came over the memory of lying on the bathroom floor with her big black bottom poised while she filled my mouth more often than anything else.

It had also been a good night's work. I'd won the prize for most spanked girl, despite being upstairs with Melody and Mr Morozov for so long, and Melody kept her word about paying me extra for keeping Mr Morozov happy.

When I got my weekly envelope there was so much in it I thought they must have made a mistake. Not that I was going to tell anybody, but for the next few days I kept expecting Mr Hegedus to ask for some of it back. He hadn't, so far, and I eventually banked most of it on my afternoon off, which meant I could walk up to the main road and take a bus into Eastbourne.

The party had even helped me to cope with being a maid, because I no longer looked at the work as a tedious and badly paid job, but as a very drawn out erotic game, so that my low status and vulnerability to men became exciting. Not that I got abused by the ordinary guests, but Mr Hegedus would take advantage occasionally, patting my bottom or pretending to adjust my uniform so that he could feel me up. Yet when it mattered, I was in control, so that when his wife was out and he told me I was overdue a spanking I simply pointed out that I was still too tender. I knew I'd get it in the end, and that denying him would mean he would make it harder and more humiliating, but that was part of the fun.

By the end of the second week after the party I was beginning to feel needy again, and wondering how to go about getting a proper punishment. That mattered, after what Melody had done, although there was nobody at the hotel I'd have allowed to do the same. A good spanking in front of the other staff seemed to be the best I could hope for and that only if Mr Hegedus could find himself an excuse; because I'd worked out that his wife would only let him do it if there was good reason, such as kicking off a party under Morris's instructions. I was also wondering if she might do it herself, because her rough manner and sheer bulk carried a horrid fascination, making it all too easy to imagine myself squealing and kicking over her knee.

On the Sunday morning I deliberately dropped a tray of dirty plates and bowls, smashing two and making a mess of milk and cereal on the restaurant floor, right in front of her. The room was full of guests, but I could imagine her taking me up to my chalet for a sound spanking where they wouldn't hear. At least, that was what I was angling for, but all I got was a sharp telling off before being made to clean up the mess. Scrubbing the floor on my hands and knees in front of all the guests while she stood over me with her hands on her hips left me feeling submissive and in need of more, but there was none to be had.

I spent the rest of the morning working, and just being in my uniform and doing menial tasks was getting to me. I hoped Mr Hegedus would catch me and deal with me then and there. Unfortunately he seemed to have disappeared, but when I went out into the yards to throw away the rubbish I'd collected from the rooms I found Stefan. He was smoking a solitary cigarette, seated on a damaged chair we'd thrown out. Mrs Hegedus was in the kitchen, but all I had to do was shut the back door and we were alone. I knew he'd enjoyed the party and was no innocent, but it still took me ten minutes of flirting before I could pop the question. 'You spanked Annabelle at the party, didn't you? I bet it was fun. Would you like to spank me?'

My cheeks were hot for my own boldness, but he played it cool, looking me up and down with his face set in an expression of amusement, even disdain. I broke before he answered, starting to babble. 'Don't you think it would be a good idea? I mean, you're supposed to be in charge of me, and so, you should discipline me, maybe? I'd like that, Stefan.'

Still he failed to answer, now openly amused by the

state I'd got myself into.

'Well? Please, Stefan, you're not being very fair! You'd love to spank me, wouldn't you?'

At last he answered. 'Vilmos said you were a slut. Come on then, over my knee, and when I've warmed your bottom you can suck my cock.'

There was no passion in his voice, just humour, as if my urgent need for a spanking was funny and that I should come to him inevitable. I went down anyway, trying to make the most of my resentment and humiliation as I got into place across his knee. He tucked up my uniform skirt and took down my knickers without preamble, again as if stripping a young woman's bottom for spanking was merely a casual amusement. For me it was anything but casual, and I was already trembling as I lifted my hips. He began to spank, clumsily, slapping me hard across my cheeks to make me gasp and kick at the sudden pain.

'Have you been a naughty girl then?' he asked, and his voice was thick with contempt.

I didn't answer, but for a choking sob for the humiliation of being spanked by a man who was only doing it because he thought it was funny and it meant he'd get his cock sucked. To him I was just a little pervert, a little English pervert who needed her bottom smacked to get off, so unlike him with his simple, masculine needs.

'Enough,' he said suddenly and it had stopped. 'Get down on my cock.'

'You've hardly started!' I protested.

'You girls take for ever. I want my cock sucked first. Then I'll finish you off.'

'You're a bastard, do you know that?' I told him, but he was already moving me down onto my knees.

70

I went, kneeling on the dirty concrete of the yard with my bare red bottom sticking out behind as he unzipped. He was already half stiff, so he obviously hadn't been completely indifferent to having my bare bottom to smack, with a small pink cock head sticking out from a thick foreskin. I took him in, sucking quite eagerly despite my ill feelings for the way he was treating me, or maybe because of them.

He was soon hard, and I was wondering if it might be nice to masturbate while I sucked. It was nice to be bare-bottom at his feet with his cock in my mouth, even if I would have preferred a proper spanking first, but there was going to be no difficulty coming over a combination of his cock and his callous attitude. I began to suck harder, the temptation to slip my hand between my thighs rising rapidly.

'Vilmos is right, you are a slut,' he drawled. 'And a fucking good cock-sucker. Plenty of practice, I expect?'

I was going to answer, but he caught me by my ponytail and began to wank into my mouth, with just my lips pursed around his knob. 'Suck it,' he demanded. 'I'm going to spunk in your face.'

I shook my head urgently, not because I didn't want it, but because I would either have to clean up at the tap in the yard and risk getting my uniform wet, or run back through the kitchen and past Mrs Hegedus with my face dripping spunk. He just laughed and tightened his grip, forcing me to attend to his knob as he tugged furiously at his shaft. I jerked back, determined to make him let me swallow.

It was exactly the wrong thing to do. His cock erupted at the instant it left my mouth, catching me full in the face with a long, thick streamer of spunk. Most of it went in my eye and I was immediately snatching at my face, only to get the second spurt in my hair and down my ear. The third went over my lips and into my mouth as he tightened his grip and shoved his cock back in, still wanking, only to let go and pull my head down hard, jamming his erection down my throat as he finished off.

'Filthy!' he grunted.

My eyes were popping before he let go, and I was almost sick on his cock, but managed to swallow it and came up gasping. He'd soiled my face and hair, filled my mouth with spunk, and I needed to get it out of my eye before I could even think about anything else, except calling him every name I could think off. He just laughed, and harder still as I took off my panties, the only piece of clean cloth I could find, to wipe my eye.

'You're a pig, Stefan!'

'You are the pig, Jemima, with your little round pink arse and your upturned nose, a pig who needs a spanking to get her kicks. That is you, Jemima.'

I was trying to get at a piece of spunk right in the corner of my eye and didn't answer. He watched, now smirking, then spoke again as I finished cleaning up. 'Now wipe my cock.'

'Do it yourself!' I snapped and threw my soiled panties at him.

They went in his face, which was funny, but he didn't seem to care, sniffing the crotch before finding a clean bit to wipe himself.

'Your cunt smells strong,' he said. 'I like a horny girl. Back over my knee then, and I'll give you what you need.'

I almost told him to fuck off, but my bum was hot and my mouth full of the taste of cock, while there was no denying he'd got to me.

'OK, but …' I began, and stopped as the kitchen door

72

swung open.

I thought we were about to be caught by Mrs Hegedus, so when I saw Penny my first reaction was relief, followed by blazing embarrassment. Stefan had my panties wrapped around his cock and my skirt was still up at the back, so that it looked as if he'd been wanking in them while I showed off my bum, making her blush and stammer an apology before disappearing rapidly back inside.

'Who was that?' he demanded.

'My aunt,' I told him. 'Look, I'd better go.'

He shrugged.

'Another time then.'

Determined not to give him the satisfaction of knowing how badly he'd got to me, although he seemed to have a fair idea anyway, I didn't answer. A hasty adjustment to my skirt and I followed, ignoring a highly suspicious look from Mrs Hegedus as I ran through the kitchen. I caught up with Penny in reception, where she took one look at me and began to dig in her handbag.

'Honestly, Jemima,' she said, shaking her head in despair as she began to dab at my face with a tissue.

'I thought I'd cleaned up,' I told her, trying not to sound sulky and failing miserably.

'It's in your hair! Where's your room?'

I took her, walking around the front of the hotel to avoid the main areas, only to find several guests sitting outside where we had some tables overlooking the sea.

'So is he your new boyfriend?' she asked as we reached the chalets.

'No,' I admitted. 'That's Stefan, the head waiter.'

She gave a little sigh but left it at that, changing the topic of conversation.

'I spoke to your mum. She seems happy. I'm sorry

about … what happened.'

'Thanks,' I answered, suddenly on the verge of tears.

She saw and quickly changed tack once again. 'I thought you might like to go out for lunch?'

'I'm supposed to be working. Wednesday's my day off.'

'Perhaps if I speak to the manager?'

'He's not here at the moment, and I know his wife wouldn't let me off.'

We'd reached my chalet and we spent a few minutes tidying up. She seemed preoccupied, and I was sure she'd heard about the party, and would disapprove, even though she sometimes went herself. Sure enough, the moment I was ready she told me she had something to talk to me about and suggested we walk up to the downs.

'What about my work?' I queried.

'I'm sure they can spare you for ten minutes,' she answered. 'And anyway, I'd far rather you came back with me.'

'What about my job?'

'Never mind your job. You can stay with me, and I'm sure we can find you something better nearby, something where you won't be risking your entire future.'

'You know about the party then?'

'Yes, Amber told me, and I know that Morris owns the hotel, and that there were a lot of new men here. We've talked about this before, Jemima. It's bad enough you attending parties at Morris's house, but at least they're discreet …'

'You go as well, and you spank me. Don't be a hypocrite.'

'Not often, and there's one big difference: I don't get paid.'

'What, nothing?'

74

'Yes, nothing. But that's not important, because if we did get exposed they'd all assume I got paid anyway and I couldn't really prove otherwise. What matters is that the papers would paint you as a prostitute.'

'What's wrong with that?'

'Please be sensible, Jemima. It's not about right and wrong, it's about how people react. The tabloids will always print whatever they think will sell the most papers. They're not interested in morality. They only pretend to be because it allows them to sound shocked, and they're definitely not interested in presenting a balanced viewpoint. Sales are all important to them, and that means presenting everything in the worst possible light, purely for the sake of sensation. They're sure to go for you as well. You're young, you're photogenic, you're from a privileged background, the ideal person to incite lust and envy in their readership, unless you were a celebrity that is, in which case they'd have a field day.'

I knew she was right, but she shouldn't have been. All I'd done was enjoy myself and make a lot of men very happy, and if society was going to judge that as wrong then it was society that needed to change its ways. It wasn't my fault anyway.

'Yeah, yeah, yeah,' I answered, avoiding the issue. 'Anyway, Morris looks after his girls.'

Penny drew a heavy sigh.

'Look, Jemima, don't put too much faith in Morris Rathwell. Yes, he does look after his girls, and that's the problem. If everything went horribly wrong, do you think he would look after you?'

'Yes, he would,' I told her, and to my surprise she agreed.

'Exactly, and that is want he wants, for you to be dependent on him, to be one of his girls. You've met

Annabelle, haven't you? She used to have a successful career.'

'She's where she wants to be.'

'Do you want to be in the same place, with a ring through your sex lips for their lead and a tattoo on your belly marking you as their property?'

'Maybe,' I answered, but I couldn't keep the sulky tone out of my voice.

'Morris is a dominant man,' she went on. 'He does have morals, but they're not conventional ones. If you're his girl he'll look after you, but he'd cheerfully wreck your career to get you. He's a sexist too, because he very definitely believes a woman's place is in the home. Even Melody.'

She'd sat down on the bank where the trees ended and paused to touch a tiny yellow flower where it poked up among the short grass; not to pick it but simply to admire the petals, then went on. 'Maybe that's really what you want, and it's not my place to stop you, but I do think you should slow down a bit. You're taking a terrible risk, with university, with your career, your whole life. At the very least you should be careful until after university. Morris is wealthy, he doesn't have to worry any more. If he gets exposed he can laugh it off, but you can't. Another thing, you can be very sure he's set up the hotel so that he doesn't have to take the consequences. For all I know he's planning the whole thing on the assumption that it will get exposed and closed down, and you ending up as his new plaything is part of the scheme. I wouldn't put it past him.'

'I suppose so, maybe ... I got sent here because Danielle convinced my dad I should work during my year off. Mr Hegedus is Danielle's uncle, and I think Morris told him to take me on.'

76

'That wouldn't surprise me in the slightest. So is there a connection between Danielle and Morris?'

'I don't know. I wish I did. I think maybe she gets spanked, or even goes to Morris's parties.'

'Not that I know of, but I hardly ever go myself. What makes you think that, anyway?'

'She ... she spanked me,' I admitted. 'And believe me, she knew what she was doing. She even threatened to do it in front of Summer!'

Penny winced, clearly understanding how I'd felt, which made it so much easier to go on as I sat down beside her.

'And she was tormenting me over having my knickers pulled down, and she knew it was making me horny, and she was playing with my bum. She's done it before, and probably been given it too.'

She reached out to give my hand a squeeze, encouraging me to continue.

'And she knows Morris, because she used to be Dad's secretary and they've worked together. I'd tell Dad if it didn't mean giving myself away about the spanking parties and stuff. Maybe ... you would? I mean, do it for me?'

She looked horrified. 'I can't do that, Jemima.'

'Why not?'

'Because it's immoral, that's why not, and also hypocritical. You and I enjoy being spanked, why shouldn't Danielle?'

'Yes, but she pretends she's so innocent, and she was a real bitch about it!'

'That's not the point, and anyway, who's to say your dad doesn't know?'

I made a face. It wasn't something I liked to think about, but I could just imagine the embarrassment of

Penny telling Dad about Danielle only to find out he did it with her and had known all along. And, far worse, if Danielle guessed I was behind it and told him about me.

'Maybe you're right,' I admitted.

She didn't reply for a long time, biting her lip and staring out to sea, only to suck her breath in and start talking again.

'It's not easy to say this, Jemima, but I think it might be for the best to accept what's happened between your parents. Kate's happier than she's been in a long time, and ...'

'I can't just let that bitch Danielle take over!'

'Maybe it would be best to make up with Danielle?'

'No way!'

She went silent, standing once more and starting to walk slowly up the hill. I followed, knowing she hadn't given up and determined to change the subject.

'Did Amber tell you that I set Mel up for a spanking from her?'

Penny laughed. 'Yes. That the first thing she told me when she rang.'

'Mel got me back though. She paddled me so hard I was bruised for over a week, and she made me give this Russian guy a blow job while she did me, and ... and something worse.'

'I can imagine. I know what Mel's like.'

I managed a shy grin, not willing to admit just now utterly Mel had humiliated me, or how much I'd enjoyed it. We carried on walking in silence, each alone with our own thoughts, up along the gently winding chalk track beside the cliff to where we could look back over the valley. The hotel and chalets seemed like a toy village, very small against the green, and I could see into the yard where Stefan had spanked me and made me suck him off.

'I ... I wasn't posing for him,' I said, suddenly eager to explain. 'I was trying to get a decent spanking and ... and it all got a bit out of hand.'

'Doesn't Mr Hegedus spank you? I know he goes to Morris's parties.'

'Only once. His wife doesn't like him paying too much attention to me unless it's a game or something at a party.'

'What about her? She looks terrifying.'

'I don't think she's interested.'

'No? That's a pity. So ... did you get it?'

'Only a few smacks, then he wanted his blowjob. He's no good at it anyway. It's not his thing.'

She didn't answer, but I could tell what she was thinking. It had been a while since she'd done me, before my last term, and it's always hard to pick up where you left off, even when you've been so intimate.

'You can ... if you want?' I offered, and was surprised at the yearning in my voice.

She just nodded and took my hand, leading me away from the cliff towards where a straggle of thorn trees had grown up, twisted by the wind. It wasn't the best place, but the down was empty but for a couple far ahead of us and walking in the opposite direction. We'd soon found a place, where an old rabbit burrow had collapsed to leave a little hollow of chalky earth with a lip just the right height to sit down on. I'd put on new knickers in the chalet and was going to wriggle out of them to make it easier for her, but she shook a finger at me. 'Uh, uh, it's best if I do that. Come here. Stand in front of me and put your hands on your head.'

I obeyed, melting into the familiar routine as she tucked up my skirt and pulled down my knickers, leaving me showing at back and front with the air cool on my bum cheeks and tummy. She leant forward a little to kiss my pussy. Turned me around and did the same to my cheeks. Then took me gently down into position across her knee. I closed my eyes, all my bad feelings already melting away as her hand settled on my bottom. She began to spank me, gently, so very different to the way Stefan had done it. Where he had swatted crudely at my cheeks, she was an artist, patting and rubbing, making sure no part of my bottom was spared and increasing the strength of her smacks only gradually.

It never hurt, my bottom warming to the point at which I was pushing it up for more, long before she'd started to use any real force. Even then she kept her pace steady, bringing me gradually higher until my glowing cheeks and the heat in my pussy had become the focus of my existence. Only then did she swap hands, slipping one between my thighs to cup my pussy and using the other to spank and to touch, pinching me and tickling my bumhole until I was wriggling with excitement and sobbing with pleasure.

She never said a word, concentrating on my bottom and pussy until at last her careful touches tipped me over the edge. I felt my orgasm building up, wave after wave of pleasure to the same rhythm as the smacks on my bottom and the rubbing of her fingers on my clit, faster, and faster still, finally exploding in my head so hard it made every muscle in my body lock tight and force a scream of ecstasy from my lips. And in that instant, nothing else seemed to matter but being over my auntie's knee with my bottom well smacked, followed by the sense of blissful wellbeing as I came down, purring with satisfaction and completely happy.

I stayed in that position for ages, until she finally eased me upright and into her arms, holding me as I sat straddled across her knees, still bare-bottomed as we hugged and kissed. When her tongue pushed at my lips I let it happen, telling myself it was no worse than letting her spank me or lick her pussy. But with our mouths open together and our tongues entwined I felt I'd revived the intimacy that had grown up between us in America.

Chapter Six

PENNY'S VISIT LEFT ME feeling a lot happier about myself but a lot less sure about what I was doing. She'd repeated her offer for me to come and live with her, and I could see the sense in her argument. On the other hand I was enjoying being a maid, especially the prospect of lots of money and lots of male attention, female too. She was still there when Morris rang to say that Mr Morozov wanted a one-to-one with me and was prepared to pay handsomely. I couldn't resist the offer and accepted, but the look on Penny's face left me burning with guilt. She'd never been able to accept the idea of sex for money, which always seems to me to be just like any other service, so it was no use trying to explain. Knowing what I'd be doing that evening didn't make her kiss any less warm when she said goodbye either, but she did try to persuade me to come with her. I declined but promised to think about it, but even the lump in my throat as I watched her little red car disappear up the drive wasn't enough to change my mind.

Mr Morozov was due at six and I was to be his personal maid for the evening, dressed in my kinky uniform and serving in the Honeymoon Suite. I knew more or less what to expect, but he had been very cruel with me, taking no nonsense when I was on his cock and utterly indifferent to my plight both while Mel was paddling me and afterwards in the bathroom. That was frightening, because until I'd lost control and stuck my hand between my legs, he couldn't have known I was enjoying myself. Also, Morris had told me only to use my stop word if I felt I had no choice, and that my pay would depend on my performance.

Mr Hegedus knew what was going on and I could tell he was jealous, but it was his wife who was in charge, hustling me to get ready and making sure none of the ordinary guests saw me in my sexy uniform. She even took me up to the room, holding me by my arm as if she was sure I'd try and make a break for it, but the really scary moment came when we were inside the Honeymoon Suite. It was already immaculate, with flowers and a bowl of fruit set out, a bottle of champagne chilling in a wine bucket and two glasses beside it, making me wonder if he wanted to spank me or seduce me, until she spoke up. 'This won't be easy, Jemima, but you must do as you are told and everything will be OK. Make sure you are busy about the room when he comes in, and address him respectfully, as Mr Morozov, or sir. Now give me a hug.'

She folded me in her arms as she spoke, crushing me to her massive breasts until I was sure she was going to crack my ribs, then kissed me and let me go. I was sure she had a tear in one eye as she hurried from the room, and she'd never shown me any affection at all before that moment, so I was left wondering what Mr Morozov was going to do to me. After all, this was the woman who had watched her husband give me a public, bare-bottom spanking with contempt, and now she was behaving like an exceptionally emotional brothel madam giving a virgin to a client.

I still had a few minutes to wait, and spent them searching the room in case he had any sinister devices.

There was nothing more suspicious than a tube of lubricating jelly in the bathroom cupboard, but I found that more puzzling than reassuring, although I was sure there were plenty of things he could do with his hands and his cock. When I heard footsteps in the corridor outside I only just managed to get into position in time, standing by the door with my feet together and my hands behind my back. He came in, looked me up and down, then shrugged off the enormous fur coat he was wearing; not like the sort of thing you might expect to see in a fancy shop, but thick and shaggy.

'Brown bear,' he explained. 'I shot it myself. Hang it up.'

'Yes, Mr Morozov, sir,' I answered and hasten to obey.

'Good. Serve me champagne.'

He sat down in one of the armchairs, waiting patiently while I dealt with the coat, opened the bottle and poured a glass. I made an effort to bend properly, showing off my froufrous behind and what little cleavage I had, but he took no notice whatsoever, sniffing at the champagne and taking a reflective sip before addressing me again.

'I am told you are an obedient girl?'

'Yes, sir.'

'But you disobeyed Mrs Rathwell, why?'

I'd thought he was playing a game with me, and didn't expect to be asked anything more complicated than whether I liked it up the bum, so took a moment to reply.

'Um ... I wanted her to punish me ... to have something to really punish me for, that is ... sir.'

'And did you feel that her punishment was fair?'

'Yes, sir.'

'Truly?'

'Um ... no, obviously not. I mean, come on! Sorry, sir.'

He made a harsh sound from somewhere deep in his throat which might just possibly have been a laugh. 'But you accepted it?' he asked. 'Why?'

'It was what I wanted,' I told him. 'No, not that exactly, but for her to push my limits.'

'For her to push your limits. I see. And you enjoyed what she did?'

'Yes ... yes, sir.'

'But not just because it gave her pleasure?'

'Not just, no.'

'So you are not a natural slave?'

'No.'

'But you are a natural slut?'

Even with him about to use me for some peculiar kink the question gave me a jolt and there was a catch in my voice as I answered. 'Yes, I suppose so. Yes, sir.'

The hard line of his mouth flickered into what might have been a smile. 'Go to the bed. Climb on and place the bolster in the middle.'

'Yes, sir.'

I obeyed, making sure he got a good show of the seat of my froufrous and I crawled across the huge bed to pull the bolster out from beneath the covers. It was long, and so thick that once I was over it my bum would be stuck high in the air, the perfect position for a whipping, but as I put it in place he spoke again. 'Along the bed, not across. Now climb onto it.'

An expression I'd heard came to mind as I adjusted the bolster, "kissing the gunner's daughter", an old naval term for a whipping delivered with the victim straddling the barrel of a cannon. My tummy was fluttering badly for the thought of what I was about to get as I climbed onto the bolster, my knees well apart, my pussy spread onto the firm, rounded surface, my skirts puffed up at the rear to show off the seat of my froufrous.

'A little further back, until your cunt is sticking out over the end of the bolster.'

Again I obeyed, wriggling down the bed a little way to make myself available not just for whipping, but for fucking as well. I was wondering what he'd use, some vicious little whip maybe, or a riding crop, but there was no doubt in my mind what he was going to do: thrash me and fuck me doggy style with my hurt bottom showing to his cock.

He stood up, and pushed a hand into his jacket pocket to pull out a hank of coloured rope. Coming to the bed, he ordered me to stay still and began to tie me in place, attaching one trembling limb after another to the four solid posts until I was helpless, strapped in place with my arms stretched out and my legs wide open. I could kick and wriggle, which was probably something he would enjoy, but I had no way of protecting my bottom or of closing my legs.

With one swift movement he tugged my froufrous down as far as they'd go on my spread thighs, leaving my pussy agape and my bumhole showing. I turned my head, to find him watching me thoughtfully, his cruel mouth now twisted up to one side, his grey eyes fixed on my open bottom.

'A very pretty bottom. A very pretty cunt too. Yes, you will do very well. Are you naturally bald?'

'Yes, sir,' I lied, sure he'd prefer to think of my hairless pussy that way.

'A very pretty cunt,' he repeated. 'A picture, I think.'

'Like this?'

'Of course, why not?'

'Well, I … OK, but can I have copies please?'

He laughed, his icy reserve finally giving way at the

thought of me wanting images of my own humiliation and punishment.

'Yes, why not,' he said. 'It will be amusing for you to see, later.'

It seemed an odd way of putting things, but then he was Russian. I pulled my back in as he extracted a small digital camera from the pocket of his bear skin coat, sticking my bottom up to give him a good show. He took several pictures, including close-ups of my spread pussy, popped my tits out of my bodice and pinched my nipples to make them stiff, then took several more. When he finally put the camera down it was to pull the case off a pillow, which he put over my head and tied off behind my neck, leaving me unable to see. Again the camera began to click and my excitement and apprehension was rising fast as I thought of how I'd look, tied and hooded, mounted on the bolster with my hips stuck high, my uniform interfered with to leave my tits and bum and pussy flaunted and vulnerable.

I was scared too, of the pain of what I was sure would be a severe whipping, but I wanted it, and to be fucked. That was what I was going to get, for certain, because when he'd finally had enough of photographing me he went into the bathroom, and a moment later I felt the cold, slippery sensation of lubricating jelly as he squirted the contents of the tube all over my pussy and up my hole. I felt it go in, and squeeze out again, dribbling slowly down my sex and falling into my lowered froufrous, but there was still plenty left; enough to ease my passage for something a lot bigger than a man's cock, a thought which had me wriggling in my bonds.

He took a few more photographs, mainly of my lubed-up pussy, and then simply left the room, or at least pretended to leave the room. All I knew for certain was that he'd opened and closed the door, so I couldn't be sure that he wasn't standing behind me, perhaps with some vicious little implement in his hand, watching my cheeks twitch and my anus wink in rising fear, before finally lashing me across my naked, helpless bottom. Nothing happened. Gradually my feelings of panic and insecurity began to ebb, leaving me with an odd sense of peace, almost detachment.

His entry into my cunt was so sudden, so unexpected, that I didn't realise what he'd done to me at first. I felt a tongue between my cheeks, lapping at my bumhole; an instant later his weight was on my back, squashing me down onto the bolster as he thrust his cock deep up me. They must have heard my scream of shock downstairs, and I jerked backwards, but it was too late. His cock was already up me, right in, and it felt too good to resist, too dirty. I was helpless anyway, being fucked at a furious pace, his erection jamming in and out of my open, slippery hole so fast and hard it knocked the breath from my body; set me gasping and panting, my fingers clutching at the coverlet and my feet kicking in the ropes that held me so firmly in place.

I just took it, because I had no option; was fucked hard with his fur tickling my back and his belly slapping on my bottom. It felt weird too, not like a normal fuck, with his balls slapping on my open sex with every thrust, like having my pussy spanked, and the moment he'd got his rhythm I knew I was going to come. I couldn't help it; not solely for the sensation of his cock in my hole and his heavy, leathery scrotum slapping on my cunt, but also for his weight on my back, the way he was holding me by my legs, the tickling of his fur on my bum and my thighs, even his rhythmic panting as he fucked me. All of it came together to produce a long, hard orgasm, making me cry out once more, only not in shock and horror, but in shame-filled ecstasy.

As I came down I managed to call him a bastard. But he took no notice, still pumping away merrily up my hole, but slower now with his meat withdrawing to the mouth of my sex after every thrust. I was too slippery and too far gone to even try to stop it happening. Then up it went deep again, the full, fat bulge; bloating my cunt to make me scream into the pillow case covering my head. The pumping stopped, and the full bulk of his meat was held in deep, the mouth of my pussy agape on thick, hard, male flesh.

I'd barely come down from my orgasm and I was still panting from being so full, and from shock too. So was he, and he'd begun to move again, his meat tugging the mouth of my straining cunt, back and forth, to set me moaning and sobbing. I could guess he was coming, his spunk pumping into my body with every short little thrust, and I wondered just how long he was going to stay on my back. It was only then that I heard the faint click of the camera and realised we were being photographed.

'You bastard!' I repeated, my voice weak with reaction. 'You utter bastard!'

'It's good though, isn't it?'

I could only nod in response, unable to deny the truth, not when he'd seen me come. He gave his harsh little laugh and his hand touched the knot behind my head, loosening it to allow him to tug the pillow case up a little, uncovering my mouth. Something firm and round pressed to my lips, his cock. I took him in, sucking willingly enough as I imagined how I'd look in the pictures, only for the motion of my head bobbing up and down to dislodge the pillow case. Then I'd found for real exactly how I would look.

The rush of shame and excitement was so strong I'd have come again with just a touch to my pussy. I began to suck more eagerly, taking him deep and nuzzling my chin against his balls, now keen to say thank you for what he'd done to me. He took me by my pony-tail to force himself deeper still, his knob wedging into my throat to make me gag and jerk as he had before. I tried my best to accommodate him, even as he began to wank on what little of his shaft was still sticking out of my mouth with his hand knocking on my nose and lips with every tug.

My eyes had started to pop and I was sure I was going to be sick on his cock when he suddenly jerked it free, pulling frantically at his shaft and calling me something in Russian that had to be filthy. I gaped wide, deliberately offering him my mouth to spunk into, but when he came it was so violent that most of it went in my hair, with two thick streamers down my face as well. Only then did he stick it back in my mouth to make me suck and swallow what was left.

Finished, he gave a long, happy sigh and stood away from the bed, grinning openly. Picking up his camera once more, he took a few more shots, laughing at the sight of my spunk-soiled face and sulky pout, before he went behind for some close-ups of my rear view. At last he sat down, poured himself another glass of champagne and relaxed back as if he hadn't a care in the world.

'What about me?' I asked.

'Nature must take its course,' he said.

I made a face, trying to look as if I was resigned to my fate, but really quite enjoying myself. It was just so unspeakably rude; a defiance of everything prudish and boring and dull, to be lying there, tied and helpless, my face smeared with my tormentor's spunk and my pussy stretched to the limit from my humping. I was even wishing he'd had a go up my bum, although for some reason that didn't feel as bad, as if it had to be my cunt for my violation to be complete.

'And now, I think, we are done,' Mr Morozov said, and it was over, as suddenly as it had began, my empty pussy now dribbling a mixture of lubricant and spunk into my froufrous.

He came across to me and smacked my bottom, not hard, but just as if to give me a gentle admonition for my behaviour. I'd have happily taken more, still horny and high on rude, inappropriate sex, while if ever a girl had deserved a spanking it was me. He began to undo the knot at my right wrist instead, but as my arm came loose the sense of disappointment had become too much for me.

'Go on, smack it,' I said, sticking up my bottom. 'Please.'

He said something in Russian, but plainly expressing surprise.

'Please,' I repeated. 'I need a spanking. I deserve one too, don't I?'

'Yes,' he admitted and I could hear the astonishment in his voice.

I slipped my free hand back and down the front of my froufrous. They were full of spunk, more than I'd have believed possible, and it was all over my thighs too, between my cheeks and in my pussy. I began to rub, revelling in the slippery, soiled feeling of my flesh and the still gaping mouth of my well fucked hole. He was staring, open-mouthed, as if he couldn't quite believe was he was seeing, but then his hand had settled on my bottom. I gave a happy purr as he started to spank me, quite hard right from the start and with a purposeful, almost mechanical motion.

It was just right, quickly bringing the warmth to my

cheeks and allowing me to feel I was being punished. As I undoubtedly deserved to be for what I'd done. Everything I'd done, from prostituting myself in the first place, allowing him to tie me and strip me, but best of all, for enjoying what should have been an experience too degrading for any woman to even contemplate, but coming while it was done to me.

I cried out as my muscles went tight. His smacks got harder and I was there, coming and coming again in a string of urgent, powerful orgasms that had me bucking and jerking in the bonds that still held me to the bed. He only stopped when he finally got fed up with applying his hand to my wriggling bottom.

Chapter Seven

MR MOROZOV HAD TAKEN me somewhere I never been before and I was completely happy about it. All the more so for the contents of the envelope he'd left on the mantelpiece at the end. That had always been a pet fantasy of mine, to have men visit me for sex and then discreetly leave me money on the mantelpiece; so it was rather nice anyway, but even in my wildest fantasies I'd never expected to be paid so much. I knew he was rich, and that high-class call girls charged the earth, but we hadn't even agreed a figure. Not that I was complaining, and the money went straight into my building society account, which was beginning to look really quite healthy. A few more clients like him and I wouldn't just be helping with a contribution to my expenses for uni, I'd have covered them with money to spare.

Among the other staff, only Mr and Mrs Hegedus knew what I'd done. He was plainly jealous and also fascinated; while she pretended to be full of sympathy. But there was a prurient touch to her questions that left me in no doubt that the idea excited her. I did wonder if Stefan and Chris might have guessed, or put two and two together. But they couldn't be sure, and it seemed to be the sort of behaviour they expected of me anyway. There was also Morris, who came down in person to congratulate me, treated me to lobster and a bottle of expensive wine for lunch, then steered me out of the hotel and up the path to the downs with his arm around my shoulder.

'There's no other girl like you,' he was saying for about the tenth time. 'There really isn't. And willing to do it again!'

'Why not? It was nice.'

'Wonderful, that's the spirit! And Karay I expect will be equally enthusiastic, which will go a long way to allowing me to cement a certain deal I've been working on. They're tricky, these Russians, you see. But I can't see him backing out now.'

'You wouldn't blackmail him, would you, Morris, because that would mean I ...'

'Jemima, please!' he interrupted. 'That is a very strong word. No, absolutely not. Let's just say that the secret we share will ensure that he doesn't feel tempted to invest elsewhere. After all, these are difficult times and banks are beginning to refuse credit to what would normally be seen as perfectly safe ventures. Hence my agreement for private finance with Morozov, which will give me an edge over my competitors in what looks like being a very tough market for several years. Now, my dear, there's something else I want you to do for me, another nice little earner.'

'What's that?'

'Well, do you remember how popular you were with the gentlemen when you were spanked by Pippa?'

'And when I spanked her, yes.'

'Exactly. It went down well, didn't it? Well, one or two of the gentlemen have been asking for more of the same.'

'That's fine. You know I don't mind playing with Pippa.'

'Not Pippa, no.'

'Who then?'

'Your er ... stepmother, Danielle.'

I stopped dead, horrified, the image of me bare-bottom over Danielle's lap in front of a couple of dozen dirty old men already burning in my head.

'No way! And she is not my stepmother!'

Morris spread his hands.

'Details, details. This is business, Jemima. You've always been a sensible girl when it comes to business.'

'I don't care! I can't!'

'What's the matter? She's already spanked you, hasn't she?'

'That's not ... How do you know she spanked me?'

'You'd be surprised at what I know,' he answered, 'and how I come by the knowledge, but in this case there's no mystery. She told me.'

'Why? How do you know her? OK, I suppose you must have met her when you were working with my dad on that Thames Vista thing. But how did you know she was into spanking?'

'My dear Jemima, do credit me with some intelligence. I've been spanking girls since long before you were born and you quickly come to recognise the willing ones; the way they dress, the way they move, a certain self-consciousness about their bottoms, a spark of interest if that all important word is mentioned. The same goes for the ones who like to dish it out, only from a different perspective.'

'And Danielle?'

'She threatened to spank your sister. Not seriously, of course. It was just a remark she made, intended to put Pippa in her place when she was getting a bit bossy, but I could tell there was real feeling underneath.'

'So what did you do?'

'I suggested she might like to come to a party, of course.'

'To the secretary of a business associate? A woman about half your age?'

'Not half my age, thank you, Jemima. And why not? The worst she could do was refuse and complain to your dad, who's hardly going to jeopardise his part in a multi-million pound contract, just to placate a prissy secretary. Besides, I knew she needed money, because her divorce still hadn't gone through and the lawyers' bills were mounting up.'

'So Danielle came to a party?'

'Yes, while you were in the States. Only the one, but she introduced her uncle to me. He was manager here at the Friston. It was in a sorry state then and about to go under. So I bought it and kept him on.'

'That explains a lot. Thanks, Morris.'

'Not at all. Now, about your spanking from Danielle ...'

'I didn't agree ...'

'About your spanking from Danielle,' he repeated firmly. 'Everybody loved seeing you and Pippa punish each other, and we could charge a great deal more if we put on a special show. We need the right woman, of course. And Danielle is perfect. Not many people know her, she looks quite like you ...'

'She does not!'

'Really quite like you,' he insisted, 'and definitely attractive, a good spanker too. You should have seen how she dealt with Annabelle ...'

'I can guess!' I interrupted. 'But look Morris, I –'

'And most importantly, she's thirty-six, so just the right age.'

'The right age for what?' I asked, and then it had sunk in. 'Oh no, Morris ...'

'To be your mother,' he carried on, oblivious to the growing horror on my face. 'I've promised them a genuine mother and daughter spanking, you see.'

'No, Morris, that's going too far,' I blustered. 'And anyway, too many of the men know me, and Pippa. They'd realise, sooner or later. Anyway, what does Danielle have to say about it? All she's interested in is getting her hooks into my dad.'

'Naturally we wouldn't have the usual crowd,' he went on, 'And one or two of them would know what was happening. I was thinking more of a select group of foreign gentlemen. As to Danielle, she is a very avaricious young lady and sure to agree if I put enough on the table.'

'So she gets to spank me and gets extra money?'

'So you're not entirely averse to the suggestion then?'

'I didn't say that!'

'You implied it, and no, she does not get more. I'll match your money.'

'And most of it still goes into your pocket?'

'Naturally. There are few things I enjoy more than seeing you spanked, my dear, but business is business. So, how about it?'

We'd reached the top of the trees and I sat down on a stile where the cliff path split in two. I was trying to tell myself it was just one more spanking, and for a lot of money, but it was no good. Having Danielle do it was too shameful, too intimate, and the thought of letting her pretend to be my mother was unbearable. I shook my head.

'Sorry, Morris. I'd do it for you, but not with Danielle. You see, she didn't tell you everything. When she spanked me it … It wasn't play, it was for real. Family discipline.'

The admission had brought me close to tears, not only for what she did to me, but for something far worse: the way I reacted. That was not something I was about to admit to Morris, who was looking at me with a mixture of sympathy and interest, but no surprise.

'So I understand, from her. But I wasn't sure whether to believe it, knowing how much you enjoy a good spanking. Genuine family discipline, eh? Why?'

'For refusing to do as I was told. And no, it wasn't just an excuse. She … she held me down, and took my jeans down to … to do it on my knickers. She's a bitch.'

He reached out to ruffle my hair, but he'd begun to look thoughtful, and I could see he was calculating how much extra he could charge if he managed to present my spanking as a genuine mother to daughter punishment, rather than one done purely for money. I made to protest, only to stop as a deliciously wicked idea entered my head; an idea that would not only be immensely satisfying, but that might make the perfect revenge.

'I've got a better idea. What if I was to spank Summer?'

Just for a moment he looked doubtful, but only for a moment.

'Summer? Now there's a thought! Would you?'

'Yes.'

'And you don't mind me saying she's your real sister?'

'No, not at all.'

'Would she let you?'

'I … I don't now. Maybe … she's fun, and Danielle threatened to let her watch my punishment, so I suppose she gets it herself. And if she's anything like her mum she'd go for the money.'

'Most girls do,' Morris remarked, 'if you offer them enough, and I expect she's no better. Hmm ... naturally you would have to present it to her in the right way, and we still need that element of reality which men find so important. Danielle might prove a problem as well, but ...'

He was thinking aloud, and trailed off, staying silent for a while before smacking his hands together in satisfaction.

'Excellent! So, if you've walked off lunch, how about a nice slow blow job to say thank you?'

Morris got his blow job, in the same hollow where Penny spanked me. It seemed only fair, and, in a funny sort of way, right. After all he was my boss and it wasn't the first time anyway, because he always had one of the girls do it after his parties. He'd been nice about my refusal to be spanked by Danielle as well, although I knew he'd have problems telling his clients it wasn't going to happen after all. Then again, the prospect of me dealing with Summer instead was sure to get them going.

It was only after he'd gone off to help arrange something that was happening the next day that I began to feel guilty for what I'd suggested. After all, it wasn't her fault that her mother was a complete bitch and it wouldn't have been fair to punish her the way Danielle had punished me. I'd have to make it fun for her, which meant not being too rough, while I couldn't imagine her being able to cope with getting it in the middle of a ring of leering men, whatever the circumstances. Not everybody is like me.

That meant I'd have to be clever, maybe seduce her first, a thought that made me shiver with anticipation. She was certainly cute, very slim with a little round bottom and long legs, so like me that nobody would be surprised to be told we were sisters, but with naturally golden hair instead of brown. To get her into bed for sex would be deliciously naughty, and a good start to my revenge. That meant Danielle would have to find out, but I could take a spanking in a good cause and that was really the most she could do to me. After all, she had to keep Dad happy, and murdering his daughter wasn't going to go down too well. Summer's spanking would be the icing on the cake; thick sweet icing in rainbow colours with lots of fancy bits. My revenge would be complete, and all the better as I'd have to be honest with Summer, which meant she'd enjoy it and have accepted money. Danielle would be furious. Arranging it was another matter, with Summer at home and me at the hotel, but there had to be some way of getting around that.

They were expecting me to go back to work, but the hotel was very quiet. There wasn't even anybody at the desk, but there was a letter for me, a thick, brown envelope written in a curious, angular hand. I guessed what it was immediately and hurried back to my chalet, my face hot with blushes just for the thought of what I was about to see.

I locked the door and shut the curtains, carefully this time as the last thing I wanted was Mr Hegedus peeping in on me. Sure enough, the enveloped contained a brief note from Mr Morozov and prints of the photos he had taken. I could only stare, mouth open in shock and delight at my own filthy behaviour as I went through them, and again, all the while with my excitement building up inside me. The first ones were just plain rude, with me tied over the bolster with my knickers down and my tits popped out of my top, bumhole and pussy flaunted for all to see. Then came the ones after I'd been hooded, less sexy and a bit scary because you couldn't tell that I was enjoying myself. Next came the really strong ones, with me mounted and the hood still over my head, which would have been enough to get Mr Morozov locked up for ever if I'd taken them to the police and claimed I'd been unwilling. The last ones were the best, once the pillow case was off, because you could see my face, with Mr Morozov's spunk in my hair and down my cheeks, my face sulky or full of bliss but quite obviously enjoying my humping. And last of all, the pictures of my fucked pussy.

By the time I'd looked through them the second time I'd pulled up my uniform skirt and was rubbing myself through my knickers. I could have finished off then and there, over the photo of my straining pussy hole with his meat in me, and his big, dark balls hanging down, but forced myself to hold back as I laid out the entire set, over fifty pictures. It was almost too much to take in, picture after picture, displaying my utter degradation to the world, because I could be very sure the bastard was going to put them up on the net and let all the other filthy perverts enjoy the sight of me getting humped; men and women too, hands on cocks and fingers on pussies as they brought themselves off over my shame.

I came on that thought with a sharp, sudden orgasm, but it wasn't enough. My head was now so full of those obscene images that I didn't need to look any more, but lay back, pushed down my panties and got to work on my bare cunt; bringing myself to orgasm after orgasm, until at last I was simply too sore to go on, with every muscle of my hips and thighs and belly aching, my fingers too, so that I barely had the strength to fiddle with myself. That didn't make the pictures go away, and I lay there for a long time, whimpering gently for the state I was in and wishing I was back in the Honeymoon Suite, bound and hooded with eight inches of thick, red cock up my cunt.

When somebody started pounding on the door I nearly leapt out of my skin, and I was very glad indeed that I'd locked it, as an instant later Mrs Hegedus called out, while trying the handle at the same time. 'Are you in there, Jemima? There is work to be done!'

'Yes, Mrs Hegedus. Sorry, Mrs Hegedus,' I babbled, frantically pulling my knickers up. 'I'm just coming.'

I gathered the pictures up fast, but making very sure I found every single one. Then I hid them under the mattress, for once glad that I was expected to do my own cleaning and so wasn't likely to get caught out. With my skirt smoothed down and my hair hurriedly sorted out, I unlocked the door and jerked it open, to find Mrs Hegedus still there, her hands on her hips and her big, homely face set in a scowl of disapproval.

'What do you think you're doing, you useless girl?' she demanded. 'There are guests. Come on!'

She finished her remark with a smack to my bottom, and for one moment I thought she was going to spank me then and there; but it was just that she, like everybody else, seemed to think that slapping my bum was the best way to make me do anything. I hurried towards the main buildings with her following, to find that the hotel reception, which had been empty earlier was now crowded with people. One of them I recognised immediately: fat Monty Hartle, computer geek and convicted panty thief, propping up his bulk on the bar with a pint of lager in one hand. The man next to him was even larger, tall as well as fat, with ginger hair in a flat top cut. Both were in combat gear, although it was hard to imagine two less likely soldiers. Chris gave me a curt signal and I went behind the bar, greeting Monty as he swallowed what remained in his glass at a gulp.

'I'll have another of those, please. Jemima, isn't it, Penny's niece?'

'I'm a cousin of sorts, really,' I explained. 'I just call her auntie. You're Monty, aren't you?'

'Yup, and this is Jeff. Jeff, say hello to Jemima, who I believe is hot to trot?'

It was a question, and he finished with a slow, heavy wink.

'Um … is there a party, tonight? If so, yes, I'm up for it, if you're good boys.'

I was being cheeky, as they were both at least twice my age, if still young by the standards of Morris's gentlemen, but I knew Monty's reputation.

'Don't think so,' he answered, 'unless we make one ourselves. We're fox hunting tomorrow. Morris has given Razorback an exclusive booking.'

'Fox hunting?' I queried.

'You know, a girl in the nude with a tail up her bum and a mask on, getting chased around by a load of guys, girls too. If we catch her we get to fuck her.'

He said it with such open relish that I found myself blushing and took a moment to reply. 'Oh, right. Who's the girl?'

'Melody's Annabelle.'

I'd half expected him to say it was me, although Morris would presumably have told me earlier, and felt an odd little stab of disappointment. Annabelle was a good choice though, very athletic, but if she was around her mistress couldn't be far away.

'Is Mel coming?'

'Sure. She's hunting. Hey, I heard what you did to her. Hilarious!'

He nudged Jeff and both of them laughed. It was impossible not to smile in response, as it seemed that tricking Melody into taking a spanking was making me a bit of a celebrity.

'Have one yourself,' Jeff offered as I put his pint down on the bar.

'Thanks. I'll have a large white wine.'

'Make it a bottle.'

I took a cold one, poured myself a generous glass and stuck the bottle back in the fridge. The press at the bar had begun to die down, and after serving one more order I turned back to Monty and Jeff. They seem just the sort of men it's fun to tease; ever eager and easily controlled, with a certain spice from Monty's reputation. All the other new guests seemed to be part of the same group too, so I knew I could say what I pleased.

'So, if you're going hunting, why are you all dressed in combats? Shouldn't you be in jodhpurs and pink coats?'

'Nah, if you do that, you get all the antis on your back, and when you try and explain you're only chasing girls they just don't get it.'

'Chasing girls, you two? I mean, how do you expect to catch Annabelle? Not exactly built for speed, are you.'

I was laughing as I said it, hoping they'd rise to the bait, but neither seemed put out at all.

'Tactics,' Jeff replied, tapping the side of his nose.

Monty, grinning, had put his hand in his jacket pocket and was about to pull something out. I caught a glimpse of a rubber ball, much like the sort you throw for dogs, but then Jeff had pushed it back.

'What is it?' I demanded.

'You'll see,' Jeff told me. 'Tomorrow.'

They piqued my interest, but before I could insist they show me another man had joined our group. He was their age, perhaps a little older, but well built and good-looking in a slightly slimy way, while his uniform was immaculate and decorated with medals and three pips on the shoulder tabs.

'Yo, Jeff, who's the cutie?' he said, his eyes flicking up and down my figure.

Jeff jerked a thumb at him.

'Jemima, meet Gavin. He runs Razorback.'

'That's me,' Gavin responded. 'I am the money man. The man whose bonus started the credit crunch. In fact, there's only one thing bigger and I've got that too, right here.'

He thrust out his crotch and gave the bulge in his combat trousers a squeeze. I couldn't resist trying to take the wind out of his sails. 'Let's see then.'

'Sure.'

He just unzipped, then and there, opening his fly to scoop a large, smooth set of cock and balls out of his trousers, weighing them in his hand for my inspection. I was staring, open-mouthed, for once in my life actually shocked, although I had to admit they were quite nice. Monty and Jeff thought it was hilarious, roaring with laughter and slapping their fat thighs.

'Not in the bar, please, Jemima,' Chris said, his voice weary.

'I wasn't doing anything!' I protested.

He just shook his head, clearly convinced that it was somehow my fault. Gavin had put himself away, but the image was clear in my mind; a vision of his big, smooth cock lying on the bulk of his scrotum, at once disgusting and immensely appealing. I tried to play it cool. 'Gosh, the last time I saw one that size was at school, down a microscope.'

He just laughed and took a swig of Jeff's lager, then made a face and ordered a bottle of champagne. I went to fetch it, feeling flustered, but quite good too. They were an odd lot, city boys and computer nerds, army fantasists and general weirdoes, but I was very much the centre of attention. And for once it looked like I'd be keeping my clothes on, at least until I chose otherwise.

Gavin, Jeff and Monty had gone to a table, and once I'd prepared the bottle of champagne I took it over to them. Mr Hegedus had come out and was talking to Chris, but I barely noticed him. I never really did any more, because he was so much under his wife's thumb, and so easily manipulated he wasn't really any fun. Gavin was far more interesting; a man I could tease until he was desperate and then charge high for a one to one. I gave him my best pose as I poured his champagne, wishing I was in my other uniform so that he could see my froufrous, but his eyes were firmly locked on my bottom anyway.

'I think you like what you see, don't you?' I said, only to finish with a squeak as a firm slap was applied to my bottom.

I spun around to find Mr Hegedus directly behind me, trying to look serious but with his mouth twitching in and out of a lecherous smile. 'Your behaviour is a disgrace, yes?' he said.

'What do you mean?' I asked, genuinely puzzled.

'To tell guests to show their cocks in the reception!' he answered in mock outrage. 'A spanking is what you need, young lady, right here and right now!'

'Hey no!' I squeaked, drowned out by laughter on all sides and voices raised in encouragement.

'That's the way!' Jeff called. 'Staff discipline, ever so important.'

'Vital,' Gavin agreed, 'and no better way to keep it than a good spanking.'

'Pull her knickers right down,' Monty put in. 'I want to

106

see her cunt.'

He was going to, because Mr Hegedus had lost no time at all, grabbing my wrist and plumping his weight down on the nearest chair. I fought back, shocked and not at all ready for a spanking, let alone in front of men I'd meant to tease. But it was a bad mistake. Seeing that Mr Hegedus couldn't handle me on my own, all three of the men came to help. Any one could have dealt with me easily, and in just seconds I'd been forced down across Mr Hegedus's knee, squealing and pleading as my legs were spread and my arms twisted up behind my back, rendering me helpless as eager hands pulled up my uniform skirt. I was trying to kick them, and calling them every name I could think of, but it only made them laugh the harder. One of them got a grip on my knickers and Monty had got his wish, my open pussy right in his face as I was stripped behind, with my scream of protest ignored.

Mr Hegedus brought a hand down on my bare bottom and the spanking had begun, fast and hard with all four men laughing as I wriggling and bucked and squealed, making a complete exhibition of myself but unable to stop. Other men clustered around, eager to watch; leering at me and passing remarks about how I looked, calling me a brat and a baby for not taking my spanking meekly, one even commenting on how tight my bumhole looked. I tried to get myself under control, knowing full well that the less dignity I showed the more they'd enjoy my punishment, but it was no good. The pain was too much, the situation too humiliating. Instead I let go completely, bursting into tears of shame and frustration; a full blown spanking tantrum as I writhed and squirmed in their grip, my legs cocked wide and my bum bouncing up and down in my struggles as the smacks rained down.

Somebody said I'd had enough, maybe because I was crying, and at that Mr Hegedus slowed down, applying a few lighter smacks to my bottom, then stopped. I slumped down, gasping, my legs still wide apart even when they'd let go of me, my pussy flaunted and my bumhole winking but too far gone to care for what I was showing. My bottom was ablaze, my chest heaving, my pussy shamefully wet. I thought they'd have me, then and there, taking turns until every single one had satisfied himself inside me.

Instead it was Mr Hegedus who took advantage, taking me by the hand and leading me from the room; my head hung and my bare red bottom wiggling behind me, the men clapping and cheering for the way I'd been punished. I felt desperately sorry for myself, but he'd got me too deep in submission and high on spanking to resist as I was led to my own chalet. Inside, I was put on my knees and his thick, dark cock flopped out into my face. The tears were still streaming down my cheeks as I took him in, but I was sucking willingly enough.

He'd soon sat down, pulling me into him and adjusting himself; his balls pulled out so he could make me kiss and lick at his fat, hairy scrotum. I did it, utterly humiliated as I served him with my tongue, unable to stop myself as I used every technique I knew to get him excited. Soon he was fully erect, rubbing himself in my face and tugging at his shaft as I attended to his balls and knob. He began to call me his baby, and to ask if I was enjoying having a hot bottom.

I nodded on my mouthful of balls and leathery skin, unable to deny it. They'd tucked my skirt up when they stripped me and my bottom was sticking out, my knickers well down to show it all, my ready pussy and my pulsing bumhole. If Mr Hegedus had wanted he could have fucked me, even put it up my bottom. I'd have given in, hating him while he buggered me, but still mewling with pleasure for the feel of his cock in my rectum, maybe even sucking him clean once he'd spunked up inside me.

Then it was too late anyway, his cock erupting in his hand; a spurt of thick white come erupting from the tip to splash down in my face and hair. A second stream into my open mouth as I struggled to catch what he had to give. The third well down my throat as I took him deep. He was done, my face and hair covered in spunk to show me up for a dirty little slut. But I wasn't done. I knelt back, my knees wide, jerking my skirt up at the front to show him my cunt, wet and ready between my open thighs.

My hand went down and I was masturbating for him, deliberately showing off and thanking him over and over again for what he'd done to me, telling him that next time he ought to fuck me. And at the very moment my orgasm kicked in, when I had no control over my desires whatsoever, and I begged him to bugger me and make me suck his dirty cock.

Chapter Eight

IF IT HADN'T BEEN for Mrs Hegedus I might have got what I wanted, although wanted isn't really the word. While I'd been frigging myself, there had been nothing I'd wanted more than his thick brown cock up my bum, and even after I'd come I was still so high on sex and spanking that I'd have let him push me into it. Maybe he would have done, but a distant bellow from his wife sent him into a panic. She gone out after fetching me from my chalet, which was the only reason he'd dared give me my spanking in the first place. She'd come back earlier than expected. He was in such a panic that he was actually trying to blame me for what had happened, calling me a slut and a tease as he struggled to escape through the window.

He nearly made it, but was still trying to squeeze the bulbous mass of his hips through, upside down with his legs waving in the air, when the door was pushed open so hard it made the chalet shake. Somebody had obviously told Mrs Hegedus where he'd gone. She showed no surprise whatsoever, but merely grunted, then let out a stream of abuse in what was presumably Hungarian, grabbed his feet and pushed. He shot out of the window like a cork, vanished from sight briefly before beating a hasty retreat, while still babbling apologies in Hungarian. I made a dash for the door.

I almost escaped, but it had swung back and she caught me before I could get it open again. There was no question about what was going to happen. Over I went, turned up with my still bare, pink bottom in the air for a firm, no-nonsense spanking that had me crying again in seconds. She really laid in too, calling me a slut over and over again; other things too, but in her own language. Once she'd finished I was dumped snivelling on the floor and told that I'd get the same again if she caught me anywhere near her husband, and that he was only allowed to spank me in her presence and with her permission.

She sent me to bed, and I didn't dare disobey, lying on the coverlets with my hot bottom turned up for maybe an hour before I finally gave in to my need. I'd been punished, again, not in play but for real, and it was impossibly exciting. Four times I brought myself to orgasm before I finally crawled into bed; still in my uniform and with my knickers rolled down the way he'd arranged them for my first spanking, and one more time before I fell asleep.

In the morning the idea of being taking Mr Hegedus's cock up my bum seemed revolting, and the fact that I'd asked for it agonisingly embarrassing. Having been spanked in public, taken away for sex and then spanked again was almost as shameful, because everybody knew; they sniggered and made dirty little jokes behind their hands while I served breakfast. But to really put the icing on the cake, I'd been told to put on my sexy uniform without knickers, so was showing off my bare bum throughout.

I got smacked, groped and pinched so often that when I finally managed to find a minute to inspect myself in the mirror I looked as if I had chicken pox. One guest had even tried to stick a piping hot sausage up me when I bent

111

to serve the next table, making me drop a full jug of orange juice in Fat Jeff's lap. He'd put me straight over his knee, just for a few playful swats, but now my uniform was wet and sticky, so I badly needed to change and to apply a little cream. I knew what that would do to me, but there was really no choice and after a quick trip to my chalet and one more shame-filled climax I was back, now in my ordinary uniform, but only to *get it* from Mel for not being properly dressed, in front of everybody and left with my skirt rolled up and knickerless, again.

By that time I was dizzy from spanking; while mistreating me seemed to have helped put everyone else in a good mood as they assembled outside for the fox hunt. Gavin had gone to his car, a jeep, painted in camouflage colours with "Razorback Paintball" stencilled on the side in brilliant scarlet and orange letters and yellow highlighting. There was a picture too, of a huge razor-backed boar pig, standing on his hind legs, his body criss-crossed with ammunition belts and a gun in his hands, or rather, his trotters. The pig was wearing shades, and so was Gavin, tempting me to make the inevitable comparison, which earned me a quick trip across the bonnet for yet another spanking. That left me rubbing my hot cheeks as he sauntered back to the rear of the jeep, rubbing his hands together in satisfaction for a job well done.

Annabelle had arrived with Melody, although there was no sign of Morris. A broad, black leather collar circled her neck, with a chain which looked like a real dog lead attached. She also had a coat on, and trainers, but that seemed to be it; at least to judge by the glimpses of her long, slender legs and taut belly when she let her coat part. I couldn't help but feel a little envious of her, when she was getting so much attention; now they'd seen every single detail of my body while I was punished, most of them had lost interest. Then again, the fox hunt sounded quite scary, as it was plain that anybody who caught her could have her, and that she had no say in whose cock she had to accommodate, or where it got put.

'One of Amber Oakley's best,' Gavin was saying as he opened a sturdy aluminium case, 'only a shame she's not here to have it stuck in her own bottom!'

Several of them laughed at his joke, which I knew would have made Amber furious, especially as she'd made him some amazing kit: two long, thick fox brushes, each of which was attached to a curved shaft with a plug at the tip, all too obviously designed to go up the wearer's bottom. Annabelle gave a delicate shudder as she leant close to inspect them.

'They look real!'

'Real?' Gavin retorted. 'Of course they're real. Do you think I'd go with fake? This is genuine fox! So are the masks, look.'

He opened a second case, in which two weird little masks had been laid out, each like the upper part of a fox's head, complete with ears but no snout, rather like Venetian masks. They looked perfectly horrid, but I was glad they'd omitted the snout and teeth, until Gavin explained why in response to a question from Melody.

'That's so she can suck cock without taking it off. The brushes come with little fishing line belts too, and some lube, so if you want to give her one up the bum you just pop the plug out and whoops, up it goes!'

Melody nodded casually, but I saw Annabelle shiver. Gavin lifted one of the brushes from the case, holding it out to Mel, who took it, examining the plug for a moment before turning to Annabelle.

'Drop your coat.'

Annabelle obeyed without hesitation, shedding her coat to stand nude but for her collar and trainers, with the tattoo declaring her the property of Melody clearly visible on her shaven pussy mound. She was very slim, but muscular too, and it was hard to see any of the men catching her, even the few that looked fit. They evidently had other ideas, grinning and nudging each other as Melody carried on. 'Stick out your bum.'

Again Annabelle obeyed without hesitation, but I noticed she had closed her eyes as she put her hands on her thighs and stuck her bottom well out, allowing her cheeks to part and show off the knot of her anus and her pussy lips.

'Lube,' Melody demanded.

Gavin handed it across, watching wide-eyed in fascination as Melody squeezed out a long, fat worm onto the plug and another between Annabelle's open cheeks. The plug went between her cheeks; Annabelle's mouth came open slightly as her anus gave way and the tail was in, held firmly up her bumhole with the shaft rising between her cheeks to project as if it was really growing from her spine. Gavin passed the belt and Melody fixed it in place, leaving the tail sticking up over Annabelle's bottom at a jaunty angle. She put the mask on herself. Melody unclipped her lead and she was ready; standing naked and nervous in the ring of men who were going to chase her down, catch her if they could and use her any way they wanted.

'Nice,' Gavin remarked, squeezing his crotch as he eyed Annabelle up and down.

'Shame not to use both sets of gear,' Jeff remarked, casually but looking at me. 'How about the maid runs too?'

Melody nodded. 'Why not? Get her.'

114

I'd realised what was coming and tried to make a dash for it, only to run straight into Monty. He might as well have been a hippo for the amount he moved, and the others grabbed me immediately. I tried to protest, telling them it wasn't fair and that I'd had enough, but my heart wasn't in my protests and they knew it. My uniform was peeled off, even my stockings, and I was held wriggling while my bottom was greased, Melody sliding one well lubricated finger deep into my rectum and wiggled it about. Her finger came out and the plug went up; pushed deep to leave my bumhole agape and the big, bushy tail sticking up from the top of my slit. I could smell fox as they pulled the mask on over my head, making me gag.

They'd barely given me a chance to react. One moment I'd been one of the crew, even with my bottom spanked and bare, and could have joined in the chase if I'd wanted; the next I'd been stripped made up into some kind of perverted fox girl, ready to be hunted down and put to their cocks. I wasn't ready at all, and if it hadn't been for Melody coming to give me a kiss and hug I might have backed out completely. They'd have had to let me, especially with Mrs Hegedus in the background, because to judge by the expression on her face she didn't approve at all.

As it was I contented myself with a dirty look for Gavin and slipped my waitressing shoes back on so that I'd at least have a chance. He had climbed onto the roll bars of his jeep and raised his hands for silence, which he only got when Melody bellowed at them all to shut up. He responded with a grin and a bow in her direction, more mocking than sincere.

'Thank you, Mrs Rathwell,' he said, 'and may your enormous strap-on dildo always find a convenient fuck hole.'

'Could be, Gavin,' Melody replied, looking right at him, 'just bend over.'

Gavin went slightly red and waited until the laughter and jokes at his expense had died down, then carried on. 'Ha, ha, very funny. Anyway, ladies and gentlemen, we are gathered her today for a fox hunt, a seriously kinky fox hunt. I always think it's rude to fuck someone without an introduction, so for those of you who haven't already met, may I introduce our two delectable foxes, Annabelle and Jemima. Both of who are going to be sore but happy before we're done. Annabelle is house slave and pet to the divine Melody Rathwell ...'

He indicated Mel, and it was only then that I realised he hadn't been joking about the dildo. She was in jeans, very tight on her full hips and cut so low that the first swell of her muscular cheeks showed behind, while at the front they hinted at the outline of a ring which could only be the fitting for a strap-on. My tummy was already fluttering badly, but the sensation grew abruptly worse at the thought of her catching me and making me kneel to be penetrated, no doubt at the centre of a ring of admiring men.

'...while Jemima is just some little slut who works here as a maid,' Gavin was saying. 'Both are fair game to anybody who can catch them, in any hole, and of course their bums are already lubed up and plugged with their tails.'

'Hey, look ...' I began, intent on negotiating, but he ignored me completely as he continued.

'The rules are simple. We all go inside, have a coffee, a beer, or in Jeff's case a second breakfast, while the girls go to earth. You can go anywhere in the grounds, you two, so long as you don't go outside the trees. Down on the beach is OK. Just don't let the proles see you, that's

116

all. But don't worry too much because the gate's locked and we've got a diversion on the cliff path. Still, when you catch 'em, boys and girls, take them somewhere a bit discreet to fuck 'em, not in the middle of the drive, please. Newbies get blooded, as usual. Game over at high noon. Right, fifteen minutes. Better get running, girls.'

'Blooded?' I queried, turning to Annabelle.

'Don't worry, it's just some initiation ceremony they do,' she answered. 'Come on, let's go!'

She sped off across the car park, ignoring the catcalls and slaps to her bum and thighs. I followed, dodging the hunters as they filed indoors. There had to be at least thirty of them, nearly all men but with a few women, all of who looked either very dominant or seriously butch. I knew they'd be worse than the men, if Melody was anything to go by, but if they did catch me it wouldn't hurt my pride so badly. That was important after the way the men had treated me; as an available little slut, many of them had taken liberties when they didn't even know my name. Better still, I could survive until noon and deny them their fun, men and women both.

Annabelle had taken off like a rocket, up the slope opposite the hotel where the trees were thickest and gave the best chance of concealment, but would still allow her to make a run for it if they got close. It seemed a sensible choice, but my shoes weren't as good as hers. I had a better idea anyway, because there was one place I knew I'd be safe: the flat where Mr and Mrs Hegedus lived. The problem was getting there without being noticed.

Instead of following Annabelle I ran down the drive. I was sure that at least some of the hunters would be watching me from reception, so I made sure I was out of sight before looping back and into the yard where I'd sucked Stefan's cock among the bins. The fire escape

117

came down to one side, invisible except from the kitchen, and while there was a risk that either Mrs Hegedus or Stefan would see me and report me, it was one I had to take. Both were in the kitchen and my footsteps sounded to me like a steel band as I climbed the steps, but neither came out to investigate.

The fire door was shut, but the window of No 15 wasn't and I was soon inside, trying to ignore the implications of the magazines lying on the bed: *Rear View*, *Guns & Ammo* and *Horse & Hound*. It was quiet in the corridor, with only the faint noise of conversation and laughter coming from downstairs. But my heart was in my mouth as I ran light-footed to the end and up the stairs. The flat was on the top floor, which wouldn't have been a bad place to hide even if the door had been locked, but it was still a wonderful relief when the handle turned under my hand.

I slipped inside, cautiously, although with so many guests and lunch to get ready there was no reason either Mr Hegedus or his wife would come upstairs, and if they did there was sure to be somewhere I could hide. For that matter, if he caught me I could easily buy his silence by sucking his cock, or worse; something that once again seemed delightfully dirty rather than disgusting. I knew I was turned on, but it was my stubborn pride keeping me from joining in the game, that and not knowing if I could cope with getting gang-banged, which was what was going to happen to me if they caught me, no question.

Nevertheless I was quickly bored. The windows looked out over both the downs and the sea, including most of the area where the hunt would be happening, but the hunters were still downstairs and there was no sign of Annabelle. I took my mask off, as it was irritating, but left my tail in place, quite enjoying the feel of the plug up my bottom and the way the brush tickled my cheeks despite the implications of having it on. There was an appeal to the thought of being caught as well, but my fear and pride were too strong to give in. I might even have masturbated, but it was unthinkable in their flat.

I took to looking around instead, wondering at their rather florid taste in decorations and the lack of books. There were plenty of pictures though, including one of Mr Hegedus outside the hotel, presumably when he'd first taken over as manager. He looked a lot younger, although just as sleazy, and immensely proud of himself, standing in front of the main building in a shiny blue suit with his hair slicked back. Behind him was Danielle, much younger and heavily pregnant, with a man beside her who was presumably her now divorced husband. Seeing her brought out my emotions, never far from the surface, and distracted me. I never even heard the door open, only Mrs Hegedus as she spoke.

'Jemima? What ...'

She sounded angry, but her voice softened immediately as she saw the tears on my cheeks.

'Oh you poor little thing! Aren't men dreadful? I mean, doing that, and to a girl of your age!'

'No, it's not that ...'

I trailed off, because I didn't really want to explain why I'd been crying. She stepped close, putting an arm around my shoulder.

'That's OK. I understand. I'm sure it's all too much for you, and you so young. What you need is comfort, at your age. A bit of discipline too, maybe, but plenty of comfort.'

There was an odd tone to her voice, making me uneasy. But I did want a cuddle, and from somebody big and strong, somebody who could hold me. I let her hug me, on the very edge of breaking down to her, and all the more so because I was in the nude. But I held back through my resentment at the way she'd spanked me the night before, even though I'd frigged myself silly over it.

'There, there,' she said, patting my back. 'I know what you need.'

I wasn't sure she did, but I knew what she wanted to do, because her pats had moved lower, to my bare bottom.

'Mrs Hegedus, I'm not sure …'

'Hush. Now let's have this silly tail out.'

She'd put her fingers between my cheeks even as she spoke, to take hold of the shaft and gently extract the plug from my bumhole. I gasped to feel my anus stretch and was left feeling more naked and vulnerable than ever as she detached the belt and put everything to one side. She took my hand and sat down on the settee, pulling gently.

'Discipline and comfort,' she murmured, more to herself than to me.

'Mrs Hegedus, I …'

'Call me Harriet, darling. Now come along, let's not have any nonsense.'

She was still pulling, and the bubble of emotion in my throat burst. I gave in to the pressure. Accepted the inevitable trip across her knee, knowing it would be a comfort spanking and not a punishment, and being really quite ready for it. Only to then be turned over and laid on my back instead of bottom up, cradled in her arms. My first thought was that she was going to give me a pussy smacking, but before I could protest she had pulled open her coat and scooped one huge, red udder from her bra, pushing the teat to my mouth.

'Suck on mama and you'll feel better.'

I tried to pull back, but my face was smothered in heavy, firm flesh, with her huge nipple poking between my lips. She pulled me closer, ignoring my struggles as she went on.

'There, there, don't fight it, just let yourself go, like you do for Mrs Rathwell. Suck on mama.'

She got her arms right round me, holding me by my bottom and back, strong and comforting for all my revulsion. And she was big, and it had felt good suckling Mel. I gave in, opening my mouth on her monstrous teat and sucking on it, deeply ashamed of myself even as I began to nuzzle her. She gave a heavy sigh and cradled me closer, stroking my hair and gently squeezing my bottom.

'That's better, isn't it,' she cooed. 'You poor baby. You're safe now. Mama won't let those horrid men get you darling, she won't …'

I was already helpless, more for my own emotions than her strength, and at her words I surrendered the last of my pride, sobbing and clinging to her massive body as she suckled me. Even when she changed her grip to ease my thighs gently apart I didn't resist, spreading to her as she found my pussy. She began to masturbate me, rubbing clumsily between my lips as she told me what a good girl I was, and only then did I realise what the sweet sour taste was. She was making milk in my mouth.

'There,' she sighed, 'isn't that lovely? That's right, have a nice suck while I play with your sweet little pussy, that's my baby.'

Her milk was coming faster, filling my mouth. I swallowed, horrified at myself for letting her breast feed me, but unable to stop. It just felt too good, and for all the crude touches to my cunt she was getting to me. I was going to come, nude in her arms with a nipple in my mouth and her milk in my belly, feeding from her like a grown-up baby, utterly pathetic and yet utterly irresistible.

I'd done it anyway, and she'd spanked me, which somehow made all the difference. Discipline and comfort, she'd said. I'd had my discipline, over her knee, and now I was getting my comfort, a bellyful of milk while she masturbated my aching, needy cunt. Before I could even try to stop myself I was pushing my belly out to her hand, while sucking greedily at her teat as I cuddled onto her. She was so big I could barely breathe for the way my face was squashed into her flesh. But I didn't care, sucking up her milk and gulping it down, mouthful after mouthful, with my thighs cocked as wide as they would go, my pussy open to her fingers as she brought me up to orgasm. My back began to arch and I was thrusting myself onto her fingers as she tipped me over the edge, still suckling as wave after wave of ecstasy swept through me, until at last I went limp in her arms, my mouth still firmly attached to her nipple and a dribble of milk running down my chin.

She held on, cradling me in her arms and calling me her baby, until at last I came off her teat to lie back, my mouth wet with milk, my body splayed out in absolute surrender. I thought she would put me on my knees and make me lick, and I'd have done it too, but that didn't seem to me what she wanted. She just wanted to hold me.

After a while she turned me bottom up and began to stroke my cheeks, then to spank me, ever so gently. I let it happen, not saying a word as she enjoyed my bottom, gradually bringing the warmth to my cheeks until at length I'd begun to stick it up. At that, her hand went back to my cunt, fiddling with me until I came again, with my smacked bottom stuck high and my face buried between her massive breasts; my mouth slippery with milk and smothered in warm, female flesh.

When I finally detached myself she wanted me to stay

until I was safe, but the hunt had only been going for half-an-hour and I was suffering from a rapidly growing embarrassment for what I'd done. It was too intimate, too personal; she was my boss and had always been quite rough with me before, save for immediately after my encounter with Karay. I did appreciate the offer, though, and her concern was obviously genuine for all that it was misplaced; at least part of her reason for keeping me away from the hunt was so that she could get her own sticky fingers on me. But what really put me off was when she told me that she kept herself in milk because her husband liked to suckle. The thought of his bristly, beanfeaster moustache and bloated face pressed to the same breast I'd just been feeding from was too much, especially when I had a bellyful of her milk.

Yet I knew that if she spanked me I'd be back on her teat in no time, gobbling down milk with my legs apart and her hand between them while I imagine him in the same position, only with his thick, brown cock getting the attention instead of my cunt. I told her I'd feel I was cheating Morris and Melody if I didn't join in the hunt – which was a lie – and that I wasn't going to let them catch me anyway, which was true, but it didn't work. In the end I just fled, taking my mask and tail with me, so dizzy with sex and spanking that I was a little unsteady on my feet as I made my way down the corridor. I needed a drink, badly, and there didn't seem to be anybody about so I risked the bar.

My bottle from the night before was where I'd left it before being so rudely interrupted by Mr Hegedus. I poured the whole lot into a pint glass and retreated to the relative safety of the first floor, sipping wine as I wondered how I could escape capture but make it look as if I'd been outside all the time. The first thing was to turn myself back into a fox girl, which was the work of a moment although easing the plug up my bum again gave me such a lovely, dirty feeling I had to forcibly remind myself that it wouldn't be nearly as much fun to have a dozen or so cocks stuck up that same slippery hole one after the other. Not that the thought didn't appeal, in a way, but I had enough experience to know that it would leave me sore and incontinent for a week.

With my tail once more bobbing above my bum cheeks and my mask in place I went to the end of the corridor, where a window overlooked the roofs of the chalets and the fields and hedges beyond. I knew I'd be visible to anybody who happened to look that way, so approached cautiously. But what I then saw left me staring open-mouthed and I was fairly certain none of those involved were going to be wasting their time staring at the hotel either.

They'd caught Annabelle, in the little field behind the first few chalets.

I had to watch. Gavin had her on the ground, his combat trousers down and his muscular buttocks pumping hard. Her legs were rolled high and her cheeks were spread; his cock plunged in and out of her gaping pussy. His balls slapped against her plugged bumhole, with her tail sticking out and to one side. I could see her face, too, with her hair spread out in a halo on the damp grass; her mouth was wide in her reaction to the cock pumping in her hole; her eyes were invisible behind the mask that made her a fox girl, and that made her available to anybody who could catch her, to do with as they pleased.

They were going to as well, no doubt about it: all thirty or so of them were standing in a ring to watch her fucking, some of the men with their cocks in their hands. Melody had a strap-on sticking up from her unzipped jeans, thick and black and menacing. Monty was one of the men playing with himself, but Fat Jeff was performing a grotesque victory dance, alternately thrusting out his belly and his huge fleshy buttocks and shaking from side to side to make it all wobble. In his hand he held what had to be one of the devices I'd seen earlier, three fist sized balls on lengths of string joined in the middle, which he was whirling around his head. I saw that another was tangled between Annabelle's well-spread ankles, barely visible in the grass, and I realised how she'd been caught.

It was impossible not to think of myself in her place, brought down as if I really was an animal, one cock already up me and another thirty or so men and women to please before they were done with me. It was terrifying, but compelling too. And I couldn't help but feel guilty for not being out there with her, taking my share. Not that I was going anywhere near them, or even outside the hotel, but it was impossible to drag my eyes away from the scene.

They took turns with her, some mounting her between her thighs, some making her go on her knees, usually with one guy up her and one guy in her mouth to get hard while he waited his turn to fuck her, so she was always entered immediately after the last one had finished. One or two couldn't hold back, so she was soon dribbling spunk front and back, her mask soiled with thick white streamers where they'd come in her face and her bottom splashed with a mixture of that and mud. It was Melody who took her tail plug out and substituted her strap-on, sodomising Annabelle to the claps and cheers of the others. After that, anything went. Monty buggered her too, in a kneeling position, and came up her bottom, so that as the next man got ready to enter her she had spunk squeezing from her bumhole. He just didn't care, entering her briefly in the cunt before using his friend's come to help lubricate her back passage.

By then I had my hand between my thighs, clutching at myself as I imagined how she would feel. When Jeff took his turn and made a point of using all three holes, her mouth last after withdrawing his cock from her now gaping rectum, I was remembering how I'd offered Mr Hegedus the same filthy service and I came close to orgasm. Then came one of the new members, who entered her and stuck a finger up her bum at the same time, before extracting it to paint a cross on his face as he fucked her, with the others calling out in delight to see that he'd been blooded. With that I came.

Chapter Nine

I ESCAPED, PARTLY BECAUSE I hid and partly because once
they'd finished with Annabelle they weren't much good
for anything else, the men anyway. One or two of the
more virile ones had her twice before they let her go,
while the women also seem content. I thought they'd be
cross with me, and made a big show of how I'd
supposedly escaped by climbing down to the beach and
hiding in a cave right out on the headland. Instead they
were congratulating me, but also demanding a return
match. With everyone's attention on me, saying how good
I looked and what a good sport I was, I couldn't find it in
myself to refuse, though I secretly hoped that something
else would come up to distract them.

Being the one who got away also seemed to make me
more desirable. They all knew I was willing, or thought
they did, and knew about what I'd done before, but not
many of them had *had* me. The evening after the hunt
Melody gave me a very public spanking, after which
every single one of the men tried to flirt with me, but it
was Melody who took me to bed, alongside Annabelle.
Unfortunately I was too drunk and too tired to really
appreciate the compliment; though I helped Annabelle
lick her mistress to ecstasy before falling into an
exhausted sleep which lasted until morning.

Once the Razorback Boys and girls had left it should

have been back to normal, but it wasn't. Everybody wanted a piece of me, Mr Hegedus, who thought he was on a promise for my bumhole, but had to be careful of his wife, who in turn wanted to feed me at her teat and had also decided I needed spanking for even the tiniest thing. Stefan was as bad, demanding his cock be sucked with the same casual assumption of authority he used when he wanted me to lay the tables or do the washing up. Even Chris had begun to look at me oddly, as if wondering if it might not be fun to take some of what was obviously on offer. I was no longer so much the hotel maid as the hotel slut.

Not that I minded, except in the odd gloomy moment, but it was hard juggling their attention and the enjoyment of being such a turn-on for everybody with their casual assumption that I was up for anything. I like men to yearn for me, and to grant or deny their wishes in such a way that their yearning becomes ever more intense. It's different with women, more playful, but from some of the things Mrs Hegedus whispered to me while holding my head to feed me from her ridiculously oversized boobs, I couldn't but wonder if she was all there.

He certainly was; a dirty, manipulative bastard who knew exactly what he wanted, nearly as bad as Morris but without the charm. I held off. I sucked his cock for him after a quick spanking one evening in the week, and let him toss over me with my bikini pants held down while we were on the beach. But I refused him my pussy, much less my bumhole. The beach was actually rather better than I'd originally thought, especially at low tide, which exposed a huge area of chalk rock pools with small areas of really quite nice sand between them. When not working or being molested it became my favourite place. On a hot day the sand would dry out and I could sunbathe

128

in comfort, topless or even nude if I wanted to, because nobody seemed to care if guests saw me naked or not.

I could at least enjoy teasing the male guests, and also the workmen who'd been hired to fit Venetian blinds to the sun gallery. They could see down onto the beach, with a clear view of my favourite sunbathing spot. But just far enough away to be absolutely sure I was naked without being able to see any details. It was great fun, especially stripping with just the right of amount of feigned embarrassment to get them going, and all the while knowing exactly what I was showing and what I chose to conceal.

There were also the caves I'd pretended to hide in during the hunt, some of them quite deep: the perfect place to sneak off to and play with myself in safety, while the smooth, water-worn flints were ideal for slipping inside myself as I let my memory run over being fucked by Karay, or the way Melody had treated me. I could be sure I wouldn't be disturbed, as the best caves were right out on the headland, and given how long it took to walk there over the flints, I could check that nobody was visible and be sure of at least twenty minutes of perfect privacy, while I could hear anybody coming long before they got to me anyway.

I went down to the beach on the Saturday morning after the regular guests had left, both to sunbathe and because it was my last chance to tease the workmen, who were putting the finishing touches to the blinds. The tide was still going out, which meant I could undress right at the edge of the sea; being deliberately awkward as I struggled to strip off and get into my bikini, twice dropping the towel to show them my bare bum. I took ages, but I still finished before the sand was uncovered and waded out a little way, watching the tiny fish in the shallows and the way the two men were watching me.

They were quite good-looking, and both young, which I couldn't help but feel would make an interesting change. Not that I was actually going to approach them, but I was telling myself that if they tried to chat me up I'd go along with my mood. I was going to have to wait until they'd finished their work anyway, so there was plenty of time. With the water now revealing the edge of the chalk flats I sat down in the wet sand, enjoying the feel of the gentle waves on my skin and the movement of the cool water between my legs. It was rather sexy, and I began to wonder how to get Summer down to the hotel, and whether a visit to the beach might not provide the perfect opportunity to get her naked and maybe even spanked.

I could picture her, naked, or with her bikini pants pulled down, and her little pink bottom stuck up over my lap, as I gave her a few playful swats to see how she took to it, and if she did take it, she'd be rosy and bare with her thighs apart while I played with her pussy. Just the thought was enough to make me shake, and tempt me to take my top off, enjoying the sun on my bare breasts and the sudden sharp increase in interest from the two workmen.

It was great fun, but it seemed to be taking for ever for the tide to go out, while a line of clouds was blowing in from the west, threatening to spoil my sunbathing. I was going to give up, and was padding back towards where I'd left my clothes when I saw that the workmen had finished and were climbing down. There was only one reason they could want to come down to the beach, and my tummy began to flutter immediately.

'Hi, boys,' I managed, now with my arms folded across my bare breasts as they came close, enjoying their embarrassed grins but feeling much the same myself.

'I'm Vince,' the shorter of the two replied and jerked his thumb at his mate. 'This is John.'

'Hi,' John responded, obviously the shyer of the two, but also the better-looking.

'So, er ... we're off today,' Vince went on.

'Yeah,' John added, 'So, um ... leave the blinds alone, yeah, in case the cords go on the wet paint.'

I nodded, fairly sure they hadn't come all the way down just to tell me to mind the paint. John was having trouble looking at me, but Vince was grinning, his eyes fixed to the little bulges of flesh where I was covering myself up at the top, then flicking down. I knew my bikini pants were pulled up quite tight, giving me a camel toe and I couldn't help but blush and smile at his attention. He saw and his grin grew broader.

'You're fucking gorgeous,' he said. 'But you know that, don't you? How about you make up for all that teasing with a nice blow job? John can keep a look out for us.'

The blood came up to my cheeks in a rush, leaving me red-faced and staring, scarcely able to take in what he'd said and wondering if I really was that obvious. He wasn't joking either, and obviously knew he stood a fair chance without going through the normal flirting and cajoling.

'You fucking pig!' I managed, eventually. 'How dare you!'

'Aw, come on, love,' he responded. 'You're a big girl. You've done it before.'

Again I was left speechless, but John, whose face was as red as mine, chipped in. 'Sorry about Vince, love. He reckons he's a bit of a player.'

Vince shrugged. 'I'm honest, that's all. You're a good-looking girl. I'm about the best thing you're going to find around here, so let's get it on, yeah? I mean, it's not like

I'm after a fuck and you're going to end up pregnant, and I'm not one of them male chauvinist sorts either. You give me a suck and I'll lick you out. Can't say fairer than that, can I?'

I slapped him. I couldn't stop myself, bringing my arm around in a long swing that connected with his cheek.

'What the fuck did you do that for?' he swore, clutching at his face.

'Because you're a pig and a bastard and a dirty little sod!' I yelled back. 'Come on, John, come with me.'

I took John's hand, leading him away from Vince, who seemed genuinely astonished that I'd slapped his face. Yet it wasn't only what he'd said to me that had made me lose my temper, but the way everybody treated me, just assuming I was up for sex whenever, wherever and however they fancied it. Vince had just been the one to catch the rough end, but it was Mr Hegedus and Stefan and the Razorback boys, even Morris as well, who I was really mad at. John had been nice.

He was trying to hold a conversation as we walked, not at all sure of himself, and I realised that for all his height and build he wasn't much older than me, if at all. That made it all the easier as I led him towards the closest of the caves, and when Vince began to follow I pretended not to notice. If he wanted to peep at us it would just leave him even more jealous than if he stayed back. That way he'd know it had really happened and that he'd been turned down in favour of his friend.

Kissing me first and not even taking advantage of me being topless, John barely knew what to do. I made up for that, squatting down in front of him and unzipping his overalls to flop out his cock and balls. He was quite big and very pale, with a thick foreskin and just the tip of his knob peeping out where my body had stared to get to him.

I kissed it, then began to lick at the underside; always a sure-fire way of getting a man's undivided attention. He responded with a sharp gasp, encouraging me to take him in properly. I lapped under his shaft as he began to swell in my mouth.

'Fuck off!'

I though he was talking to me for a moment, and then realised that Vince had caught up with us and was watching from outside the cave. He ignored John, and the V-sign I gave him, but it was only intended to make him keep his distance. I wanted him to watch, and began to get really rude, rolling John's foreskin back with my lips and suckling at his knob, squeezing his balls at the same time, and with my back dipped to show off my bum in the tight scarlet bikini pants that barely covered me at all.

John's hand found my head, pulling me closer and forcing me to take him deep. I didn't mind at all, quite happy to let him make me gag on his erection, even fuck in my throat, just so long as it made Vince jealous to see how dirty and how compliant I could be. He'd seen, swearing under his breath and squeezing his crotch. I got busier still, blatantly enjoying John's now straining erection, tickling and squeezing at his balls, wanking him into my mouth and performing all the dirty little tricks I'd been taught in America.

'That's so good,' John sighed. 'You're lovely, Jemima.'

'Lovely, yeah. A lovely little tart!' Vince exclaimed, his voice thick with envy.

I pulled back long enough to stick my tongue out at him before taking John in my mouth again, as deep as I could to make him sigh once more and tighten his grip in my hair. He began to push into my throat, making me gag, but I was determined to be a good girl and didn't even try

133

to pull away, watching Vince sidelong all the while. It was too much for him. His hand went to his fly and he'd whipped out his own cock, long but skinny, and already erect. I just had to taunt him, and pulled back once more.

'You dirty bastard!' I mocked, laughing. 'Here, have something to wank over.'

I thumbed down the back of my bikini pants, baring my bottom, then shifted a little to give him a good rude view of what he wasn't going to get, never once letting go of John's cock. Having him getting so horny over me was almost as good as sucking on John's erection, and the temptation to stick a hand down my half-lowered bikini bottoms and bring myself off while I sucked was growing fast. It would have been the final insult for Vince too, watching me get off over his friend's cock when I'd rejected him.

I gave my bottom a wiggle, taunting him, but he got the wrong end of the stick, stepping close with his erection in his hand, obviously intent on taking me from behind. John swore, but didn't let go of my hair, and I was forced me to grab Vince's cock, because it was the only thing I could to do stop him putting it up me. I pulled hard, meaning to hurt him, but he merely grunted and closed his hand over mine.

'Not so hard, love,' he gasped. 'There, like that, over your tits.'

John's grip had tightened and I knew he was going to come, his fist twisted in my hair and his cock jammed down my throat, too deep for me to pull off, while Vince was using my hand to wank himself, squatted down with his erection pointed at my bare chest. I squeezed John's balls, hard, and felt his cock jerk and fill my mouth. The next moment I was gagging, with spunk exploding from my nose and around my lips, again and again, all over my hand and his overalls too.

'You filthy bastard, John!' Vince crowed. 'Get it out. It's my turn.'

I'd given in, wanking Vince's cock of my own accord as I struggled to swallow John's spunk, although most of it was dripping down my face and chest. The moment he'd withdrawn Vince put his in, sticking it deep without the slightest thought for me. I tried to take him, but he was so long and so thin it had gone right down my throat, making my stomach lurch violently.

'You suck like a pro!' he sighed, an instant before I brought my breakfast up all over his cock and balls. 'Jesus shit, you dozy bitch! Oh who gives a fuck …'

He trailed off with a sigh, wanking furiously at his cock as I sank down, coughing and retching. My tits were covered in John's spunk and my own sick, then Vince's spunk too as he came in my face and down my chest, milking his erection with his hand squashing in the mess I'd made over him, right down to the last few drops, which went in my hair before he shook his cock in a vain effort to get it clean.

'You're a dirty pig, do you know that?' he snapped.

I couldn't speak, but managed a half-hearted V-sign before climbing unsteadily to my feet, dripping filth. John looked concerned, but I could see he was trying not to laugh, while Vince was only worried about himself.

'Look at my fucking overalls!'

'That'll teach you to stick your cock down girls' throats!' I managed. 'Give me a hand, please, John.'

'What do you want me to do?' he asked, obviously reluctant to touch me.

I threw my hands up in despair and started down the beach for the nearest decent sized rock pool. Behind me, they'd begun to argue. I ignored them, getting down in the

135

sand at the bottom of the pool and splashing water in my face. I still wanted to come, but I wasn't going to give them the satisfaction of watching me, especially Vince. It would have to be later, but I knew what I'd be thinking of when I came, not John with his gentle but masculine style, but the moment Vince had jammed his cock so deep that I'd been sick down my tits.

He'd started back for the hotel, but John waited for me, apologising for his friend as we walked back towards where I'd left my clothes and towel. I hadn't bothered to put my top back on, because he'd seen just about everything anyway, which meant that I was in nothing but wet bikini bottoms and flip-flops as a woman jumped down the last couple of rungs of the cliff ladder and started towards me, a woman I recognised immediately – Danielle.

'Oh shit, it's my stepmother … I mean my … whatever. Say we were swimming, please.'

'Yeah, but …'

No doubt he wanted to point out that he was in his overalls, but as he hadn't bothered to clear up it was pretty obvious what we'd been doing anyway, and the smirk of contempt on Danielle's face as she approached made it very clear that she'd realised.

'There you are, Jemima,' she began. 'Aren't you supposed to be working instead of flirting with the workmen? Although flirting isn't really the right word, is it? You really do need taking in hand, don't you?'

For one ghastly moment I thought she was going to spank me, then and there on the beach in front of John and Vince watching from the cliff top, but she merely shook her head and picked up my towel for me. 'At least have the decency to cover your breasts.'

'What are you doing down here?' I asked, wishing I

could speak to her without sounding like a sulky little brat.

'I came down to see you, of course,' she replied, 'and uncle Vilmos.'

'Is Dad with you?' I asked hopefully. 'And Summer?'

'No. He's taken her to the London Eye. Summer gets on very well with your father, and I think you might make a little more effort to get on with me. We're a family now, Jemima.'

'What did you send me here for then?'

'Because I wanted you to do something productive and sensible in your year off, something that would teach you about life.'

John had wandered off, no doubt embarrassed by our conversation, allowing me to give free rein to my outrage as I replied. 'Oh, I'm learning about life all right, getting spanked and molested by your pervy old uncle! And the rest.'

'Oh what nonsense! I'm sure uncle Vilmos treats you very well.'

She knew it was a lie. I could tell from the tone of her voice, and I wasn't going to let her get away with it.

'Yeah, right, Danielle. I've spoken to Morris, so I know!'

For just a moment she seemed discomfited, then quickly changed the subject. 'You don't know what you're talking about, but I came down here to see you, and to treat you to lunch, so you can stop behaving like a brat and show a bit of gratitude.'

I responded with a grunt and followed as she turned for the ladder. Whatever reason she had for coming down, I was sure it wasn't just to treat me to lunch, and I was on my guard as we went inside, even wondering if she was looking for an excuse to spank me. Mr Hegedus was in reception and I was ready to run rather than get done in front of him, or by him in front of her. Nothing happened, and she was actually quite nervous, sticking close to me and going out to her car when I went to shower and change. I was just about to get into my uniform when she knocked on the door. 'Jemima?'

'Hang on. I'm just out of the shower.'

'Oh for heaven's sake, it's only me!'

'Yes, and ... oh never mind.'

I pulled my knickers up, wrapped a towel around myself and opened the door. She was holding a parcel, which she gave to me.

'This is a present for you. I'm hoping we can be friends, Jemima.'

I couldn't help but smile, and quickly tore the paper off. It was a dress, bright red and very light, just right for a summer's day, also very short.

'Thanks!'

'Put it on. No, let me do your hair first.'

'I'm all right.'

'No, come on. I want to.'

I've never been good at going against people when they're being nice, so I let her, and sat on the bed while she dried my hair and brushed it through. She had her own brush in her handbag, one with a handle, which had my tummy fluttering at the thought of what else it could be used for. But again she behaved perfectly normally, expect for insisting on putting my hair in bunches fixed up with little red plastic flowers.

'That's very pretty,' she said as I went to look in the mirror.

'I look about twelve!'

'Nonsense, and don't be in a hurry to grow up too soon. When you're my age you'll wish you did look twelve.'

'You're beautiful, actually.' I couldn't stop myself blushing as I said it, and I felt as if I was betraying myself for doing so, but she was trying so hard to be nice to me.

'Put your dress on then.'

I let my towel slip off, no longer worried about being naked in front of her, and slipped the dress on over my head. It was pretty, although a bit embarrassing because it made my nipples look really prominent and it was so short and light that the slightest breeze was going to leave me with my knickers on show. So was bending over too far.

'It's lovely, thanks. A bit short maybe.'

'I wasn't quite sure about the size, but you've got the legs for it. And anyway, you were topless on the beach just now!'

It seemed ungrateful to argue and I kissed her to say thank you, feeling better about our relationship than at any time since she'd shacked up with Dad. I didn't mind showing off either; there were no guests about, the workmen had been packing things into their van when we'd been in reception, and the staff had seen everything I had to show anyway, several times.

'Lunch then,' she said. 'I'm starving. Let's eat in the sun gallery.'

'It smells of paint, and we're not allowed to put the blinds up.'

She ignored me, chattering blithely about shoes as we made our way down to the main building. It was rather nice in the gallery, especially as the sun had gone in behind the clouds I'd seen earlier; cool and dim after the heat of the beach. I was hungry too, after being sick on Vince's cock, and it was amusing to have Stefan serve me. We were the only people there, and it was strangely quiet after the usual bustle of a Saturday lunchtime, making me wonder if Morris had a party planned for later. Again I considered whether there might be something going on, something Danielle knew about, but if so it wasn't happening at that moment and so I was content to eat.

'Shall we have a bottle of wine?' she asked. 'I don't have to drive.'

'Are you staying the night then?'

'I thought I might. Jeremy won't mind, and then I could take you shopping in Eastbourne this afternoon, if we go by bus.'

'That would be great! If you're sure it's OK?'

'Of course. A mum ought to spoil her daughter now and then.'

I bit down on my instinctive response, not wanting to start an argument, but those few words had completely destroyed my sunny mood. She carried on as if nothing had happened, ordering a bottle from Stefan before picking up the menu. 'How about the lobster? Is it fresh?'

'Mrs Hegedus buys them from a fisherman just up the coast and keeps them in a tank at the back, but it's terribly expensive.'

'Oh I think we can cope.'

'OK then, thanks, Danielle.'

'Shouldn't that be "thanks, Mummy"?'

I shook my head. She was looking right at me, and her voice had been kind but firm, growing firmer still as she spoke again. 'Jemima.'

There was a lump growing in my throat as I struggled to find the right thing to say. She was trying to be nice, and I did want to respond in kind, but that was one thing I could never do. 'I'm sorry, I can't!' I pleaded.

'I thought we had this out?' she said, her voice soft

'Bastard! Make him go away, Danielle, please?'

'Language, Jemima,' Danielle chided. 'If he wants to watch, he can. It'll do you good. Right, dress up.'

I snatched back with my free hand in a desperate attempt to stop her lifting my dress, but it was already up, the seat of the big white panties I'd put on now on show to her and to Stefan. My bottom felt huge, bulging in the cotton and I was calling both of them every name I could think of until Stefan spoke.

'So that's why you like it, you get it from your mum.'

'Piss off!' I screamed, still fighting to get my dress back down.

'Stop it, Jemima,' Danielle warned, 'or I'll have Stefan hold you down.'

'No, come on, please, that's not fair!' I babbled in rising panic. 'No!'

'Then let go,' she ordered.

I stopped fighting but kept my grip on my skirt, still trying to bargain.

'I'll be good if you make him go away, or at least let me keep my knickers up!'

'No,' she answered. 'You let go now, or I'll hold both your wrists while he gets you stripped.'

'No!'

I released my grip, sobbing bitterly as I put my hand back on the floor to steady myself. The tears were running down my face and it felt as if there was a huge bubble in my throat as she adjusted my dress to leave me bare from the waist down, save for my panties.

'Good girl, that's better,' she said. 'Now, how about those knickers? I said they'd come down, so down they come.'

'No, Danielle, please!' I begged. 'Or if you really have to, make him go away, please …'

'I said they'd come down, so down they come,' she repeated. 'Knickers down, Jemima!'

I'd caught hold of them, because I couldn't stop myself, but her last two words were a stern command and she'd already got her thumb in my waistband, with half my bum already on show. I was clinging on as hard as I could, but only succeeded in pulling them up into my slit to spill my cheeks out at either side. My flesh was wobbling crazily as I began to struggle again, kicking and squirming and cursing her as we fought over the tiny scrap of cotton that was my last barrier against complete exposure and the unbearable humiliation of a panties-down spanking from her. Stefan was laughing, and suddenly the most important thing in the world was to get rid of him.

'Please, Danielle,' I gasped as I slumped back over her lap. 'Don't let him watch. I'll be good!'

'Then let go of your knickers.'

'Only if you promise.'

'Oh very well, I suppose it is a bit inappropriate.'

I let go, relief flooding through me, only for her to immediately whip my panties right down. As my bum came on show, I screamed and tried to throw myself off her lap but she clung on. He was laughing louder than before as Danielle got me properly bare, dragging my panties off my kicking legs and hooking one calf around my ankle to spread me out, so my pussy was gaping and my bum cheeks wide open to show every rude detail between.

'You fucking bitch!'

'Temper, temper, Jemima,' she panted, 'You're only making it worse for yourself. When I say knickers down I mean knickers down, and that's that. You do not argue!'

'OK! But make him go away, please!?'

'No. In fact, I rather think he should watch. Perhaps then you'll learn your lesson? Anyway, he knows you get it. He's seen you at Morris's parties. Maybe he's even done you. Has he?'

'Yes,' I answered, the word a barely audible sob.

'I thought so,' she said. 'So what can it possibly matter if he sees you get it from me? It's all right, Stefan, you can spank her whenever you feel it's appropriate as far as I'm concerned. It'll do her good.'

He was looking doubtful, and no surprises there if he really thought she was my mother. But she was obviously enjoying my humiliation too much to care one way or the other. She was certainly keen on him getting a good look, holding me with my bum spread as she got her breath back. I hung my head, defeated, about to be beaten and burning with humiliation; for the position I was in, for being done in front of him, but most of all for being done by her. Finally she found her voice. 'Right, Jemima, you are going to learn a lesson, a hard lesson.'

As she spoke she had leant down to where she had placed her handbag by her chair. I knew what she was doing immediately and began to wriggle again, and to beg.

'No, Danielle, not the hairbrush! It'll hurt!'

'It's supposed to,' she answered, and brought it down with a heavy smack, full across my open cheeks.

'Ow! Danielle! Ow! Please, not so hard! I'm sorry, I really am … I'll be a good girl, but not so hard!'

She took no notice at all, spanking me with firm, deliberate swats to the crests of my cheeks. It hurt crazily and I could barely move, but to kick my one free leg up and down and thump my fist on the floor in a futile effort to dull the pain, all the while cursing and pleading with her to stop or at least slow down. At last she spoke, her

145

voice punctuating the smacks of wood on my bare flesh.

'This is a punishment, Jemima, not play. It's supposed to teach you a lesson.'

My answer was an incoherent wail as she continued to lecture me and apply the hairbrush, a word and a smack, another word and another smack.

'You will show me respect and you will show me gratitude. You will do as I tell you and you will do it promptly. Otherwise, you will be spanked. Do you understand that, Jemima? Spanked! Spanked! Spanked! Spanked!'

The last four smacks were even harder, and delivered to both my cheeks and the backs of each of my thighs, which stung so badly I lost what little remained of my control, thrashing wildly in her grip with my hair flying in every direction and my fist thumping a furious tattoo on the floor as she carried on with the beating; now on the back of my legs as well as my bum and faster than ever.

I thought I'd go out of my mind with the pain, because she was spanking so hard and she just wouldn't stop, peppering my bottom and thighs with blows, until everything had merged into one, hot ache, taking me over the brink. Suddenly I needed fucking; my cunt the centre of my body, a wet hole at the heart of my beaten flesh, was desperate for a long, fat cock while I was held shaking in the arms of the woman who'd beaten me. I couldn't help it, but that didn't stop me feeling desperately ashamed of myself as I began to stick my bottom up and my squeals and yelps turn to cries of pleasure. It stopped.'

'Oh no you don't!' Danielle laughed. 'I know your game, you little slut. Now get up.'

I couldn't; I was too well beaten to respond until she helped me, and even then I had to support myself on the back of a chair. Stefan gave a single, amused grunt and walked away, leaving me alone with Danielle.

She offered me a handkerchief. 'Wipe your face. You look a disgrace.'

She was right: my cheeks were wet with tears and snot hung from my nose and chin. I wiped it up, glad of the excuse to do something because I felt dizzy and confused; not sure if I hated her more than ever, or whether I needed a cuddle and my head put between her thighs. I was hurt and humiliated, but on a spanking high so strong I could barely keep my fingers away from my pussy. She knew; I could see it in her eyes and the faint smirk on her lips.

'You should give in to it,' she suggested. 'Come on, how about a hug for Mummy?'

It took all my willpower not to give in as she held out her arms. Her nipples were stiff, showing through her blouse, and I knew what I wanted: to be held to her chest and suckled while my bottom was soothed and my pussy masturbated.

'Piss off!'

'Jemima.'

It was all she said, but it was so firm, so full of authority, and she had taken me very gently by the hand. Something inside me seemed to snap. I went down, curled into her, my legs open and my face nuzzling at her breasts. She gave a little sound of amusement or surprise, but she understood and quickly tugged my dress up to leave my chest bare. Then she opened her blouse and lifted one breast free of her bra. I took her nipple in my mouth, hating myself even as I began to suck, with my cunt spread to her hand and the tears pouring down my cheeks. She knew she had me, smiling in triumph as I fed at her teat and her fingers rubbed on my pussy.

My tears were running free as I was masturbated, but I

147

couldn't stop myself. She was far more skilful than Mrs
Hegedus, flicking and rubbing at my clitty until I'd started
to arch my back and push myself into her hand, all the
while suckling urgently at her nipple and rubbing my face
on her breasts. My head was full of thoughts of my
spanking: how firm she'd been with me; how she'd stood
no nonsense about my knickers staying up; how hard
she'd beaten me in a really thorough punishment spanking
given with the flat of her hairbrush to leave my bottom
and thighs sore and aching; how she'd driven me to
complete surrender; made me lie in her lap with my titties
bare, my mouth fastened to her nipples and my thighs
cocked apart as she fiddled with my cunt.

When my orgasm came it was so strong I nearly
passed out, but before my head had even begun to clear
all my resentment came rushing back. I pulled away from
her, trying to get up, but my legs were shaking so badly I
fell on my bottom, which hurt and made her laugh. It was
all I could do to roll over onto all fours and pull myself up
on a chair, with her chuckling as she watched me. I knew
I was pouting, but I couldn't help it, because if it made me
look like a spanked brat then that was exactly what I was.

'What a sight!' Danielle laughed. 'Go on, in the
corner, hands on your head and leave your bum bare
while you think about learning a bit of respect.'

'You can't make me do corner time, Danielle!'

She picked up the hairbrush.

'OK, OK!' I promised. 'I'll go in the corner, but for
goodness sake!'

'Just do as you're told.'

I was going to go, but first I craned back to inspect my
bottom, which was one huge bruise, the backs of my
thighs too. But as I tucked up my dress so that I'd be
showing, I caught a noise outside and realised there were

people on the terrace. They'd probably heard, because I hadn't exactly been quiet, and I was blushing again immediately but very grateful John had told me to leave the blinds down. Dropping my dress, I poked two fingers between the slats, opening them to peep out and see who it was, because all they'd have to do was look down through the slats and they'd be able to watch me doing corner time.

'Don't …' Danielle began, but it was too late.

There was a man looking in at me; an elderly Chinese man with a completely bald head and a face like a big moon. He'd been watching, peering down through the slats as I was stripped and spanked by Danielle, and he wasn't alone. There was a whole line of them, the Chinaman, three who looked like American tourists, a pair I guessed were Turkish or Greek, an Arab in full traditional dress, a big, greasy looking individual who might have been Spanish or Latin American, Mr Hegedus and Morris Rathwell.

It took a moment for the truth to sink in. They'd watched my spanking, no doubt from the start; everything, including my surrender to Danielle. And it was no coincidence they were there. I'd been set up, and as all the pieces gradually came together in my brain my mouth had dropped open and the blood was rushing to my face in a blush so hot I must have been purple. The Chinaman had stepped back, and said something to Morris which I didn't catch, then laughed.

At that my paralysis gave way, a blinding humiliation welling up inside me as I dashed for the door. Tears streamed down my face, only for my grief to give way to anger before I got to my chalet. I turned back, choking with fury, to see Danielle already outside with Morris and Mr Hegedus shepherding the men away towards the car park.

'You ... you utter, fucking scumbags!' I screamed as I approached them. 'They were watching, weren't they? They saw everything! How could you, Danielle, you ... you let me suck ... you ...'

'You came,' she interrupted, her voice full of laughter.

I flew at her, going for her face with my nails, but Morris caught me, holding me around my waist as I clawed at Danielle. She had stepped back, well out of range as she went on.

'Get a grip of yourself, Jemima. You're a submissive little slut, and the sooner you accept that the better!'

'Ladies, Ladies!' Morris urged. 'There's no reason to argue, not when you have both earned a very substantial sum for a little fun. Now calm down, Jemima.'

I'd been trying to kick him and elbow him in the gut, but he was too strong for me, holding on with no real difficulty. Danielle put her hands up in a calming gesture, but I spat at her, catching her on the leg. Her face went dark and I thought she was going to slap me, but Morris turned me away, putting his body between us.

'Ladies!' he repeated, and now his voice was harsh. 'Calm down! For goodness sake, it was only a spanking.'

'Only!' I stormed. 'They think I was getting it from my Mum, don't they? You had it all worked out, didn't you? I suppose you even had the blinds put in just so that bunch of filthy old perverts could watch! You bastard, you fucking pig, you ...'

'Of course,' he responded, without the slightest hint of shame. 'Planning is everything. Why, even the two young gentlemen you treated to blow-jobs knew what was going on. I leave nothing to chance.'

Vince had appeared around the corner of the gallery, grinning, and I realised why he'd thought he could

150

squeeze a suck out of me so easily. John followed, and at least had the decency to look embarrassed. But that hadn't stopped him taking advantage, and they'd probably watched my spanking too.

'Bastards!' I spat.

'Come, come, my dear,' Morris urged. 'You were planning exactly the same for Summer, weren't you?'

'No, I ... I ... not like that!'

'Oh yes you were,' Danielle put in. 'And that alone more than earned you what you just got. But if you touch my Summer you'll think that was nothing, I warn you!'

'Just piss off!'

It was all I could think of to say, because in a sense she was right. I stopped struggling and Morris let go, leaving me to flop down in one of the cast iron chairs, unable to face them but staring out to sea. They left me to my thoughts, Chris handing out cold beers as Morris spoke to Danielle.

'That was good, very good in fact. Most of the men are delighted. But one or two did feel you overplayed it a little, especially letting Stefan watch, and you were so obviously enjoying yourself. They were expecting a bit more maternal authority and a bit less lewd delight, I think. Not that I'm blaming you, with little Jemima over your knee, who wouldn't have a bit of fun, eh? Still, we need to take everything into account. And you know how picky spankers can be, expecting every little detail to be perfectly suited to their fantasy. They're keen for more though, and prepared to pay, which is what matters. It really would be a good idea to have Jemima spank Summer, you know, or if not, how about doing her yourself?'

'Absolutely not!' Danielle gasped and there was real outrage in her voice.

My mouth had twisted up into a crooked little smile.

Chapter Ten

I'D THOUGHT MORRIS HAD given in a bit easily when I refused to let Danielle spank me and now I knew why. Looking back, I could see how he had planned the whole episode, right from telling Mr Hegedus to have the Venetian blinds installed. That had been a master stroke, allowing the men to watch undetected from just a few feet but ensuring that the conversation between Danielle and I couldn't be heard properly through the double glazed windows, because that would have been sure to give the game away. He had taken a few risks, and he'd been lucky the sun had gone in, or I might have seen the men's shadows against the blinds, although even then I couldn't have stopped them looking in while I was spanked and I wouldn't have known I'd been set up until afterwards. As it was, he'd got away with it; everything working perfectly save for the fussy old gits who'd felt the spanking was too rude and not disciplinary enough, and as they'd paid in advance his only concern was to provide them with another spanking more to their tastes at some future date.

They'd paid a lot too. I don't suppose it matters to rich men, not when they are used to throwing money at a problem until it goes away. When the problem was wanting to see a mother spank her daughter they could appreciate that they were at the top of the market, like maybe, egg collectors paying top dollar to have somebody raid the nest of an osprey. They had no more morals than egg collectors either, not only willing to go along with Morris's scheme, but thinking of it as the height of entertainment. It was followed by a lunch that lasted most of the afternoon.

I'd flatly refused to waitress and they made Danielle do it, but that was small consolation for what she'd done to me and the way I'd been tricked. The spanking was bad enough, and she'd really laid in, leaving the whole of my bum and most of my thighs black and blue. Having them think she was my mother while she spanked me was worse, but nothing to the appalling humiliation of having surrendered to her, so that the perverted old gits genuinely thought they had watching me suckle at my own mother's breast after a punishment spanking. That was what stuck in my head, creating emotions so strong and so muddled I couldn't even think straight.

Seeing the envelope on the mantelpiece in my chalet just made my feelings stronger still, and it was three days before I could bring myself to pay in the money. I did no work at all, and Mr and Mrs Hegedus left me alone, no doubt on Morris's instructions. When Chris told me there was another spanking party at the weekend I flatly refused to attend. As before, we were going to clear the hotel of ordinary guests on the Saturday morning, with a show at lunchtime and games in the afternoon leading up to the main event.

My bum was still a mess, but I knew that Melody wouldn't take any nonsense, and that even if she decided to leave me alone some of the other girls were sure to want to talk to me, and would inevitably try to persuade me to come along and watch if not actually join in. I was determined not to, and walked up onto the downs in the morning, meaning to stay out all day.

For the first hour I was all right, enjoying the open air and the bright summer sunshine despite my black thoughts. Unfortunately there's not a lot to do on open downland, except to sneak off into the bushes and play with myself, and I didn't dare for fear of where my thoughts might take me in the weakness of orgasm. By half past eleven curiosity had got the better of me and I had come back to where the hill overlooked the hotel.

Most of the grounds were hidden by the trees, and I could see why it was such a good place for their kinky fox hunt. I could also see the car park and the front of the hotel. Morris's gold Rolls Royce was there, which was no surprise, also the Razorback Jeep, which meant Gavin and probably Jeff were in attendance, maybe Monty too. There was also a big, black car just pulling in, almost certainly Mr Morozov's Mercedes.

My Russian gentleman and lover, who had taken advantage of me just as surely as Morris and Danielle, but who I found it hard to resent. That set me thinking about my own motives, and how what Danielle had done was so much worse. It all seemed to come down to pride, really, because both had mistreated me, but both had brought me to ecstasy as well, and society would have found their behaviour equally unacceptable. It wasn't even Morris who was the real problem, but Danielle, who claimed she wanted me to think of her as my mother, but had been happy to accept money to spank me in front of a paying audience.

Not for the first time I swore that I would get her back, even as an involuntary shiver ran through me at the memory of what she'd done, both the spanking and the suckling. I called her a bitch, out loud, but my voice was swallowed by the empty downland, making me feel utterly insignificant, my problems trivial. They were, really, in the great scheme of things; a thought I found more comforting than depressing, leaving my head clear for the first time in a week.

Far below me in the car park I could see Karay, prompting a truly wicked thought. For him to fuck Danielle, preferably with her strapped up tight after getting a well smacked bottom, would be delightful. To let Summer watch would be better still, a perfect and well deserved humiliation, but unfortunately impractical. Even if Karay agreed, and I could somehow set it all up, it was sure to end in disaster, with Summer completely freaked out and me in Holloway.

It was better to concentrate on Summer, if only to teach her to enjoy having her bottom roasted and maybe licking pussy. Danielle would be furious, and yet there would be nothing she could do unless she wanted her own behaviour to get a very public airing. Besides, the thought of spanking Summer and teaching her how to lick was deliciously horny. I was fairly sure she'd go for it too, just from the way she behaved with me, and after all, she was her mother's daughter.

Another car had arrived at the hotel, a taxi which left immediately after dropping its passengers, two girls. I didn't recognise either of them, although they might have been at the first hotel party, but they walked into the hotel with complete confidence. Both knew what was coming to them, any number of bare bottom spankings dished out by other girls and a load of dirty old men. Morris's girls knew, at least in general terms, if not the particulars, and once spanked they'd be leaving the next morning with several hundred pounds in their pockets, while I'd be sulking in my chalet.

I bit my lip, thinking of my savings account and the

three years at university ahead of me, starting in just over two months. Another few hundred would be very useful indeed. While if Mr Morozov wanted me to do him a special favour it might be a great deal more. They'd go easy on me too, because they were bound to want to see my bruises they'd spare me anything heavy. That meant only hand spanking, and perhaps not so very much of that, while Morris was sure to show his appreciation for my return. All I had to do was swallow my pride.

Half-an-hour later I was still thinking about it, although my meandering footsteps had taken me a fair way down the hill. I knew they'd be in lunch, which would mean a display spanking for somebody, just as Mr Hegedus had used me the first time. Chris had told me how they were going to do it as well, making the girls draw straws and the loser getting it over Melody's knee. The draw would already have been made, I was sure of that, and I was also hungry, having forgotten to take anything with me. All I had to do was turn up, make my peace with Morris, watch some hapless girl get her bottom roasted while I ate my lunch and then, if I decided I couldn't cope, I could easily escape.

I set off towards the hotel, my tummy fluttering and unable to shake the feeling that I'd given in too easily, but driven on by hunger and the thought of the envelope of cash that would be on my mantelpiece that evening if I just allowed a few men to spank me one more time. It really was the sensible choice, or so I was telling myself all the way down the hill. I said hello to Karay, who was still outside reception, and went in. Everybody was in the dining room, and to judge by the slaps, laughter and girlish squeals, whoever had drawn the short straw was suffering the consequences. I poured myself a glass of wine and joined them.

The girl being spanked was Jade, a close friend of Penny's, and she was over Melody's lap as I'd expected, with her jeans and knickers in a tangle around her ankles and her jumper and bra pulled up to bare her huge breasts, which were bouncing to the same rhythm as the slaps being applied to her chubby bottom with a leather spanking paddle. Everybody was concentrating on the show, some horny and eager, others laughing at the state Jade was in, or just mildly amused. Gavin, Monty and Jeff were at a table near the door, and as they'd always been nice to me, however dirty, I pulled up a chair, trying to sound confident and chirpy as I greeted them. 'Hi boys.'

Monty didn't notice, his eyes glued to Jade's wriggling bottom, but Jeff gave me a brief thumbs up and Gavin leant close to kiss me.

'Hey, Jemima. How's it going? We wondered where you'd got to.'

'I wasn't going to come. Bruised bottom.'

He gave an understanding nod and turned back to watch the action, but Melody was just finishing up with a last few swats before offering the paddle to Jade's mouth. Jade took it obediently, the leather gripped between her teeth. Mel told Jade not to drop the paddle or she'd be getting a dose of the cane, then slipped a hand between the plump thighs. I thought Mel was going to masturbate her and see if she could keep the paddle in her mouth while she came, but she had something much crueller in mind. Sticking both hands up Jade's already lifted jumper, she began to tickle her under the armpits. Jade went wild, completely unable to control herself, even less so than during her spanking, with her body absolutely writhing in Melody's grip, while she was squealing like a stuck pig.

She looked so funny I was having trouble not laughing out loud, for all that I'd been in equally ridiculous situations myself many a time, with an audience finding my pain and humiliation amusing as well as a turn-on. The boys had no reservations at all, laughing out loud and yelling for more, only for delighted cries to break to gasps and cheers as Jade lost control of her bladder. I heard her despairing cry, begging Melody to stop before she wet herself, and then it was too late. She had her legs cocked wide and she'd slid forward on Mel's lap, leaving her bottom stuck up so that as the pee erupted from her pussy it went almost straight up, in a great, pale yellow fountain that came down all over her bottom and legs and back, in her hair and on her jeans and knickers. Mel got wet too, with Jade's pee spraying in every direction as she wriggled in her frantic efforts to escape the tickling, but it didn't seem to bother her. She just carried on, with spurt after spurt of urine squirting from her victim's open cunt until they were both dripping with it and the spanking chair stood in a growing pool, which Jade sat down in when Melody suddenly let go

Everybody began to clap, and Mel stood up and took a bow before making for her room to clean up, but the show wasn't over. Jade was left sitting in her own puddle, looking thoroughly sorry for herself. The paddle had long since fallen out of her mouth, and no doubt she thought she had at least been spared the cane, but it was not to be. Mr Hegedus appeared, waving his arms and ranting about how he'd been running the hotel since nineteen ninety-one and nobody had ever pissed on his dining room floor, but it was all show. He made Jade kneel on the chair with her bottom stuck out to the audience and gave her six hard strokes of the cane across her wet bum cheeks. Then set her to mopping up her pee puddle with her own clothes, while she was nude with a striped bottom wobbling behind her as she scrubbed.

'Great stuff!' Gavin declared.

'Fucking ace!' Jeff agreed. 'I love the way her tits hang. I swear they're a big as footballs!'

Monty merely gave a connoisseur's nod, then turned to me.

'Hi, Jemima. I hear you got fucked by Karay?'

I was blushing immediately, and while I couldn't really deny it I immediately found myself making excuses.

'Yes … I was tied up though, and I had a pillow case on my head. I didn't even know until … until it was too late, and … anyway, he was more of a gentleman than any of you lot.'

'Be cool. I think it's kind of horny. Do you think he'd hunt with us?'

I choked on my wine.

'No pressure,' he went on, 'But if you're up for it that would be great, and there'd be a grand in it for you.'

'I'll see,' I managed.

'Cool. So what's with the bruised bum? Old Vilmos get a bit carried away with the staff discipline, did he?'

'Something like that,' I admitted, not willing to tell admit the truth or anything close.

'Let's have a dekko,' Jeff demanded.

He sounded interested, but sympathetic too, so I stood up and unfastened my jeans, pushing them down to show off my bruised thighs.

'Ouch!' Gavin commented, with both the others nodding their agreement. 'On the thighs too! I bet that hurt?'

'A lot,' I confirmed.

'I don't get the thigh thing,' Monty said. 'I mean, a bum's a bum's, so obviously it's good to smack it, but thighs?'

'So it hurts more,' Jeff pointed out. 'It's more for

sadists than perves like you, Monty.'

Monty nodded, clearly quite happy to be called a pervert.

'Drop your knicks, Jemima,' Gavin demanded.

Quite a few other people were beginning to show an interest, but I quickly popped my knickers down the back to show him the state Danielle had left my cheeks in.

'Colourful,' he said, 'very colourful. No spankies for you tonight then?'

'Maybe a bit of OTK,' I said as I covered up, 'But most men prefer the girls to start fresh anyway.'

'That's true,' Monty agreed. 'There was one guy Morris was telling me about, who thought that once he'd done a girl she was spoiled, so he'd only go for the ones who'd never been spanked before.'

'Who he thought had never been spanked before,' Jeff corrected. 'This is Morris we're talking about.'

All three of them laughed and I found myself smiling. I knew they were as bad as any of the other men in the room, maybe worse, but they were treating me better than before, as a person and not just a pretty toy. All of a sudden I was on the very edge of tears, but managed to hold them back, distracted by Gavin.

'Right, lads, lunchtime. You in, Jem, or do you have to serve?'

Nothing had been said, so I accepted his offer, tucking into fish and chips followed by a big slice of chocolate cake. Gavin kept the drink flowing too, so that by the time we'd finished I was feeling really quite good about myself, enough to want to make sure that I didn't miss out on the brown envelopes at the end of the party. Morris was at the far end of the room, with Mr Morozov, Lucius Todmorden and various other important clients. I went over, seating myself on Lucius's lap in a deliberate snub

161

to Morris. As usual he seemed indifferent, beaming happily.

'Ah, Jemima, good to see you! I am sorry about last week, but business is business. No hard feelings, I trust?'

'I'm here,' I said, unwilling to commit myself any further.

'But not, I see, ready to perform,' he went on. 'At least not if the sweet little exhibition you just gave to the Razorback boys is anything to go by?'

'Yes, you poor thing!' Lucius put in as he cupped my bottom, stroking gently.

'I don't mind hand spanking,' I offered.

'That's the spirit,' Morris responded, 'but we have seven girls this evening so I think we can spare your bottom.'

'And I still get paid?' I asked hopefully.

'I don't see why not,' he replied. 'I always feel it's unfair if a girl takes a severe punishment and then can't work for a couple of weeks, although I would like you to do me a little favour in return.'

'Oh. Does it involve Danielle?'

'Danielle's not here. I did ask her, but she doesn't dare risk a spanking in case your dad notices. No, there are two things I want you to do for me. The first is to persuade Amber Oakley and Kay to come to the next party. She's rather wary, as you can imagine, because she knows that Mel will be out for revenge. But I happen to know that both she and Kay fancy you more than a little bit. If they were on a promise I think we could get them down here. Not a word to Mel though. She doesn't trust you, and frankly I don't blame her.'

'Well I don't trust you,' I responded. 'How do I know you're not going to get Amber and Kay and me into bed and film us or something?'

He laughed. 'What an excellent idea, and a fitting revenge! Mel would enjoy that immensely, especially if you two were to top Amber. But no, I have something else in mind.'

'Um … let me think about it. What's the other thing?'

'Very well, but don't take too long. The other thing is that I have a little problem with Senor Juan Márquez y Lucientes over there.'

He gave a gentle inclination of his head and I followed his eyes across the room to where a big, greasy man with his napkin tucked in under his chin was making short work of a plate of pasta. I recognised him immediately as one of the men who'd watched Danielle spank me, making my tummy go tight as Morris went on.

'For some reason best known to himself, he doubts that Danielle is really your mother …'

'Morris …'

'And that you're a virgin.'

'But I'm not!'

'Yes, I know that, but he has a thing about virginity and he was making a fuss over my charges for watching the spanking so I told him you were. All he wants to do is ask you a few questions and inspect you.'

'Inspect me!? But Morris, that's not going to work, is it?'

'Now that's where you're wrong. All we need is a little liquid skin – you know, the sort you put on cuts – and there you are, *virgo intacta* once more. Mel's been practising on Annabelle and it's very convincing, but we'll make sure he's drunk too.'

I glanced at the man, who noticed and gave me a little wave.

'After lunch then?' Morris asked.

For a moment I was going to rebel, but it was five

hundred pounds, just to let some greasy old perve stare up my pussy, and not so much as a pat to my tender bottom.

'OK,' I said and sighed. 'What a bunch of weirdoes!'

'Many cultures attach great significance to virginity,' Lucius began. 'And I imagine that our friend is a Roman Catholic, in which case ...'

He carried on, still gently pawing my bottom as he lectured us. I cuddled into him, enjoying being held but not really listening. Mr Morozov disagreed on some point and they began an earnest discussion; Lucius breaking off occasionally to spoon feed me sticky toffee pudding from his bowl. Morris had lit a cigar, indifferent to the large no smoking sign directly above his head, and continued to puff until Melody came over.

'She's up for it,' he announced. 'Get her ready and I'll tell the Tradesman.'

'Good,' Mel replied. 'Come on, Jemima.'

She held out a hand, which I took, allowing myself to be led from the dining room, only not up to the Honeymoon Suite as I'd expected, but into the kitchen. Stefan was doing the washing up, which should have been my job, and gave me a filthy look. He was going to say something too, but Mel got in first, jerking her thumb towards the door.

'Out, you can do that later. Jemima, strip.'

'What, naked?'

'Jeans and knickers off will do, then get on the chopping block.'

Stefan left, but Mrs Hegedus came in as I was unfastening my jeans, watching me with a disturbing intensity as I peeled off and climbed on the heavy wooden table we used for chopping meat. There was no time for modesty; Mel pushed me back and spread my thighs to leave my pussy gaping to the room. She peered close, one finger probing my sex as she began to speak. 'The problem is that we're not sure how good a look at you Juan the Tradesman got while Danielle was spanking you, but I've been looking at hymens on the net and they vary a great deal in size and shape. I'm going to give you just a little one, but it needs to look right.'

'Why do you call him the Tradesman?' I asked.

'Because he always enters round the back,' she explained, using her little finger to tickle my anus. 'At least, when the front entrance is blocked, as yours is about to be. Hmm ... Harriet?'

'Yes, Mrs Rathwell?' Mrs Hegedus answered.

'Do you have a raw chicken breast handy?'

'Certainly, Mrs Rathwell.'

'A raw chicken breast!?' I demanded. 'What for?'

'The texture is about right,' she explained as she eased my hole wide. 'We need that glossy pink look.'

'I thought you were going to use liquid skin?'

'I am, to hold the piece of chicken meat in place. Now stay still.'

Mrs Hegedus had given her a chicken breast and I could only lie back and think of men who liked to put it up girls' bums in order to preserve their virginity, presumably for later. I could barely feel it as Mel splayed out the mouth of my pussy and put a tiny piece of chicken meat in place, but the liquid skin was cold, making me gasp.

'Stay still!' Mel repeated. 'Hmm ... not bad, not bad at all. Still, it will help if you make a bit of a fuss over being inspected.'

'That won't be difficult!' I promised, now feeling thoroughly put upon with my pussy blocked with a piece of raw chicken and some randy old bugger about to inspect me for virginity.

'I'll stay with you, of course,' she promised. 'Come on then, he thinks you're already upstairs.'

I hurried back into my clothes and followed her up by the fire escape to the Honeymoon Suite and that same bed where I'd been had by Karay. That had been strange, pure filth and seriously horny, but there was something disturbing about what I was doing now, and it was beyond kinky.

'He wants you naked,' Mel told me, 'and bottom up.'

That was no surprise. Men generally do. I peeled off quickly and Mel took my clothes, hiding them out of sight to leave me stark naked and without protection. We talked for a while before there was a knock on the door, Morris, with Senor Juan Márquez y Lucientes behind him. To my surprise Mel addressed him in Spanish and he answered in the same language, then glanced at me, his little fat mouth pursed in speculation and his piggy eyes flickering over my breasts and hips.

'Get on the bed,' Mel told me. 'Crawling.'

I obeyed, only remembering to make a fuss at the last second and trying to give the briefest possible flash of my pussy. Mel spoke a sharp word, slapped me and took me firmly around the waist, holding me tight as she spread my hole to the men. I was wriggling as they both peered close and the Tradesman said something in Spanish. Again Mel slapped me, but I kept wriggling and began to snivel, at which the Tradesman made an odd clucking sound which might have been disapproval for my lack of obedience, amusement at my reluctance, or just plain lust. Again he spoke, and he sounded satisfied, then to Morris in heavily accented English.

'She is intact. I extend my apologies for doubting you.'

Mel let go and I hurriedly turned over, covering my tits and pussy in best outraged virgin style. He was smiling

166

now, which made him look even creepier than before, and had sat down on the edge of the bed.

'Say to me, Jemima,' he asked. 'Does your mother spank you often?'

What with having bits of raw chicken glued into my pussy and having to stick my bum in the air for an intimate inspection, I'd forgotten all about Danielle, so that for an instant I thought he meant Mum. That made it such a nasty shock that even when I did realise, all I could manage was a feeble nod. It seemed to be exactly what he wanted; the excitement rising in his voice as he went on. 'Does she always pull your panties down?'

Again I nodded, because the image he'd planted wouldn't go away, of me over Mum's knee with my knickers turned down at the back and Pippa sat giggling on the sofa as she watched me get my bottom smacked.

'Ah, yes,' the Tradesman was saying, 'it is so important that a girl should take a spanking with her panties down; but do you mind?'

I tried to concentrate, wondering what answer he'd expect: yes, that I hated going bare bottom, or no, that I accepted it as necessary for my discipline. The truth was somewhere in-between, that it was just something that happened when I was spanked, like Dad having a whisky when he got home from work. He didn't have to do it, but he always did; in much the same way my panties came down. But if Senor Juan Márquez y Lucientes liked virgins he probably liked good girls too, fairly good ones anyway.

'A ... a naughty girl should always be spanked bare bottom,' I said. 'So no, I don't mind. I know they have to come down.'

He gave a sigh of such profound ecstasy that for a moment I thought he'd come in his pants, only for him to carry on.

'And your mother, she takes down your panties always, or sometimes she makes you take them down?'

'She always takes them down herself,' I answered automatically.

This time he looked disappointed and I hastened to correct myself. 'Except sometimes, when she makes me take them off in front of her, and gives me a lecture before my spanking.'

This time I imagined Danielle, telling me off as I stood in front of her, bottomless with my hands on my head and Summer watching. I was going to kill Morris.

'A wise woman,' the Tradesman commented. 'And I have seen that she spanks you hard, as a bad, bad girl should be spanked. Still you have the blemishes.'

I nodded, not sure if he expected an answer.

'But then,' he said, 'why does she put you on her udder?'

Mel burst out laughing, then quickly apologised as he threw her a filthy look.

'Her breast,' I supplied.

'Not when it's Harriet,' Mel said quietly.

This time the tradesman's look was questioning.

'Harriet, Mrs Hegedus,' Mel explained casually as my face flared crimson. 'She takes over Jemima's discipline when Danielle's not about, and she lets her suckle too. She has big breasts.'

As Mel spoke she held her hands under her own boobs, which were hardly small, indicating even bigger ones. The Tradesmen smiled.

'Senora Hegedus? She does, yes, *muy grande*.'

He laughed, then turned to me again. 'So why?'

'To … to comfort me,' I managed, now as red as a beetroot. 'To make me feel better after my spanking, but ... but to make me feel small too, like I'm a baby.'

'This is good,' he replied, 'and now I understand. Yes, you should not forget you are her baby. So last, into the corner you go to show your red bottom?'

'I have to do corner time, yes.'

He clapped his hands and turned to Morris.

'She is perfection. Never should I have doubted you. I wonder, does she need sodomising?'

You don't often see Morris Rathwell taken by surprise, but his eyebrows rose at least a quarter of an inch.

'Um ... well,' he began, glancing at me as I gave a squeak of alarm. 'Perhaps later?'

'You must excuse me,' the Tradesman responded. 'My English is not perfected.'

He went on in Spanish, addressing Mel, who then turned to me. 'He wants to pay you for a bum shag.'

'I gathered that! Um ... look, I ...'

He'd got me impossibly flustered: my stomach churning and my pussy hot, my head full of confusing thoughts about spanking. I didn't know if I was ready to be prostituted to the Tradesmen, or how easily I'd be able to accommodate him up my bottom for that matter; an idea that seemed to be utterly revolting and irresistibly exciting at the same time. Mel was talking to him, maybe selling me, a thought that made me want to spread my legs then and there.

'OK,' I said very quietly. 'But Mel stays in the room.'

She spoke, he spoke back, and I'd been sold. He paid then and there, placing the money on the mantelpiece. Morris left the room and I was put on my knees to suck him erect while Mel poured him a drink and got my bottom ready. His cock was thick and dark brown, a bit like Mr Hegedus, but with an enormously fat head, so big it was like sucking on a golf ball; something Hudson had

169

made me do as part of my blowjob training. Like a lot of older, fatter men, he took his time as well and was still only half stiff as Mel came out from the bathroom with the same lube Mr Morozov had used, and a slim pink butt plug.

'Stick your bum out, Jem,' she said happily as she got down beside me. 'You have a lovely cock, Senor Márquez y Lucientes.'

'And you, you have lovely udders ... no, breasts,' he replied. 'May I see them, perhaps?'

Mel shrugged and began to unfasten her blouse. He watched, one hand resting lightly on the back of my head to control the rhythm of my sucking as she peeled off, first her bloused and then her bra, to bare her heavy, black breasts. She held them up, stroking her nipples to make them stiff. He gave a please sigh and began to push himself in and out of my mouth.

I'd stuck my bottom out as ordered, and closed my eyes, concentrating on the taste and feel of his cock in my mouth, and I tried to relax as Mel put one well lubricated finger to my bumhole. She teased me for a moment, tickling my hole before easing her finger gently inside and up my bottom. I stuck it out a bit more, thinking of how I was being prepared for a buggering from the man whose cock was growing in my mouth and how the woman doing it had sold me to him.

'That's right,' Mel said softly. 'Just take it easy and ...'

She trailed off as she removed her finger, replacing it with the butt plug. I felt my ring start to spread as she pushed for the first time; a little more the second time, to leave me feeling open and loose as she pulled back, only to then push more firmly, easing the plug all the way in to my bumhole stretched taut and open.

'Up it goes. There, you do look cute.'

Senor Márquez y Lucientes still wasn't fully hard, maybe because I'd been concentrating on accepting the plug up my bottom, so I took his balls out and into my mouth while tugging on his shaft. Mel saw and began to play with her boobs, cupping them in her hands and rubbing them on my back. I was getting horny for her, eager to suckle on her lovely big breasts or have her sit on my face, but I'd been paid for a buggering and carried on playing with his cock, until at last he had a thick, stiff erection rising from his open trousers into my mouth.

'Now I am ready,' he said. 'Show me that little bottom, and your virgin cunt … kneeling.'

I didn't need telling, and quickly turned from the chair to lay my upper body over the bed with my bottom presented. He gave a grunt of effort as he heaved himself out of the chair, but he was eager enough, shuffling over to me on his knees with his cock aimed between my cheeks. Mel came and sat down on the bed, stroking my back as he got behind me. His cock touched my pussy and for a moment I thought he was going to ram it up, bursting my fake hymen for the supposed thrill of taking my virginity, only for him to start rubbing his huge knob on my clit. My mouth came wide in a gasp of pleasure, and he chuckled to see hear my helpless response. I really couldn't help myself, pushing myself back onto his prick, only for him to stop rubbing and just for one instant press his knob to my hole as if to fuck me.

'One day, little one,' he said. 'What do I do with this?'

His fingers had found the base of my plug as he spoke, to pull it free, none to gently, and leave my bumhole agape for his cock.

'Give it to me,' Mel said. 'Open wide, Jemima.'

'Hey, no! Mel.'

171

'Hush,' she said firmly and the plug had been pushed into my mouth.

He gave a lewd chuckle to see me made to suck on something that had just been up my bottom and I hung my head as his cock pressed to my open, slippery rear hole. Mel began to stroke me again, cuddling close so that her naked breasts were pressed to my side. I twisted around, smothering my face between them as he pushed and I felt my anus start to spread.

'Is this the first time?' he grunted, and pushed.

My answer was a gasp as my anus gave to the pressure, his bloated cock head now up my bum with my ring pushing in on his shaft. I couldn't have answered him anyway, with the butt plug in my mouth and my face smothered in Mel's boobs.

'I think it is,' she said, and he made an animal noise in his throat as he jammed another inch or so of prick into my rectum.

I felt as if I was going to split, my ring straining wide on his shaft and pulling in and out as he continued with my buggering, forcing himself gradually deeper with his hands locked on my hips and his thumbs spreading my cheeks to show off my buggered anus. I took it gasping and shaking, clinging onto Mel and rubbing my face in her cleavage for comfort, until at last she took pity on me, pulling the butt plug free of my mouth and substituting one hard black nipple. He said something in Spanish as I began to suckle, gave another push and I could feel his belly pressing to my bum cheeks. Another and his balls were touching my pussy, the full, fat length of his cock now bloating out my rectum.

He buggered me hard, grunting like a pig as he rammed his cock in and out of my bum hole with his fat belly squashing against my cheeks, and his balls slapping on my empty cunt. I'd soon reached back to masturbate, all thoughts of pretending to be shy and reluctant forgotten, my head full of how I'd been sold and buggered, but that wasn't what I needed to come over. Any other time, yes: for the sheer, filthy, sleazy delight of remembering how I was, bent over the bed with my bumhole speared on his erection and my cheeks open to his eager gaze, his cock pulling my straining ring in and out while the money I'd been paid for the use of my bottom lay on the mantelpiece, while the woman who'd sold me gave me comfort by stroking my hair and letting me suck on her nipples.

As my fingers worked my clit my thoughts had gone elsewhere, to what he'd said and the pictures he'd conjured up, first of me standing bottomless in front of Danielle for a lecture with Summer watching my humiliation. That put tears in my eyes, because I didn't want it to turn me on, but I couldn't stop myself, yet even that wasn't the final indignity I needed for my orgasm. The Tradesman saw the wet of my tears on Mel's breasts and grunted something, obviously getting off on my crying as he buggered me, but in my head I was far away, lying across Mum's knee with my skirt tucked up and my knickers pulled down while Pippa giggled over the sight of her little sister getting a spanking.

Chapter Eleven

I WAS A LITTLE sore after my buggering from the Tradesman, and very ashamed of myself for what I'd come over, but that didn't stop me enjoying the rest of the party. Once I'd got in my little uniform, but leaving my froufrou knickers off, everybody was admiring my bruises and it was fun watching the other girls get spanked while nobody was allowed to touch me. My resentment was still there, but now focussed on Danielle save for a lingering spark that made me want to get back at Morris, so I stuck to the people who were friendly to me as well as pervy – mainly Lucius and the Razorback boys. I got very drunk too, and ended up treating Monty, Jeff and Gavin to blow jobs in my chalet before having my false virginity ritually taken in a game of cards that lasted until dawn.

The next day was a write-off. My head hurt and so did just about every other muscle in my body. I stayed in bed, with the door locked, ignoring Stefan's angry demands to come and help with breakfast. He went away in the end, after threatening to get me sacked and spanked, neither of which bothered me in the slightest. I went back to sleep and didn't wake up again until well into the afternoon. By then all the guests had left, except for Mr Morozov, Mel and Morris, who told me he'd had arranged another party two weeks later on the Saturday evening with the fox hunt the following day.

I went for a walk with Karay to clear my head, both of the fumes from the night before and my muddled emotions for the way I couldn't help growing aroused over what should have been the most inappropriate thoughts imaginable. In the end I got so turned on that I let him fuck me, enjoying every second for all my aches and pains, with his fur coat tickling my bum and his lovely big cock working in my hole until he'd spunked up inside me. I rubbed myself off in the mess while he obligingly licked my bum, bringing me to a truly wonderful orgasm that left me feeling a great deal better as we made our way back to the hotel.

Mel was waiting for me in the bar, to check that I was really up for the hunt and to make sure I was willing to call Amber and Kay. I wasn't particularly happy about being the bait for her intended revenge, but the thought of being taken to bed by them was highly intriguing. I knew Amber's reputation for needing to find an excuse before she could enjoy her submission, so in the end I agreed to do it. But with a warning, calling her to say that though I'd love to play with them at Morris's party, Mel would be after her. She said she'd call back.

The next two weeks passed quickly. I'd got so used to being a maid, it had become automatic; serving and cleaning, being told what to do by everybody, even being spanked now and then, though all that bare bottom discipline is hardly recommended treatment for employees in the service industry. But after over a week without it, I was getting needy before my bruises had even gone and gave no resistance when Mr Hegedus used a broken cup as an excuse to turn me over his knee in my chalet, and then made me suck him off.

After that it was business as usual, with my uniform skirt getting turned up several times a day for my bottom to be smacked, while I seemed to spend half my life down on either cock or nipple for a mouthful of spunk or milk from my bosses. I preferred Mrs Hegedus, because while they'd both spanked me, at least she had the consideration to rub me off while she fed me. She'd begun to make me lick too, with my head clamped between her huge thighs and my hair in her fist to keep me in place until she was finished.

Amber didn't call back until the Saturday morning, to tell me she and Kay would come, while making it very clear that they wanted me in bed with them that night, which left my tummy fluttering and my mouth dry as I went about my work. As usual we had to clear the hotel, and I was still carrying suitcases outside for the ordinary guests when I saw a small red car coming down the drive. It was Penny, two hours earlier than she was supposed to arrive; although as she never looked anything but completely respectable it didn't really matter. I finished what I was doing and joined her in the bar, only to be steered outside and along the cliff path.

'I've got you a place,' she said as soon as we were clear of any flapping ears. 'As a lab assistant in my own department. But I can't hold it for very long and we should really have advertised the post. It doesn't pay all that much, but it'll be more than you're getting here.'

'For being a maid, yes. But I'm getting five hundred just for tonight's party, and more tomorrow.'

'Jemima!' she sighed. 'Must you?'

'Yes, I must. I want to pay my way through uni.'

'I know, but still … I just wish you wouldn't, not for money.'

'We've had this out before.'

'Yes, we have, haven't we, and look what happened with Danielle.'

'How did you know about that!?'

'Melody told me, while offering me five hundred pounds to give you an aunt-to-niece spanking. I refused.'

'Oh. I wouldn't mind, not with you.'

'Jemima!'

'Oh all right, I suppose you're right about Morris. But how about if I leave here, stop going to the parties, but keep my private gentlemen?'

'I'd rather you didn't, but … maybe. Where would you entertain them, or whatever you call it?'

'At your house, maybe?'

'At my house!'

'Why not? There's plenty of room. I could even stay with you, and that way I wouldn't have to live with Danielle, and it would be better for getting into work, and you can spank me.'

I added the last bit quietly, knowing she liked to and hoping the offer would be too good to resist. She wasn't so easily taken in. 'I intend to!' she assured me. 'Hard, and often. But you cannot bring your clients to my house, Jemima! It's not a brothel!'

'It's only spanking.'

'It's not a spanking brothel either! For goodness sake, your grandmother lives across the road! Anyway, it's not only spanking, is it? You suck them off afterwards, don't you?'

'Usually, but so what? You get up to far worse, and it's not as if I'll be bringing random nutcases home, only my private gentlemen. How about Lucius Todmorden?'

'He's safe, it's true, but …'

'And even if Grandma walks in she'll just think he's come to visit about your will or something.'

'Oh right, while he's spanking you upstairs?'

'Well, we'll have to be a bit clever about it, obviously.

But it would only be once a week or so, twice maybe ... three times tops, and we'd agree who I could bring, and ...'

'Jemima,' she interrupted, 'you are not using my house as a spanking brothel and that's that!'

'If you want me to quit on Morris you're going to have to let me.'

She didn't answer and looked pretty cross as we walked on, up the hill to the very top, not far from the hollow where I'd let Karay fuck me two weeks before.

'Just three men,' I urged. 'That's all, I promise.'

'Who?' she demanded, weakening.

'Lucius,' I said quickly, 'and Mr Morozov, and maybe this Mexican guy I met, Senor Juan Márquez y Lucientes. They're rich men, and very discreet.'

She was staring out to sea, biting her lip, and spoke suddenly, her voice far from confident. 'OK, but you're to give notice today.'

'Tomorrow,' I pleaded, 'after the hunt, but you're coming aren't you, so I can just leave with you. Nobody's going to stop me, are they, not after the way they've treated me?'

'That's true,' she agreed. 'OK, have it your way.'

I kissed her and we walked back down the hill hand in hand. Other people were beginning to arrive: Morris with Melody and her entourage, Fat Jeff, then Mr Protheroe and Mr Judd, whose eyes followed me and Penny as we walked across the car park as if glued to our bottoms. Jeff was even less reserved, coming up between us and taking a cheek in each hand as he spoke. 'Ah! Nothing like a handful of nice, bouncy girlflesh. So what's Morris got lined up for us tonight, eh?'

'We're having a lottery, sort of,' I told him. 'It's called Joker in the Pack. Amber wouldn't come unless Mel told her how it works and she told me. Everybody's name goes in a hat on a piece of paper and the girls have to nominate somebody to pull one out on their behalf. Whoever's name is chosen gets to spank them, or they can have another go, but it's a spanking and the cane. Or a third go, but it's a spanking and cane again, and whoever they pick last gets to take them up to his room, or her room, which is why it's so clever. Mel knows Amber will keeping picking in the hope of getting a girl, but the odds are she'll end up getting spanked, caned and taken upstairs by somebody like Mr Protheroe. Mel would love that.'

'She'd prefer to punish Amber herself,' Penny put in. 'And anyway, we'll probably have to go more than once each so Amber's almost certain to get done by a man.'

'Sounds good either way,' Jeff said. 'So what's the joker?'

'If you pick your own name you get passed around,' I told him. 'Just for spanking, but from everybody, and no backing out.'

He laughed. 'Who're the girls, other than Morris's crew and you two?'

I didn't know, and told him so, leaving him to talk to Penny because what she'd said had made me think. Amber was sure she knew what Mel was up to and had decided to take her chances, accepting a spanking from whoever she picked. There was still a risk of picking Mel, or getting passed around, but Mel was taking the same risk. Somehow it had to be fixed, perhaps by having a second hat in which every piece of paper had Mel's name written on it, or worse, Amber's. That also explained why the girls weren't allowed to do the draw themselves, so that if Amber challenged her result, Morris would have a chance to switch hats. I was sure I had it, and was smiling

179

to myself as we entered the hotel, only to be brought up short by Stefan.

'Better get that skimpy uniform on, Jemima,' he ordered. 'You're serving lunch.'

I didn't argue, but apologised to Penny and made for my chalet. It was for the best anyway, because while everybody was in the restaurant, I could look for the second hat and either just pinch it, or if I had time, change all the names, maybe to Penny, who would be the softest option for Amber, not Kay, because I knew she found it almost as humiliating to be spanked by her own, very submissive, girlfriend as by Mel.

It had been a while since I'd worn my sexy uniform, and as I pulled my froufrous up I realised that I'd put on a little weight, no doubt partly made up of Mrs Hegedus's milk and her husband's spunk, although with so much food available all the time it was hard not to pig out. My bottom did look a little plumper in the mirror, especially with my froufrous pulled tight across my cheeks.

I told myself I'd still be the slimmest girl at the party, but that didn't make me any less conscious of the way my bottom bulged in my froufrous as I hurried back to the restaurant. And I was wishing I'd refused Mrs Hegedus's offer of bacon, eggs, black pudding and beans that morning, which had left my tummy bulging ever so slightly as well. Not that I need have worried, with the men paying me more attention than anybody else over dinner, with hands on my bottom every time I bent to serve.

Amber hadn't arrived and I was kept too busy to ring her mobile and warn her, but there was a big cardboard box on the front desk, which I was sure would contain the gear for the evening, including the hat, or hats. It was only going to take a second to check, but Mrs Hegedus and

Stefan had me running around like a mad thing, while there was a constant trickle of people coming in and out of reception.

I even suggested that Mr Hegedus spank me and make me do corner time by the front door, so that everybody who arrived could see, but it would also mean I was right next to the box. To my surprise he told me we were too busy, not to be such a slut, and that I could count on all the spanking I could handle later on. He was right too, because just about every table was full and we'd served sixty-three covers by the time the last guests were finished.

There were ten girls, twelve including myself, Amber and Kay, to go around fifty-two men plus the other four staff, which meant that I'd have to go up for the draw at least four times, more likely five. That was going to mean a very hot bottom indeed, and I knew that once I was warm I'd be unable to resist turning down my first and second picks so that I ended up being taken upstairs with no say over who got to have me: as scary and as exciting a thought as I could have wished for.

With lunch over Stefan made sure I did my share of the washing up, keeping me away from the box, and when I was finally allowed to mingle it was gone. I knew where it would be though, the Honeymoon Suite, and waited until both Morris and Melody were busy before dashing upstairs with the spare key from reception clutched in my hand. Sure enough, the box was on the floor by the window, but there was only one hat in it: a big glossy topper.

It didn't take a genius to work out that it was a magician's hat, and sure enough, the top part of the lining came away to reveal a shallow compartment underneath. With a little sleight of hand Morris could make sure that when Amber's turn came she was sure to get her own piece of paper, but I couldn't fix the draw another way for the simple reason that the names hadn't been written out. I hesitated, wondering what I could possibly do and not paying attention, so that the first I heard of Melody was a cough from directly behind me. The hat was still in my hands and the expression on her face told me she wasn't going to be accepting any excuses.

'Very clever, Sherlock,' she said. 'You figured it out, which leaves me with a little problem.'

'What's that?' I asked. 'I won't tell Amber, I promise. I was just curious.'

'I don't trust you, Jemima. I know you fancy Amber, and why not? She's just the woman to cope with a little slut like you. And so am I.'

'I … I know. I love what you do to me, Mel.'

'I'm very glad to hear that, Jemima. Come here.'

I hung my head, put the hat down, and crossed the room with every expectation of being whipped across her knee for a good spanking before being made to lick. Instead she took me by the hand and led me into the bathroom, making me realise she had something else in mind. 'If you're going to pee on me at least let me strip off!'

'Shut up. Get on the floor, kneeling.'

'But, Mel …'

'Shut up, I said! I'm not going to punish you, Jemima, not yet. I just want you safely out of the way until I've had Amber. Now kneel down and put your wrists together behind your back.'

'But Mel …'

'Do it!'

I obeyed, pouting badly as I was left on the floor while she collected a hank of rope, which she used to tie a tight cinch between my wrists; locking them together and pulling on the spare cord to force me to bend lower and stick out my bum.

'Ow! That hurts!' I protested but she ignored me, tying the cord off on the exit pipe from the sink. 'Mel, this isn't fair!'

'Who says I play fair?'

She tested the knot at my wrists, then the one securing me to the pipe. I was sure I could twist around and get my teeth to the second one, but she realised and put a loop in the cord to leave me splay-legged with my bum stuck up in the air and completely incapable of getting at the rope.

'You should be able to move around enough to keep your circulation going properly,' she remarked. 'But I don't see you escaping in a hurry. Yes, not a bad job if I say so myself. See you later.'

'But, Mel ... Mel! It's ages until the party!'

'Tough.'

She was gone, leaving me helpless. I knew I couldn't get at the rope, but I tried anyway, only managing to leave myself hot and frustrated, while my wriggling had pulled the knots tighter still. There was a bubble of panic welling up inside me, and I wanted to cry, but shook my head, trying to concentrate on the way Mel took my control away so easily instead. It would have been OK, if she'd been there to do things to me, or if she'd been coming back fairly soon, but she wasn't. Before I could stop myself I'd begun to sob, and when I heard the door open I burst into tears of relief.

'Mel? Oh thank you, Mel ... Oh, Mr Hegedus.'

He was stood in the doorway of the bathroom, looking down on me with an all too familiar expression. 'Has baby been naughty?' he drooled. 'Has baby got a hot botty?'

'No I haven't!' I answered. 'Mel put me here, because … because she doesn't want me around this afternoon.'

'I know,' he said. 'She sent me up to check on you, but do you really mean she forgot to spank you? And such a naughty baby!'

He'd squatted down as he spoke, quickly checking my knots.

'Would you loosen them a bit?' I tired. 'Or at least undo the loop so I can move around a bit more.'

'Oh no, I do not think so!' he answered. 'Mrs Rathwell warned me you'd try your little tricks.'

'Please!?' I begged. 'I … I'll suck your cock, nicely.'

'And what it I just pop it your mouth anyway?'

'I'll bite.'

'Naughty baby!'

'Ow!'

He'd smacked me, not hard, but right under my cheeks, catching my pussy lips where they bulged out between my thighs with only the thin, see-through material of my froufrous to protect me.

'She really didn't spank you?' he went on, his tone of voice suggesting it was an impossibility that anybody could have me helpless without smacking my bottom.

'No. Please, Mr Hegedus. Mr Hegedus!'

He'd pulled my froufrous open, peering down the back to inspect my bum, then, apparently unsatisfied, pulled them right down to leave my bottom showing bare beneath the frills of my underskirts. 'Well, well, all smooth and pink,' he said, and he'd begun to stroke my bottom. 'Now that will not do at all, will it? Naughty babies should have hot botties, shouldn't they?'

'Mr Hegedus, please.'

I gave up. He'd begun to spank, squeezing his crotch

as he slapped at my bottom, left handed because it was the only way he could get at me.

'Just loosen my knots when you've finished,' I asked. 'Then you can do it, and you if put your cock in my mouth I promise not to bite.'

His response was to unzip himself and pull out the thick, dark penis I'd got so used to sucking. Again he began to spank, all the while tugging at his cock, before shuffling forward and presenting it to my mouth. I took it in, closing my eyes as I sucked him, with his hand still on my bum, stroking and squeezing and slapping, until I'd began to react despite myself. His cock was already swollen, and grew quickly in my mouth, while I knew I was getting juicy, but I was still determined to bargain and pulled back as soon as he was fully erect.

'That's nice, isn't it? Loosen my knots and I'll do it properly, the way you like it, and … and I'll suck on your balls. Please?'

'Mrs Rathwell said –'

'She needn't know! Come on, Mr Hegedus, please? Haven't I been a good girl for you? I always suck you nicely, don't I, and you get to spank me as often as you like, and I never tell.'

It was meant to be a veiled threat, and he seemed to take the hint.

'You promised me one thing, yes?'

'I … I don't remember, but OK, if I promised.'

'You did,' he assured me, and he'd stood up. He turned the tap on and I craned back, wondering what he was up to, to find him washing his hands.

'What are you doing?'

'You promised, remember?' he said. 'Baby promised me I could fuck her bottie.'

'Oh God! You filthy old perve! Fuck me, but not up

185

my bum, please!'

'You promised, yes?'

'No! Not like that, I … I … Oh God, OK. But get me ready properly.'

'Nice and slippery, yes?' he answered, and I realised what he was doing with the soap.

'Not soap! Soap stings! There's some lube in the cabinet if you really have to, but … Mr Hegedus!'

He'd stuck his soapy finger up my bum, popping my ring and pushing in as deep as he could go. My mouth had come open in a wordless gasp as he began to wiggle his finger about in my bumhole, and wider still as my anal flesh began to sting.

'Ow! Mr Hegedus, that stings so much!'

He merely chuckled, enjoying my bottom hole with my cheeks held apart so he could watch his finger going in and out. I took it panting and shaking my head, my anus on fire and my helpless fingers clutching on air in reaction, while I could feel my ring growing quickly slack. He put more soap up, rubbing the tip of the bar on my already open hole, then his fingers again, two this time.

'You are ready, yes?'

'Yes,' I admitted, my voice a weak sob.

He kept his fingers inside, but I could hear the fleshy slapping of his cock as he gave himself a quick toss to get properly hard again. I shut my eyes and put my face to the floor, lifting my bum in surrender, telling myself that I was tied and helpless, that he could do what he liked and so I might as well try to enjoy it. His fingers pulled out and I farted, giving me a sharp stab of humiliation and drawing a tut of disapproval from him even as he pressed the head of his cock to my bumhole.

The soap stung so badly it was making me crazy, and

as my ring spread to the pressure of his cock I was drumming my feet on the floor and wriggling in my bonds. I'd started to shake too, really badly, and I couldn't stop my sobbing either, or the little mewling noises that escaped my lips as my bumhole stretched out around his knob. He had my cheeks open again, spreading them with his thumbs, and I knew he was watching it go in, with my anus a straining pink ring on the thick brown shaft of his erection. I thought he'd stuff it right up, the way the Tradesman had. But no sooner had he got the head up, he began to pull at his shaft, his knuckles tickling between my cheeks as he wanked up my bottom.

'You dirty pig!' I sobbed. 'At least stick it in properly. Ah! Fucking Hell, you … you bastard! You … you …'

He'd done as I'd asked, but I hadn't been expecting the full length of his cock to be rammed up my slippery bumhole with one hard push, or for him to take off at a frantic pace, buggering me so hard and so fast I was left speechless, my mouth open and spittle dribbling down my chin, lost to everything but the furious pumping of his prick in my rectum. I might have come, with his balls squashing to my cunt with every thrust like that, but before I could fix my mind on the filthy way he was using my helpless body he stopped; panting for breath with his cock held in as deep as it would go. It felt as if I'd got a baseball bat up my bottom, thick and hard and heavy in my straining rectum, while my anus was a ring of fire and my cunt hot where soap fluid had trickled down into my hole.

'Carry on,' I panted. 'You... you nearly made me come. Carry on … and finish off up my bottom, please, Mr Hegedus!'

'No.'

'Please! I want to come … I want you to spunk in me.'

187

He began to move again, drawing a moan from my lips and at last it all began to come together, the helplessness of being tied with my hands behind my back, the humiliation of having my bottom molested and spanked, and fingered, and finally stuffed with cock. I began to beg for him to go faster, to reduce me to the same shivering, gasping mess as before, only for him to stop before he'd even got a decent pace up.

'Now in your mouth,' he grunted.

'What!? No, Mr Hegedus, I ...'

'That's what you promised, yes?'

He was right, but that had been when I was on the edge of orgasm.

'Not that!' I begged. 'Do it up my bum, or wank off on my cheeks, even in my face, but not –'

My voice broke off in a squeak as his cock pulled from my bumhole, which stayed open, stinging badly. I was dizzy with arousal, struggling to fight my own desires as he shuffled around to present his slimy, glistening erection to my mouth, but I couldn't stop myself. My mouth stayed open and in it went, filling my senses with the taste of soap and my own bottom; strong enough to make me gag, but that didn't stop me sucking, or swallowing, or revelling in my own degradation as I gobbled urgently on a cock pulled straight from my anus. He came in an instant, adding a mouthful of spunk to my woes. My own body went into orgasm, with no more that the faint tickling of my pulled-down froufrous to stimulate my cunt, but with my mind overwhelmed by the sheer, filthy ecstasy of what he'd made me do.

'That's my baby!' he sighed as he drained himself down my throat. 'Dirty baby.'

Spunk erupted from around my lips as my body rebelled against the abuse, unable to cope with the powerful contractions of my orgasm and having a cock stuck halfway down my throat at the same time. More came out of my nose and I was forced to pull back, my body still shuddering as I fought for breath, wracked with spasm after spasm, and I never even realised that my bowels had come open until it was too late.

It just came out, squeezing from my buggered anus in time to the unstoppable contractions of my muscles, to drop into my lowered froufrous in a thick, heavy coil. I could feel the weight of it growing as they bagged out behind, hanging under my still urgent cunt, a sensation at once so disgusting and so unutterably, deliciously dirty that I cried out in ecstasy once more before the appalling shame of what I'd done got the better of me.

That didn't stop it coming, my bumhole too well buggered to close properly, so that everything that was in me just came out, into my panties and on to the floor, to leave the swollen pouch hanging heavy below my pussy and a big pile on the tiles beneath me. All I could do was let it come, with my head hung in shame and his mess still dribbling from my nose and mouth, until at last he spoke.

'You dirty girl!'

'I couldn't help it!' I wailed. 'It just happened!'

He'd stood up, craning over my back to look at what I'd done, shaking his head.

'You dirty girl,' he repeated.

'I think you're going to have to untie me now,' I said, trying to make a joke of it, but failing to hide the pleading note in my voice.

'Perhaps.'

'Oh come on! You can't leave me like this!'

'Mrs Rathwell, she said ...'

'Yes, but she didn't know you were going to bugger me and make me poo myself, did she? All over her bathroom floor as well! She's not going to be best pleased, is she?'

He gave a thoughtful nod, frowning down at my dirty bottom and the pile underneath me for a long moment before speaking again.

'Most of it went in your knickers.'

'I know that!'

He pulled up his sleeve.

'What are you doing?' I demanded. 'Hey, no ... Mr Hegedus! No ...'

My words broke to an inarticulate grunt of shock and disgust as he dumped what I'd done on the floor down the back of my already bulging knickers, and pulled them up, snug around my bottom with the mess inside pressing between my cheeks. I couldn't even speak, my mouth agape in utter horror for what he'd done, and for the feel of the now huge load hanging in my panties; so heavy it had tugged them back down a little when he let go.

When he opened the door of the bathroom cupboard to find some new loo paper I even got to see, my rear view briefly reflected in the mirror: my bound wrists, the puff of my skirts, my bottom straining in my froufrous, all very girly and clean but rendered filthy and obscene by the big, round bulge in my panty crotch, so fat it had pushed the material out and was showing at the sides.

'I will tell her you soiled your knickers, yes?' he said, as he began to clean up the floor. 'Maybe then she will come to untie you.'

I had no words to answer him, my head hung in shame and the load in my panties wobbling gently to my sobs. My self-control was almost gone, panic welling up inside me as I imagined not just Mel coming upstairs, but Morris, maybe Annabelle and Harmony, Mr Morozov, Lucius Todmorden, a dozen other men and women, two dozen; all staring down at me as I squatted on the bathroom floor with a couple of pounds of shit bulging out the back of my panties.

He was going to leave, flushing the loo and making a last, critical inspection of the floor and my rear view before walking from the bathroom towards the suite door. I had to stop him, whatever it cost, if it meant letting him bugger me and then come in my mouth every day for the rest of the summer. 'Don't go! No, Mr Hegedus!'

As I spoke I lurched towards the closing door, giving way to my panic, the cord binding me to the waste pipe taut on my wrists, then suddenly slack. I went down, flat on my face, just as the door closed, crying out in pain and then again, in shock, as a sinkful of cold, soapy water burst from the broken pipe, all over the seat of my froufrous, my skirts, my legs. I jerked back, a really stupid thing to do, as I realised as my bum touched the floor with a thick squelch, to leave me sat in my own mess at the centre of a gradually expanding puddle.

'Bugger!'

Nobody answered me, which was just as well, because if I'd been in a sorry condition before, now it was worse. At least, it was more humiliating, if that was possible, but I was no longer securely tied. I'd played bondage games with Pippa and others often enough to know that I could get my bound wrists under my bum and feet, which would mean I could get my teeth to the knot on the cinch.

Chapter Twelve

IT SEEMED TO TAKE for ever to get free, and it left me, my uniform and the bathroom floor looking like an accident in a pigsty. After about the same time again, plus a large quantity of cleaning products, and everything was as it should be except for the broken pipe and the fact that I was stark naked. The pipe was easy, because I managed to fix it in such a way that the break didn't even show, although whoever used it next might be in for a bit of a surprise. I hoped it was Mel.

Being in the nude was a bit tougher, but not much. The guests weren't going to be even slightly surprised to see me running around with no clothes on, and the only real problem was escaping Mel's attention. If Mr Hegedus had told her about my accident she was obviously content to leave me as I was, which was an awful thing to do but useful in the circumstances. That meant I could run to Amber, tell her what Mel was up to and beg for her protection. She fancied me and was sure to help.

I left the room with my heart in my mouth, expecting Mel to appear at any moment. Nobody was about, but as I came down to the first floor I could make out voices and laughter, then the unmistakable meaty smack of a hand being applied to a girl's bottom. Somebody was being spanked, which probably meant they'd started the game. I moved cautiously on, wondering how best to reach

Amber in safety, my tummy fluttering at the smacks and squeals coming from the restaurant.

Morris and Mel would be by the door between reception and the restaurant, which meant I had to sneak out through the kitchen, praying that both Mrs Hegedus and Stefan had gone to watch the spanking. I made it, padding barefoot around the back of the chalets to my own, where the chance to put some clothes on was too good to resist. A pair of panties, my red summer dress and flip-flops were all I needed, which made me feel much less vulnerable for all that I knew I could be stripped as fast as I'd dressed.

That was going to happen anyway, but by Amber, not Mel, or so I thought until I reached the back door to the restaurant. I was too late. The tables had been arranged in a ring and Amber was standing at the centre of the room, looking beautiful and very dominant in full riding gear but staring about her in utter horror, with all fifty-five men and eleven women looking back. I realised at once that she was going to be passed around, and Mel was smirking openly, her full mouth curved up into a wicked smile, until she saw me.

'Two seconds,' she said and dashed over, grabbing me by the arm as she hissed into my ear. 'Don't say a word, Jemima, or the next time you mess yourself your face goes in it, and I mean that! How did you get out anyway? No, don't answer that. Just sit down, and when your turn comes to spank Amber you'd better do it properly, or else. OK?'

'You're hurting me!' I squeaked, but she only tightened her grip. 'OK. OK! There's no need to be such a bully.'

She let go, throwing me a final warning look before turning back to the room, now smiling as she spoke to

Amber.

'You can choose who goes first, of course.'

Amber responded with a dirty look, obviously close to panic but too proud to back down, with her lower lip caught under her front teeth as she glanced around the motley collection of sybarites, perverts, sex maniacs and dirty old men she had to choose between. I knew it would be a girl first, and I was fairly sure who.

'Penny, please,' she said at last.

Penny responded with a sympathetic smile and patted her lap. Amber went to her, and I could see the shaking of her fingers as she laid herself into position across her friend's knee with her full bottom bulging out the back of her jodhpurs, so tight I could see the outline of her knickers beneath. Penny tried to be gentle, starting off with a few playful pats to the seat of Amber's jodhpurs, only for Mel to interrupt.

'Do it properly, Penny, harder, and get her bare, because if you don't somebody else will.'

'The rules do say bare bottom,' Harmony added.

Penny hesitated, her hand lifted in mid smack, then gave a little shrug.

'Sorry, Amber,' she said and her thumbs had gone into her friend's waistband.

I could see Amber's flesh trembling as she was stripped, her smart jodhpurs pushed down, knickers and all, to leave her full, pale bottom bare to the room, with just a hint of honey-coloured pussy hair showing between her thighs. Mel's face had set in an evil smirk as Penny began to spank once more, harder now, to make Amber's bottom quiver and show off teasing glimpses of the tight brown star between her cheeks.

Amber tried to control herself, but as the pink flush spread slowly across her bottom you could tell it was getting to her. First she'd began to toss her head a little, then to kick one foot up and down, while her breathing was getting deeper and a little ragged. Penny stopped as soon as she reasonably could, but as Amber stood up I could see that her face was flushed, the skin of her face cheeks much the same colour as those of her bottom.

'Who's next?' Mel demanded. 'How about me?'

Amber shook her head and quickly covered herself. The glance she turned around the room showed that she was a step closer to panic. I could understand why, when it was going to take an hour to get her properly spanked, and I knew full well the state that would leave her in.

'We're going to have to choose for you,' Mel warned.

'Annabelle,' Amber said suddenly.

'My slave?' Mel echoed, her voice rich with sadistic contempt. 'You want to be spanked by my slave? How very appropriate! Go on then, Annabelle, smack her fat arse for her.'

'Yes, Mistress,' Annabelle responded.

Amber stood limp in the centre of the room until Annabelle had seated herself in the spanking chair, her naked body and the collar around her neck incongruous as she patted her lap.

'Over my knee, please, Miss Amber.'

For the second time Amber got into spanking position, and for the second time her jodhpurs and the big white panties beneath were pulled down to bare her bottom to the room. Annabelle spanked hard and well, setting Amber's legs kicking and bringing a rosy glow to her bottom. But she was very methodical about it, spanking for spanking's sake without any of the little humiliations the men would have used, or Mel for that matter. Morris was grinning as he watched, and after a while clapped his hands together in satisfaction.

'I can see this is going to take a while,' he said, 'so let's get on with the game. Who's next?'

'Jemima,' Mel said without hesitation. 'She hasn't had a go yet.'

'How true,' Morris answered. 'Jemima, who would you like to pick for you?'

'Amber?' I suggested, hoping to provide her at least a moment's relief.

'She's busy.'

'Penny then.'

Penny gave me a sympathetic glance as she walked up to Morris's table, where the hat stood at the exact centre. Like Amber, I couldn't but help glance around the room as she pushed her hand in among the pieces of paper, knowing that in a few seconds one of the men or women was going to have me across their knee, and that I had little say in the matter.

'Mr Judd,' Penny announced.

My heart sank. I'd been hoping for a girl, or at least one of the Razorback boys, not the balding, middle-aged Judd. I still managed a curtsey, and as I started towards him Mel spoke up.

'Hang on, let Amber choose hers and we can do them face to face.'

Amber had already stood up, holding her jodhpurs and panties halfway up. Her bottom was quite red and she looked a little dizzy as she once more inspection the eager faces around her.

'Pick one for me, Penny,' she said.

Penny dipped her hand into the hat.

'Senor Juan Márquez y Lucientes.'

The Tradesman stood up, beaming. Amber gave him a look of utter despair and hung her head. Judd had already pulled a chair forward, next to the spanking chair, so that as Amber and I laid ourselves across our men's laps we were face to face. I could see the look in her eyes as the tradesman began to fondle her bottom; deep humiliation undercut by a helpless acceptance of what was going to happen to her. I tried a smile, but she'd shut her eyes as her jodhpurs and panties were peeled off her bottom once again.

'There's not much point in pulling them up, really, is there, Amber?' Mel remarked, causing a ripple of laughter.

'Oh yes there is!' Mr Judd responded. 'Because if the girls don't pull their knickers up, then the boys can't take them down again. Isn't that right, poppet?'

'Yes,' I sighed.

He'd began to stroke my bottom through the seat of my dress even though it was so short my knickers showed anyway.

'Yes,' he went on, 'but what happens first? Come on, poppet, what happens to naughty little girls before their knickers come down.'

'Their skirts come up,' I told him, knowing full well what he wanted to hear.

'That's right,' he went on. 'Skirts up and knickers down, that's the drill.'

He'd suited action to word, raising my summer dress onto my back as he spoke, but he paused with my knickers halfway down.

'And what do we say?' he demanded.

'Um ...,' I began, no longer sure what he was on about.

'We say "thank you", don't we?' he chided. 'We say "thank you" to the nice man who's taken the time and trouble to discipline us, don't we?'

'Thank you,' I answered.

'Properly,' he demanded. 'Come on, poppet, you can do better than that!'

I shook my head, choking with humiliation for what he was making me do.

'Thank you, Mr Judd,' I managed, and then I'd broken. 'Thank you for giving me a spanking. Thank you for taking my knickers down and for giving me a spanking, sir.'

'That's better!' he said happily, and my knickers had been peeled off my bottom, leaving me showing it all behind and ready for my punishment.

Amber was already getting hers, sobbing and biting her lip as the Tradesman applied his hand to her bottom. I could see the helpless pleasure rising in her face, but she was still fighting. Not me, I was already lost, all the feelings I'd had building up in me since Melody had first hauled me upstairs rushing back as Mr Judd set to work. He was every bit as rude with me as I'd expected, pausing every few smacks to grope my bum, first weighing my cheeks in his hand as if I was a piece of prime steak, then holding them wide to inspect my bumhole and show me off to the entire room, lastly cupping a hand under my pussy to rub me as he went back to spanking with the other.

I thought he was going to make me come, and I couldn't help myself, sticking up my bottom to his hand and wriggling my hips to encourage him. It was just so rude, to be spanked by a dirty old man in front of a huge audience, and to show how utterly incapable I was of resisting him would have been perfection. I thought he'd like it too, getting his kicks out of bringing me off across his lap, but he was a bigger bastard than I'd guessed. When my muscles had begun to contract and I was gasping in ecstasy, trying to kiss Amber and begging him to spank me harder, he stopped.

'I do declare you are enjoying it!' he said. 'Now that won't do at all, will it?'

'Carry on,' I sighed. 'Make me come!'

'Uh, uh!' he chuckled. 'Oh no you don't. Into the corner with you, young lady, and keep those hands on your head and off that sloppy little cunt of yours.'

He'd helped me to my feet as he spoke, leaving me with no option to do as I was told, going to the corner to stand with my bare red bum on display and my hands on my head. That didn't stop me watching the spanking though, or fantasising about what I was going to get; although whatever they did to me it couldn't be as bad as what Amber was already suffering. The Tradesman had finished with her and had simply passed her on to the next man, not even bothering to ask her opinion. She was too far gone to resist, meekly draping herself across his lap and sticking her bottom up for his attention.

I was surprised she'd given in so easily, but I remembered what Mel had said about her needing an excuse to show her submissive side. It seemed to be true, but there was no mistaking the misery and shame in her face as she was dealt with, despite her obvious excitement. She was crying too, for all that her pussy was juicing nicely, making me want to rescue her, to bury my face between her beautiful big cheeks and lick her better, and to spank her myself.

Not that I was likely to get my turn for a quite a while. They really set to work on her punishment, every one of them determined to get his fill of her lovely bum and to show off to the rest. Before long she'd been made to take off her boots and jodhpurs, but they left her with her panties in order to add to her humiliation. They were pulled up and down, knotted around her ankles, taken right off, stuck in her mouth, put back on again, pulled up tight between her cheeks, pulled down again, and finally stuck up her pussy by Monty Hartle, and all the while with her bottom being spanked and spanked and spanked.

Her tits had been out for quite a while before Monty got to her, but he was the one who took her bra and blouse off, to leave her nude with just a wisp of damp white cotton showing between her thighs where she'd been stuffed. By then she barely seemed to know what she was doing, unsteady on her feet. And after Fat Jeff had spanked her and put a finger up her bum, she was crawling on all fours from man to man with her cunt on display, the hole stuffed with her wadded panties.

The game continued, girl after girl obliged to go over the knee; Penny and Annabelle and Harmony and the others, bottoms bared and smacked, one by one until at last it was my turn again. Mel chose for me and I got Lucius, who made me straddle his lap with my bum to the room so that my pussy was spread over the bulge of his cock while he spanked me. I'd have happily let him fuck me, in front of all of them, and I was left wanting more, far more. But most of all, I wanted to be the centre of attention.

Amber was maybe two-thirds of the way through her punishment, rolled up on a table in nappy changing position, which has to be the most humiliating way to spank a girl there is – nothing hidden at all, and ideal for any man who wants to slip a cock in once she's done. I didn't know the man who was spanking her, and I don't think she did, but her mouth was open in ecstasy and she was masturbating as he slapped at her cheeks. Mel was watching, her face alight with cruel pleasure, and paying no attention at all to the table with the hat on it. Nor was Morris, busy roasting Penny's bottom on the far side of the room, and the opportunity was too good to resist.

Nobody even noticed what I was doing, much less tried to stop me. I reached the hat just as Amber came, gasping and sobbing her way through an orgasm with tears streaming down her face, even as she rubbed her cunt and wriggled in pleasure for the smacks being applied to her bottom. Everybody was watching, even Morris, who looked well pleased and was fingering Penny's bumhole in a casual fashion as he watched Amber disgrace herself. It even took them a moment to realise what was going on when I spoke up. 'Hey, look. All these pieces of paper say Amber. Melody cheated!'

I had to repeat myself, a lot louder, before they really began to take notice. Heads began to turn, one by one, including Morris's. His finger was still up Penny's bottom, but his expression changed from amusement to annoyance. The last person to notice was the man spanking Amber, so that for a few seconds the only sound in the room was the slap of his hand on her cheeks and her soft, panting responses. When he stopped there was absolute silence. Every other pair of eyes in the room fixed on me; my own met the full glare of Melody's fury.

'You cheated, Mel,' I insisted. 'You ought to be passed around, not Amber.'

'Oh, you think so do you?' she answered, indifferent to the justice of my accusation.

'Yes,' I managed, digging myself in deeper. 'You should, and not just for spanking either. A good caning from Amber would do you the world of good. Then ... then you can suck Mr Enos off in front of everybody.'

'Good idea,' Mr Enos agreed, but he was the only one who spoke up.

Melody was shaking her head slowly from side to side

as she began to walk forward, and from the look in her eyes I knew that unless the others held her back physically, I was for it; maybe even for what she'd threatened earlier. I panicked and ran, out of the door and across reception, followed by her bellow of rage and Fat Jeff's gleeful, high-pitched yell.

'Game on, boys!'

I went through the door at full speed, sprinting across the car park and up the hill, but without the slightest idea of where I was going, because the truth was that I didn't want to escape. My panic was already giving way to that weird mixture of fear and excitement that drives my need. I wanted to be caught and to get what was coming to me, from the Razorback boys, from Morris and Mel, and from Karay. Maybe I didn't have my mask and tail on, but the hunt was for real and I knew there'd be no mercy. I didn't expect any, but if they wanted me they were going to have to catch me first.

When I finally risked a glance behind me it was to find my pursuers spilling out from the hotel. A few were coming for me, a hundred yards or more down the slope, but most had stopped to get their gear, and were clustered around the Razorback Jeep or Morris's car. I ran on, heedless of the rules, taking the bank where I ought to have stopped, before bursting out onto the open downs with my legs burning and my lungs feeling as if they were about to burst. Another hundred yards and I turned again, to find Annabelle coming over the bank, stark naked. The others were still someway behind.

For a moment I thought they might have put her out for extra sport, but she was coming right at me and she looked determined. I made for the clumps of thorn and bramble inland of the cliff, dodging among them in the hope she'd loose sight of me and wishing my dress wasn't quite such a brilliant scarlet. Twice I thought I'd lost her, and twice she got a sight of me, calling out to the others that I was headed up the valley. I was cursing her as I ran, and she was gaining too, just yards behind me as I reached the fence that divided the public land from the fields.

It was barbed wire, four strands high, but the fence posts were thick and strong. I vaulted, clean and easy until my dress snagged, tearing wide and spilling me into the lush grass. A squelch and a sudden earthy reek told me that wasn't all I'd gone in, adding a dress covered in cowpat to my worries, but I didn't dare stop. Annabelle was right behind me but lost her nerve at the fence. I was laughing as I sprinted away across the field, only to stop dead in my tracks as I realised why she'd backed off, and it wasn't because she was in the nude, or scared of catching herself on the barbed wire.

The mess I'd gone in wasn't a cowpat, not exactly a cowpat, at least to judge what was swinging between the hind legs of the huge, reddish brown animal in front of me; not an udder, but a truly gigantic pair of testicles. Even as I realised it was a bull I heard Annabelle's voice from behind me.

'Come on, big boy, how about some nice fresh grass?'

She was holding it out in one hand as she called to the bull, which had noticed, his huge head turning slowly to look at us out of great brown eyes. I ran, not towards Annabelle, but down the field, praying that bulls really were colour blind and that the stories about them going for red weren't true. Behind me I could hear her laughter, then the bellow of the bull and she'd changed her tune, urging me to run. I didn't need telling and I was suddenly certain that bulls could not only see red, but that it drove them wild as well. My dress was off in seconds, leaving me in nothing but shoes and panties as I fled on, making the gate at the bottom of the field and hurling myself across it before I dared look back.

The bull was with Annabelle, munching contentedly on the grass she was feeding it, while my dress lay halfway between us, a limp, dirty rag showing red against the green of the grass. I yelled out to tell her she was a mad bitch, at which she gave the bull a pat on his head and disappeared among the bushes. She would be coming for me, I was sure, either that or she'd gone back to tell the others where I was. If I moved towards the cliffs they'd get me. I was in a country lane in nothing but my shoes and big white panties, but not big enough to conceal the fact that I'd recently been spanked.

I was still panting for breath as I tried to work out what they'd do, but it wasn't obvious. Morris was an old hand at hunting girls, and the Razorback boys spent their free time playing war games. They'd break the rules, now that I had, and they were better dressed for a chase as well as not having to bother about being seen. Not that I really care who sees me topless; that and my speed were my only advantages. So I made for the main road, cautious, but intending to wait until there were no cars visible, before sprinting to where I could get back into the other side of the hotel grounds.

Nobody saw me, leaving me smiling for the thrill of my streak as I once more returned to safe ground. It was only a couple of hundred yards to the hotel, and I could have come in the back and rejoined those who'd stayed inside, so that when the frustrated hunters finally returned they'd find me happily bent over the knee of one of their less adventurous fellows. The only problem was Melody, who'd then have free rein to do with me as she pleased, whereas if the Razorback boys caught me she'd have to

204

wait her turn. Not that I'd escape either way, but at least I'd get fucked first, which would make her treatment easier to take.

I decided to keep running and turned up the hill past my chalet. From a safe spot among the trees I could see the opposite hillside, with the tiny figures of the hunters spread out in a long line, presumably hoping to flush me out from among the bushes. I couldn't help but laugh, and decided to be really cheeky by nipping into my chalet to change into jeans and a long-sleeved top, pushing open the door to have my wrist taken in an iron grip.

'Hello, Jemima,' Mr Morozov chuckled. 'You are ready for Karay, I hope?'

As he caught me, he'd twisted a cord around my wrist and in seconds he'd got both tied behind my back, taking advantage of my surprise as much as his greater strength. I didn't even manage to answer his question, or say anything beyond a squeak of surprise until he'd got me tied off and pushed me into a sitting position on the bed.

'Are you ready for Karay?' he repeated.

I nodded weakly, wondering if he was going to tie me into a crawling position again so I could be fucked from behind, or so he could try some different perversion; perhaps with his cock fed up my bum as I lay helpless on my back.

'Good,' he said. 'So then, I must call the others, just as they promised to call me should you be caught up on the down. I knew you would come here though, and so I must surely deserve you first?'

He'd unzipped as he spoke, to flop his cock and balls out of his trousers. Two steps forward and he was in front of me, his legs braced either side of my knees as he pushed himself at my face. 'Suck it, Jemima.'

I didn't need telling. I let my mouth open and fill with

thick, heavy cock, then began sucking eagerly. He began to toss into my mouth, squeezing his balls and tugging on his shaft, already swelling. I closed my eyes, enjoying the sensation of being tied and helpless while I sucked my captor's penis – my fear and excitement soaring for what was coming to me over the next hour or more.

He was hard in no time, and as merciless as ever, fucking my throat to make me gag and wiping his slimy cock in my face, pinching my tits and pulling my hair, squeezing my jaw and slapping my face until I was hot and dizzy with sensation. When he came he was very deliberate about it, pinching my cheeks to force me to hold my mouth open, then spunking on to my tongue, in my face and hair next, before finally ramming his cock as deep as it would go down my gullet to finish off in my throat. I was left gasping, with a mixture of spunk and snot hanging from my nose and chin, my face and mouth badly soiled. He pulled off my panties to clean his cock and left me lying on the bed as he phoned Morris, assuring him that I'd be ready and waiting in the area behind the chalets.

'Up,' he demanded, and lifted me to my feet. 'Now stand still.'

I waited, not daring to run and knowing I'd be caught in seconds even if I tried, as he took a heavy duty dog lead and collar from the bag he'd concealed behind my bed. The collar was studded brown leather, old and smelling faintly of dog; making my nose wrinkle as I was put into it and led from my chalet. All I could do was follow him as we walked around to the area of grass where I was to meet my fate, and obey orders as he got me ready.

First I was made to kneel with my ankles well apart as he tied each off and fixed a bar between them to force me

206

to keep them wide and my cunt available. Taking two big metal pegs from his bag, he drove one into the ground to either side of my feet and fixed my ankles to them. My hands were untied, then retied with me in a crawling position and with two more pegs hammered in to leave me completely helpless, in the nude, tied up and staked out for the use of my captors. Lastly he brought the chair out from my chalet, poured himself a glass of brandy, lit a cigar and sat back to watch in comfort as the rest of the hunt arrived.

They wasted no time. Gavin was first to arrive and had his cock out of his trousers and in my mouth before he'd even got his breath back. One of his friends got down behind me, rubbing his soft cock in the slit of my bottom and joking with Gavin for the state I was in and how much fun they were going to have with me. Others were clustering around, mainly the Razorback boys, but also Annabelle and Harmony, while I could hear shouts from the main body of the hotel as Mr Hegedus called for the last few people to come and join in.

Before Gavin was even hard, I was surrounded by a ring of eager men and women too; Lucius with his cock in Penny's hand as she got him ready to enter me, Stefan feigning disgust but squeezing his crotch, Vince the workman gloating openly. I could hear still more: Monty and Jeff complaining that they couldn't see, Mr Enos asking wheezily if somebody would mind fetching him a chair and his Viagra tablets, Kay saying she hoped I'd be OK and almost in the same breath asking to borrow Amber's strap-on dildo.

The man who'd been rutting between my bum cheeks stuck it in the moment he was hard; holding me by my hips, he pumped away to make my body rock to the same rhythm, rowed back and forth on his cock and Gavin's.

Somebody got down and began to grope my tits and rub his cock in my armpit, with Harmony on the other side, fiddling with my pussy and my spare tit. Her touch was more than I could take, bringing me to my first orgasm before either of the men inside me had come.

Neither was far behind: Gavin filled my mouth with sticky, salty come before whipping his cock free to show off by doing it in my hair. Then his friend imitated the gesture by pulling free to spunk all over my upturned bottom. Two others replaced them, the man who'd been fucking my armpit and Mr Judd, both rocking me back and forth on their cocks. Somewhere in the background I was vaguely aware of the Tradesman complaining that my virginity had been ruined, but nobody was taking any notice of him, me least of all.

I'd got what I wanted, caught and used by everybody. But now that I was staked out with a cock in both ends, I wasn't sure if I could take it. Not that it mattered what I thought, because none of the men and not many of the girls even bothered to check that I was OK before taking their turn. They just got stuck in, even the shyest of them determined to get his share, man after man entering me mouth or cunt. Harmony was the first woman to take me, holding me by my hair as she forced my face to her sex, and Monty the first to bugger me, using the spunk dribbling from my pussy to lube me up without a second thought and ramming himself home until I could feel his balls.

By the time he'd finished with me I was gaping; my bumhole as easy to fuck as my cunt. And when one of the Razorback boys slid in underneath me so I could mount his cock, I got another up my bum at the same time, with a third in my mouth. I couldn't even see by then; my eyes were closed beneath the sticky coating from all the men who thought it was fun to come in my face, so a beard of spunk and saliva was soon hanging from my chin. I'd drunk so much my belly was swollen, and if I ended up pregnant there were going to be twenty or more men who might be father, while after the third man had spunked up my bum it was starting to come back out in little squirts. Melody must have fucked me at some point too, but I could no longer tell the difference between dildo and cock; my cunt was too hot and slimy, and my senses were reeling from what seemed to be an endless supply of shafts pumping into my body. I'm lost count of how many times I'd come as well, from people fiddling with me, men and women both, from balls slapping my pussy lips as they used me, and from Annabelle, when Melody made her lick me out from behind and swallow what she got in her mouth.

She rubbed off while she did it, and she was the last, or so I thought, only to catch a rustle of movement and a ripple of voices as they made space around me. I knew Karay was going to fuck me, because none of them had that much respect for each other. The flash of a camera through my spunk sodden eyelids and I was doubly certain. I couldn't stop it happening, and I didn't want to, but that did nothing to calm my sobbing or to stop my aching limbs starting to twitch as I waited for it to happen.

I felt him touch me, and an instant later I'd been mounted, his long, bulbous cock rammed home in my slippery cunt, his weight on my back, his hair tickling me between my bum cheeks. The others began to clap and cheer, watching me humped with ever rising enthusiasm, egging Karay to fuck me harder and faster still, and breaking into catcalls and delighted laughter as I came. I just couldn't help it, the orgasm rising up to break in my head for the sheer joy of my fucking, for what was being done to me, and for all the people watching – an audience who'd just used me themselves and were enjoying the sight of my supreme degradation.

My vision went red as my climax tore through me, and with my cunt in violent contraction on his cock, Karay came too, filling me with so much spunk that it exploded out of my straining hole. There were wild cheers and a second peak for me, more powerful than the first at the exact same moment that he stuffed everything he had up me with one furious shove. I screamed, my climax bursting inside me in mingled agony and ecstasy, my vision red again, then black.

Chapter Thirteen

I CAME TO FACE down in a puddle of mud and spunk after Harmony threw a bucket of water over us, which was one of only a few clear memories when I awoke the next morning. The first thing I saw was the dark bob of Penny's hair nestled on the pillow beside me, which brought back vague memories of being over her knee and then head-to-tail in bed. I snuggled up to her, still more than half asleep, so that it only dawned on me very gradually that I wasn't in my chalet.

With that it all started to come back; being staked out and used, with Karay mounting me last of all while everybody cheered him on and took photos; me passing out and coming around again still full of cock; Mel ordering the boys to turn me over and stake me out on my back for her to fill my mouth; Amber telling her it wasn't going to happen. They'd argued, but in the end Mel had backed down. We'd left, Amber and Kay and Penny and I, driving north with me nursing a half bottle of brandy in the back.

I could barely remember the drive at all, or arriving at Amber's although I now realised I was there, but I could remember what had happened. We'd been sitting around her kitchen table, laughing and swapping stories and teasing each other, with the inevitable result that Kay had ended up over Amber's knee. She'd been passed on to

Penny, and to me, before demanding her revenge. We'd gone upstairs, to Amber's bedroom, after which everything dissolved into a blur of smacked bottoms and breasts and pussies and orgasm after orgasm; first the four of us, then Penny and I. My body was sore and stiff, not surprisingly when I'd been used so thoroughly. There'd been sixty-nine of them after all, a few of them twice, and that didn't include playing with the girls later, yet I couldn't help but smile as I lay staring up at the ceiling.

It was already late in the day, but it had been nearly dawn when I finally got to sleep so that was no surprise. I wasn't the first to wake up either, because I could hear Amber and Kay downstairs, their voices mixed with the occasional clatter of crockery, but it was only when the smell of frying bacon began to waft up the stairs that I manage to drag myself out of bed. Penny followed shortly after and the four of us breakfasted together as we talked of this and that, but mostly of how I should learn to assert myself with dommes, specifically Melody and Danielle.

Penny and I left at teatime, driving back to her house in Berkshire, where we spent the night together again, but this more for comfort than for sex. In the morning we took the train into town together and I was introduced to my new job. It was very different, far more interesting than being a maid, with lots to see and lots to learn both in the department and the small museum where all the biological specimens were kept. There were no students about, but there was plenty to do with only a few weeks left until the start of the new term.

I knew that what I was doing was very much a taste of what was to come. It would be a different university and I'd be reading a different subject, but it was still far closer than what I was used to. In no time at all I was missing the constant sexual attention and the feeling that I was the focus of so much desire, even the way men and women used me as their plaything. At the university I was treated with friendly respect, which was nice in a way, but I quickly came to understand why Penny took such delight in her punishments. To me spankings had become a way of life, administered daily, but to her they were a treat, or really rather more, because she didn't just like to be spanked, she needed to be spanked. By the end of the week I was already beginning to feel the same way.

Not that I was doing without, because I got it every bedtime, but it wasn't the same. The constant threat of ending up with my hot bare bum stuck in the air, whether I liked it or not, was gone; and although I had an appointment with the Tradesman coming up on the Sunday as well, I knew that wouldn't be the same. He liked to spank, but it wasn't his favourite thing. The same was true of Mr Morozov, and even Lucius saw it as a prelude to getting his cock inside me. What I'd always thought I needed was discipline: firm, authoritarian discipline from somebody older than me who understood how I felt across their knee. And that was what I was getting, but for my full satisfaction I also needed a touch of something else, something compounded of fear, resentment and real shame, as I explained to Penny on the Friday night after dinner.

'Like when Mr Hegedus used to do it, or his awful wife. I mean, I love being over the knee for you, and knowing that my Auntie's giving me a spanking. But it's too ... too loving, I suppose.'

'You've really got the bug, haven't you?' she laughed. 'Oh well, once a spanked girl, always a spanked girl, but we're all different in subtle ways. Who would you like to get your spankings from then?'

'I don't know,' I told her. 'It would have to be a

woman, I think, for it to really feel like discipline. Pippa's quite stern about it, more than you are, and I suppose a big sister's almost as good as an aunt, but there's something missing.'

'Melody? Amber?'

'They're both good,' she admitted, 'in slightly different ways. Mel's harsher, and she does scare me, but Amber's more … motherly?'

'Mel likes to suckle me,' I told her, but I knew that wasn't what she meant.

She didn't answer, sipping the wine she was drinking and looking thoughtful, only to suddenly speak up. 'Don't take this the wrong way, but maybe you should accept Danielle's right to do it?' she suggested.

I shook my head. 'I couldn't, not after the way she betrayed my trust, and anyway, I'd feel bad about Mum.'

Again she didn't answer, frowning as if trying to reach a tough decision, and again when she did speak it was very sudden. 'That's who you really need to spank you, isn't it, Kate?'

All of a sudden I could barely breathe or speak for the lump in my throat and the gathering tears in my eyes, but I wasn't going to admit what I feared to be the truth. 'You're as bad as Morris!' I managed, trying to make a joke of it. 'Worse, if anything, because he only wanted me and Danielle to pretend!'

'I wasn't suggesting she do it in front of a bunch of dirty old men,' she laughed. 'But seriously, maybe that is what you need? I sometimes wonder if I do.'

She'd spoken very quietly and I didn't answer. We sat in silence for a long moment, each lost in her thoughts for the guilty secret we shared. She was blushing and kept fidgeting with the stem of her wine glass, while I was struggling to hold back my tears. At last she smiled.

'Well, nobody can deny we deserve it, can they? Come on, Jem, over Auntie's knee.'

I didn't hesitate for a second, crossing to where she was sitting on the sofa and draping myself across her lap with my bottom slightly raised to let her get at the button of the jean-shorts I'd put on when we got home. Most of my bum was sticking out of them anyway, but I knew that wasn't going to stop her taking them down, or the panties beneath. Sure enough, her arm came around me, to open my button and zip before my shorts were eased gently down off my bum. She spent a moment stroking my bottom and I stuck it up a little more to get the pale blue cotton taut across my cheeks.

'Beautiful,' she sighed, 'and so spankable. Now then, panties down.'

She took hold of them by the waistband, my eyes closing in bliss as my bottom was unveiled and those thrilling words running through my head over and over again – *panties down*. Now they were, with my bottom bare to her gaze, lifted just enough to show off the rear of my pussy lips and the little, tight pucker of my bumhole between my cheeks, ready for spanking.

'That's right,' she said. 'Stick that little bottom up, show me everything. Not that it matters what I see, but you have to be bare bottom to remind you of your place, don't you? That and the smacks have to sting properly.'

As she spoke she'd begun to spank me, using just the tips of her fingers to make my skin sting and tingle. It felt lovely, as it always did from her. But for all her words there was none of the resentment and helplessness that I needed. I was still going to enjoy it, and I would still come, but it wouldn't be perfect.

'Imagine I'm Kate,' she said softly. 'We're in your bedroom and you're going to be spanked for being naughty, maybe for wearing such cheeky shorts in the street?'

My answer was a sigh and to lift my bottom a little more. Now she was starting to get to me. The smacks grew harder and she took me around my waist, holding me firmly in place as she applied her hand to my bottom, never pausing to soothe my reddening cheeks, nor to touch me up; making it impossible to resist the fantasy she was trying to provoke. I'd done it before anyway, with the Tradesman, thinking of lying spanked across Mum's knee with Pippa giggling at me for my plight.

'Yes, that's right,' Penny went on. 'Spanked for going out in shorts that leave half your bum sticking out. What a disgrace, Jemima!'

I moaned and pushed my bottom up a little more, thoroughly ashamed of myself but unable to tear my thoughts away from that awful scene.

'Pippa ... Pippa's watching,' I managed. 'And she's laughing at me. She thinks it's funny ... she thinks it's funny that I'm getting a spanking ...'

'It is,' Penny took over, 'for her. What could be funnier than to watch her little sister spanked over Mum's knee, with her little round bottom all bare and her legs kicking up and down, with her bottom hole showing to all the world and her cunt too ... your cunt Jemima, showing between your thighs while your mother spanks your naughty bottom and your big sister laughs at you.'

I couldn't hold myself back any longer. The picture was just too vivid in my mind, of my own rude rear view over Mum's lap, my bottom cheeks all red from spanking with my bumhole showing between, and my thighs pumping in my pulled-down knickers and frayed shorts with the lips of my pussy peeping out between, swollen and moist in the middle. I cried out in shame as my hips went up and my hand went back, raising my bottom to Penny's hand as I found my sex. She began to spank harder, full across the cheeky swell of my bum, bringing my pleasure up with astonishing speed as I rubbed furiously at my clit.

'Oh you little disgrace!' she laughed. 'Rubbing your cunt when you're over my knee. Would you do the same, Jemima? Would you do it in front of your sister and your mother, playing with your dirty cunt because you'd had to have your bottom smacked? What an utter disgrace!'

She'd gone too far, but her words had got into my head and I couldn't stop myself. As I started to work myself towards orgasm I was thinking how it would have been, not over Mum's lap, but afterwards, if I'd rubbed myself off in the bathroom the way I had after Danielle dealt with me. Maybe I'd even have done it in front of Pippa, with her giggling crazily because I'd been turned on by a spanking from Mum. It was unbearably shameful, so shameful it was going to make me come while I was spanked, but as my climax built in my head Penny spoke again. 'Kate would understand, Jemima. She knows what girls like you and I are like.'

'No!' I sobbed, but it was too late.

I'd started to come, and as my orgasm rose the picture in my head had changed. Pippa was still there, but watching solemnly as Mum held me in her arms, comforting me by stroking my hair and whispering in my ear with my bare red bottom showing behind and my fingers between my legs, fiddling with my wet and greedy cunt.

'You bitch, Penny!' I screamed and I was there, bucking up and down on her lap in an uncontrollable orgasm as she spanked with all the force of her arm and my fantasy took on one last, awful detail: of Mum lifting one breast from her blouse to let me suckle as I masturbated.

Afterwards Penny told me everything, a story going back years which left me astonished and removed any lingering trace of that ubiquitous adolescent assumption that your own generation is the first to really discover sex. She'd known she'd wanted to be spanked for a very long time indeed, but the first time she'd got it was from Grandma, when she'd been a bridesmaid at Mum's first wedding. Kate had done her too, in the greenhouse behind Grandma's house with her knickers full of rotten peaches, peaches from the same tree I'd feasted from a hundred times when I was little. She'd played with Aunt Susan too, although that didn't completely surprise me, and I knew about Pippa, but the biggest shock was to learn that Grandma still spanked her.

They'd had an understanding for years, ever since Penny had admitted she needed it in response to Grandma commenting that she'd often been tempted to dish it out even before the first time. Now it happened once a week, usually before Sunday lunch if they were alone, with Penny put across Grandma's knee for a hand spanking or a dose of the hairbrush, sometimes sent upstairs to masturbate, sometimes allowed to do it the way I had, while still over the knee. Sometimes it had even happened when the rest of the family had been coming to lunch, which meant that I'd been sitting at the big dining room table, completely in awe of my highly-respectable, academic aunt while all the time she'd had a hot bottom in her knickers courtesy of my even more awe-inspiring Grandma.

I've never been exactly shy about my feelings, but what she had told me helped me let go in a way I never had before. Knowing that so many people I'd always felt would disapprove were no different to me was wonderfully liberating. If anything they were worse, because I'd been introduced to the joys of spanking by Pippa and Penny, but it was in their blood. When we'd gone to bed and head to tail, as we did most nights, I came over a fantasy as delicious as it was kinky, in which I was initiated by being passed around for spanking between Mum and Pippa, Penny and Aunt Susan, losing a little bit more clothing with each time and finishing up in the nude to have my bottom roasted by Grandma.

The next morning I felt strong in a way I never had before. I was keen to talk more, and not just to Penny but to the others. She wasn't keen, pointing out that not everybody knew all the things which had happened and that Kate had always done her best to shield Pippa and I. I let it go, but promised myself that at the very least I would speak to Pippa, who would be back from Australia for a while until the start of her term, and as she didn't want to be in the same house as Danielle, was going to stay with Grandma.

Having been so open with me, Penny had to completely swallow her objections to my gentlemen visiting, and on the Sunday I entertained the Tradesman before going over to Grandma's to join Penny for lunch. He was full of sympathy for my supposedly broken virginity, despite having taken his turn with the rest when they had me staked out. After making me a very generous present indeed to assuage the guilt he felt, he fucked and buggered me, but even with my body shaking to the thrusts of his cock up my bumhole I was imagining what I knew to be going on in the house across the road, where Penny would be lying bare across Grandma's knee for her weekly spanking.

When he'd gone and I went over to join them, it took all my willpower not to say something. I was even a bit jealous, because she'd got a hot bottom and I hadn't; she looked pleased with herself and I was feeling frustrated. She dealt with me later, once we'd got home, and it was a blessed relief once my knickers were down with my bottom warming to the slaps, which seemed the most natural and satisfying thing in the world.

She was right. I'd got the bug, and with a vengeance. All through the following week I could think of nothing but my next spanking, to the point when I came up to Penny's room at the university and suggested she lock the door and put me over her knee then and there. She told me to be patient, pointing out not only that the huge windows looked directly across to the language centre, but that old Dr Hobbs next door was likely to have a heart attack if he realised what was going on. I had to wait, which made it all the better when I got it that evening.

By the end of the week one other thing had managed to intrude itself into my mind: the need to go home and get my stuff. It wasn't that I really needed it, but I wanted to make a gesture of moving out in order to make it very clear to Danielle that she had no influence over me. There were several reasons that I didn't want her to be there when I visited, not least that I might end up over her knee again, or worse: getting myself turned on by my punishment. So I rang Dad and after a few careful questions managed to discover that they were going down to Poole at the weekend for a day on a neighbour's yacht.

I drove over in Penny's car, a little naughty when I was still on a provisional licence, but the only practical way for me to get there. The house looked just the same as it had always done, putting a lump in my throat as I parked; because for all that I'd only been gone a couple of months, it felt like a lifetime. It seemed oddly silent though, which the rustle of a fresh breeze in the trees only seemed to make more intense. Inside it seemed quieter still, and I found myself going on tiptoes for no real reason. Dad's car wasn't there, which meant they'd definitely left, but I still found myself checking the living room and kitchen before going upstairs.

Danielle had tidied my room up, not just picking up the way Mum always did, but packing everything away as if it was going in storage. Logically that made perfect sense when I was moving out and would shortly be going up to uni, but, as it was, just the knowledge that she'd been through my things left me burning with resentment. I'd been thinking about what she'd done to me at the hotel anyway, and soothing myself by dreaming up complicated and impractical ways of getting my revenge, which took on new colour as I began to work out what she'd put where. One sack was labelled "charity". When I pulled it open I found all the old toys I'd never been able to part with; my old dolls and bears, even the big red elephant Mum had bought for me when I was born.

'You bitch,' I mouthed. 'You wait.'

I took the bag down to the car and was coming back when it occurred to me that she might have done the same with Pippa's things. Her room was in the same state as mine, but as I came in I caught a movement from the window. Looking out, I found that I wasn't alone after all. Summer was in the garden, on the old swing Dad had bought for Pippa and me, rocking gently back and forth with her long skinny legs kicked out to either side and her golden hair turned to a cloud by her motion and the breeze. In front of her was the old teak table liked to have beside him when he sat out in the garden, and on it was a camera.

It was perfectly obvious what she was doing, because I'd done it myself many times, although never on the swing, which would have felt wrong. She was taking rude pictures of herself, with her knickers showing up the tiny yellow and green miniskirt which was just about all she had on, aside from bright green flip-flops and a yellow crop-top. I knew what she'd be doing with the pictures she took as well, posting them on the net, maybe to show off to a boyfriend. But if she was anything like me just for the joy of being naughty.

I watched, intrigued but also with some very wicked thoughts building up in the back of my mind. She was obviously having trouble with the self timer on the camera, because when she went to check the picture she wasn't satisfied and reset it before going back to the swing. I could guess what she was up to, trying to get a shot that looked accidental, which meant she had to be swinging rather than just posing on the swing. That way she could pretend that it was just chance that she was showing her knickers, assuming she had any on and wasn't being really rude.

She did: little white ones pulled up so tight they gave her a camel toe cunt. I saw when she deliberately cocked her legs as wide as they would go as she swung forward. This time she seemed pleased with the result, but that didn't stop her trying again, only this time with her crop-top adjusted so that one nipple was half showing, as if by accident. I couldn't let it be, and as I hurried downstairs I was telling myself it was just because I wanted to play with her and not to find a way to get revenge on her horrible mother.

I came around the back and watched for a moment, hoping she'd go further so that I could catch her in the act. If it had been me I'd soon have had my top up, and probably my knickers off too, but she seemed happy with just flashing her panties and a little bit of tit, so I soon lost patience, waiting until she was making a very obvious show of her knickers before walking out around the corner of the house.

'Hi, Summer!'

She fell off the swing. That wasn't quite how I'd been imagining the opening to our encounter, but it meant I could get to the camera before she did. The last picture she'd taken was a beauty, with her leant right back as the swing came forward, her hair streaming behind her, looking as if butter wouldn't melt in her mouth, and with her legs wide open and the front of her panties on full show up her skirt, so clear and so tight that I could pick out the twin bulges of her sex lips even in miniature.

'You bad girl!' I laughed.

Her face was crimson as she snatched for the camera, but I darted behind the table.

'You've been taking self shots for the net, haven't you?' I teased.

'No!' she squeaked, and made another grab for the camera.

I danced away, laughing, and she gave chase. Halfway across the lawn I pretended to stumble and she caught hold of my T-shirt. We went down together, tumbling on the grass.

'Give me the camera, Jemima!'

She'd got hold of it, stretched out next to me. I let go of the camera and swung a leg over her, mounting up on her thighs before she could recovering and bracing myself to keep her pinned down. Her skirt had come up a bit, showing a small slice of creamy smooth, pink bum cheek and the edge of her knickers. I simply couldn't resist. One flick and her skirt was right up, her beautiful bottom on show, two firm little cheeks wiggling in her panties as she struggled to get free. I wanted to pull her knickers down and deal with her properly, a full on bare-bottom spanking the way I like it myself, but I knew it would be too much too soon.

'Naughty, naughty, Summer!' I laughed, and smacked her across the seat of her panties. 'You need spanking, you do!'

'Jemima!' she squeaked, but there was a giggle in her voice and I knew I had her.

I gave her another smack, not hard at all, knowing I had to keep it playful, and find an excuse to sit on her other than wanting to get her out of her knickers.

'Who are the pictures for?' I demanded. 'Come on, tell me!'

'Just for me!' she said, an obvious lie.

'Yeah, right!' I answered her. 'Come on, tell me, or I'm going to spank you some more.'

I began to smack her bottom, playing pattacake on her firm little cheeks as she wriggled underneath me, but she wasn't trying very hard.

'Jemima!' she protested.

'Tell me, Summer,' I demanded.

'No! It's … it's private!'

'Some boy then, or are they going on the net because you like to show off to all the dirty old men who surf for porn. I bet that's it, isn't it?'

'Jemima! OK. OK, they're for my boyfriend. He … he asked.'

'I don't believe you.' I did, though, because I'd met him briefly and he was just the sort of dirty little sod who'd want photos of his girlfriend flashing her panties on a swing, but I couldn't admit it or I'd have to get off her.

'It's true!' she squealed.

'Yeah, right! Come on, admit it. You're going to put them up on a picture site, aren't you?'

'Jemima!'

'Admit it, Summer, or I'll pull down your panties.'

'Jemima!'

I was still spanking, quite a bit harder now and her cheeks had begun to go pink where the flesh stuck out around the edge of her panties, but she was still playing at being helpless.

'Come on,' I urged. 'Or do you want your panties pulled down?'

I was sure she did, sort of, despite her protests, because I'd played the same game with Pippa a thousand times. 'I think you do!' I laughed. 'I think you want your panties pulled down, don't you Summer? Hey, everybody, Summer likes her panties pulled down for a smacked bottom!'

There was nobody to hear, but to judge by the squeal she let out in response you'd have thought she had an audience to put one of Morris's parties to shame. She stayed where she was though and I stopped spanking to take a firm grip on her waistband.

'Come on, Summer, admit it, or down they come.'

'Jemima!'

I decided to be firm with her, knowing from my own experience that it's often OK once your knickers are off.

'Stop saying "Jemima", you sound like a parrot. OK then, if you're not going to admit it, down ... they ... come.' I spoke the last three words slowly, and as I did so I began to pull, peeling the tiny white panties slowly down over her bottom. She went wild, squealing and thumping her fists on the grass, but it was all fake. I was only sitting on her thighs, and she wasn't that much smaller than me. She'd still be scared and uncertain, I was sure, but her bottom was bare and I'd won.

'Now I'm going to spank you anyway,' I told her, 'just for fun.'

'Jemima ...' Her voice had trailed off this time, and her tone had changed; it was doubtful, pleading, but far from being angry.

'Hush, it'll be nice, I promise.'

'But, Jemima.'

'Hush.'

I pulled her panties down properly and took a good grip on her skirt, just to make sure she stayed in place. She had a lovely bottom, all the better for being naked, her cheeks little firm eggs of girlflesh, so neat her bumhole showed between them, even when she was face-down, with just a hint of pussy peeping out below. It was a joy to spank her too, from the way her cheeks wobbled to the little cries and sobs she gave with every smack, and even though she was still wriggling I could feel her melting into it as her flesh warmed up.

With every smack my need for her grew, and I could easily have buried my face between her cheeks, or just stuck my hand down my knickers and come over the sight of her now rosy bottom so sweetly framed between panties and skirt. I didn't know if she was ready though, and forced myself to hold back, now peppering her little pink bottom with gentle smacks and hoping I'd bring the heat to her cunt and that she liked girls. Even if she didn't, I had to have a photo, and the camera was lying just by her head. I grabbed it, but she realised I was going to take a photo of her smacked bum and gave a sudden lurch.

'No, Jemima, don't ...' she gasped, but I'd gone over, off balance but with the camera in my hand.

She struggled up, tripped over her panties and went down again, into a crawling position, just as I got my finger to the button. The picture was perfect, with her on all fours, her skirt still up and her panties in a tangle around her knees, one tit showing where her crop-top had come up, and her bottom a small red moon right in the middle of the picture with both the tight star of her bumhole and her neat little pussy on plain show.

I was laughing as I rolled away, with her after me, crawling along the ground and grabbing at the camera. She looked so funny that I couldn't stop laughing, and I pushed the button again but only got a picture of half her face, and a lot of sky as she came down on top of me. I grappled her, trying to get on top so that I could carry on with her spanking, but the feel of her body in my arms and the scent of her hair and the heat of her pussy where her legs were cocked open across my hip was all too much. Her face was next to mine and I kissed her. And kissed her again, pressing my mouth to hers as she tried to pull away briefly before giving in.

Our mouths came open together and all the feelings I'd been bottling up since the moment I met her came flooding out. She met my kisses and even helped me as I quickly pulled her out of her crop top and skirt. Then she was suddenly eager: her thighs opened as my fingers burrowed between them. I held her close, masturbating her as we kissed, too turned on to stop, but determined to give her so much pleasure she'd never look back once I was done.

She came in seconds, arching her back and squirming her cunt onto my hand as I rubbed, her kisses now more passionate than my own. I clung on, praying she wouldn't get a sudden fit of guilt once she'd finished even as the shivers of her climax ran through her. She didn't, her cuddles growing gradually bolder as I soothed her, and when I pulled my own top up her mouth went straight to my breasts. I let her suckle, holding her tight and stroking her hair, until at last she pulled away, her mouth open and her eyes wide, her face framed in a halo of golden hair as she looked down at me.

'Do you want me to ...' Her question was left unfinished, but it was obvious what she was offering. I giggled as I tugged down my jeans and knickers, stripped eagerly and helped her off with her panties, before we rolled back together, now both stark naked. Our inhibitions were gone, our mouths and fingers touching everywhere as we explored each other, breasts and bottoms and pussies. She put a finger in me, began to rub at my clit with her thumb and I gave in to the pleasure, lying back with a sigh. She was giggling as she began to masturbate me and turned a little to let me see her bottom, the cheeks pink with spanking, her pussy swollen and wet.

'My bum feels all warm!' she giggled.

I reached out to touch, stroking her hot skin and making her giggle again.

'You can do it a bit more, if you like?' she offered.

'Come a bit closer then.'

She obliged and I began to spank her once more, only now with her fingers working on my pussy to bring me gradually higher. For once I wasn't going to need a fantasy, because I had one then and there: Summer's beautiful naked body with her lovely little bottom red with spanking while she brought me off; the girl who'd sat on her and pulled her knickers down; the girl who'd spanked her bare bottom and made her masturbate me, now kneeling with her bum stuck out and every rude detail on show for me to come over.

I grabbed her, hauling her bodily onto me, to bury my face between her thighs. She squeaked in surprise, but didn't try to stop me, her fingers till busy with my open sex as I began to lick her. I couldn't stop myself, lapping at her clit and trying to get my tongue up inside her hole, past the tight arc of her hymen, kissing her hot cheeks as I babbled apologies for being rough with her. She giggled, still rubbing, and I lost control completely, sticking my tongue in up her tiny pink bumhole as far as it would go as my body went tight in orgasm.

My hands were on her hips, my face held tight to her naked bottom as I licked her anus, my head full of conflicting emotions as my body jerked in orgasm; I revelled in sheer joy over her body, delighted in the heat of her cheeks from the spanking. And experienced a sense of contrition for doing exactly that, which made having my tongue up her bumhole perfectly appropriate. Only when I ran out of breath did I collapse back on the grass.

'You licked my bottom!' she gasped, her voice full of shock, but also delight.

She was still sitting over my face, her bottom cheeks open to show off the tiny pink star between. I pulled up my head just long enough to plant a kiss full on the little wet ring and as I lay back once more she burst into giggles, then said, 'You, Jemima. You're the one who needs spanking!'

I got it later that same afternoon, over her knee in the living room in-between her own sessions from me. She was like a wild thing, eager to explore everything she knew about and to learn what she didn't, including lots and lots of spanking. Three times I made her bend over, and the third time I used a hairbrush on her, leaving her bruised and feeling a little sorry for herself until I kissed her better, on both cheeks and on the hole between. She loved having her bottom licked, something she'd never done before, and made me do it after my punishment, reaching what must have been her fifth orgasm of the afternoon while sat on my face with my tongue up her bumhole and her fingers busy with her cunt. I felt it was only fair that she returned the favour, which led to a lot of pouting before she did me, as I was bent over the very same chair her mother had spanked me across, with her tongue flicking at my pussy and bumhole while I brought myself to orgasm under my fingers.

By then I was beginning to worry that Dad and Danielle would come back, to catch us running around the house naked and red-bottomed. There would have been hell to pay, so I finally persuaded her to get dressed and to help me carry my things down to the car along with a few of Pippa's. It was only then that she really opened up to me, saying how sorry she was about the situation with our parents and almost begging me not to hold it against her. I told her not to be silly, considering what we'd just done, and promised she could come and see me whenever she wanted; with the strong implication that we'd both end up with hot bottoms and well-licked pussies.

The hug she gave me before I left was tight and long, and it was her who pushed me to open my mouth to her kiss. As I drove away I was singing, exalted by what we'd done together, and also because Danielle would have been utterly furious to know that I'd not only spanked her precious little Summer, but included some very dirty lesbian sex into the bargain. Not that I had any intention of revealing our secret, satisfying though it would have been. It was hardly sensible, or fair on Summer.

Penny was in an almost equally good mood, having just had her weekly dose of domestic discipline from grandma Elaine, and I couldn't resist telling her. She was a little doubtful about the way I'd made Summer take it, but she couldn't help but enjoy the details, or get aroused, with the inevitable consequence that we spent the rest of the day in bed together. It was gone midnight before I got to sleep, sore but happy.

The week went painfully slowly. Summer and I had been swapping texts and trying to work out how to meet with her mother getting suspicious, while Pippa was coming back on the Friday night. I'd also had a call from Mr Morozov, asking for an appointment, which meant more money and some extremely kinky sex too. It was impossible to concentrate on work, knowing all the things that might happen that weekend, and I made a complete mess of the seed boxes I was supposed to make for Botany practicals, which meant I had to stay late on the Friday.

When Penny came to pick me up she told me that Morris had called, but had been evasive when she asked him what he wanted to talk to me about. That almost certainly meant he was back on his mother and daughter spanking kick, as I couldn't think of anything else he wouldn't have been able to tell Penny, who'd been going to his parties off and on for years. He'd also said he might call in, but no matter how much money he offered or how persuasive he was, I was determined not to end up back across Danielle's knee.

Pippa's plane was due in very late, but I wouldn't have missed meeting her at the airport for anything. I hadn't seen her in months, and an awful lot had happened since we last met, while for all the support I'd been getting from Penny and others she was the only person who would share my feelings completely. When the passengers from her plane finally started to come into

231

arrivals I was close to tears, and she came straight to me, dropping her hand luggage to hug me and kiss me before greeting Penny. She had changed a lot in so short a time: her skin was darker and her arms and legs were cut with long, hard muscles, while she'd had her hair cut back to a fuzz of tight, dark curls and was dressed as if she'd just come in from the outback.

We were talking constantly as we drove back, about all sorts of things, but it was the following morning before we had the serious conversation, over toast and marmalade at the breakfast table. Pippa's attitude was the same as Penny's, that our parents had been growing apart, that we were grown up and so should try to accept their choices. I could see the sense in what she was saying, but found it hard to take in and moved on to vent my feelings about Danielle as quickly as possible. Pippa was horrified, not only by the way she'd treated me, but with Morris and Mr Hegedus too, I did, however, explain about the money and how much I'd enjoyed the spankings.

'But that's not the point is it?' she was saying. 'No, I take that back. It is the whole point. They're taking advantage of your sexuality, Jemima.'

'Yes, but it's what I need, and besides, a few more appointments with my gentlemen and I'll have enough saved up to pay my way through uni.'

'You do have a trust fund, Jemima.'

'Yeah, which is worth about half what it was last year.'

'It's still enough. Look, why not just admit it, you get off on being paid for sex. That's OK, I'm not judging you, but Morris is way over the top, and as for this Danielle!'

'I did try to tell her,' Penny sighed. 'And to be fair she did come away from the hotel before anything disastrous happened. Anyway, I have to go in to make sure the seed trays are correctly labelled this time, so I'll see you two at lunchtime.'

'I ought to do that,' I volunteered.

'You stay here,' she insisted. 'Keep Pippa company.'

She left, but the sound of her car had barely faded before building again, to end with a crunch of tyres outside the front door. I got up, thinking she'd forgotten something, only to open the door not to Penny, but to Danielle. Her face was set in cold fury and she was dragging Summer by the arm. 'I want to know what you did, and I want to know now!' she demanded, pushing inside.

'What are you –' I began, and stopped as she threw a printed out photo onto the hall table.

It was the picture I'd taken when she'd tripped over her panties, showing her crawling across the lawn with everything she had on full show, including her very obviously well spanked bottom. I looked up at her, but she wouldn't meet my eyes, turning a hang-dog expression to the floor instead.

'Did you think I don't monitor her computer?' Danielle demanded. 'Well, I do, and now I want to know what the fuck you thought you were doing!?'

'We had sex, big deal,' I mumbled.

She lashed out, catching me a stinging slap across the face. I went back, clutching my cheek, and she had grabbed my wrist before I could react further, pulling me towards the straight backed chair next to the telephone table. It was obvious she meant to spank me, in front of Summer, and with nothing on but my pyjama bottoms and a bathrobe it wasn't going to take a lot to get my bottom bare either. I fought back, kicking and scratching as she dragged me close. But she'd already got my wrist in the small of my back and I was going down, over the knee, bum in the air, my robe flipped up and my pyjamas jerked down to leave me bare-bottomed as I let out a wail of despair, cut through by Pippa's voice.

'What are you doing!?'

'Oh it's you is it?' Danielle snapped. 'Well, you'd better stay out of this, because I'm just in the mood for this and I can spank two little brats as easily as one.'

'You're not spanking anybody,' Pippa answered and waded in.

I suppose all sisters fight now and then, and I suppose the little one nearly always loses. Pippa had always beaten me anyway, and I'd always been in awe of her strength, or maybe it was the way she'd toughened up in Australia, or the hard biker girls she goes around with. I was still amazed by the way she handled Danielle. She just grabbed her under the arms and lifted her bodily off the seat, tumbling me onto the floor, and before I'd managed to get my pyjamas up it was all over, with Danielle in some sort of arm lock, spitting threats and struggling furiously but obviously helpless. I was shaking with reaction for what had been about to happen to me, my eyes full of hot tears and my mind burning hotter still, for vengeance.

'Spank her, Pippa!' I shouted. 'Go on, spank her!'

Pippa hesitated, but only for an instant.

'Get another chair,' she told me. 'We'll do this together.'

Danielle let out a scream of fury and consternation that must have been heard in Reading, and if I'd thought she'd been fighting before, it was nothing to her kicking, screeching fury as she realised she was about to get a dose of her own medicine. I ran for a chair, picking the twin to the one in the hall and quickly setting them facing each other.

'Down you go!' Pippa hissed, seating herself and

taking the frantic Danielle with her, across our interlocked knees as I too sat down. 'I'll hold her. Jem, you get her stripped.'

'Don't you fucking dare!' Danielle yelled.

'And what are you going to do about it, exactly?' Pippa answered, and tightened her grip.

Danielle gave a grunt of pain, but she hadn't given up, her body jerking in Pippa's grip and her legs thrashing up and down in her efforts to kick us. I hooked one of my own around the back of her knee and as Pippa followed suit we shared a grin. Danielle was helpless, her bottom pushed out beneath the short blue summer dress she had on, round and tempting, far too tempting to hurry over. Summer had seen everything, standing speechless by the door, her mouth and eyes had come wide in horror as I looked up to her.

'I'm sorry, Summer, but she deserves this. She did it to me, and she wanted to do it in front of you. In fact, you were going to, weren't you, Danielle, you vicious bitch?'

'Fuck off!' Danielle screamed. 'Don't you dare touch me, Jemima, or –'

'Or what?' I broke in. 'Or you'll get your own back when Pippa's not around. Fine, do me. I like it, and even if I didn't I'd gladly take the cane just for this moment.'

I lifted her dress, very slowly, to expose the smooth flesh of her thighs, the muscles twitching; her desperate attempts to kick her way free; then the seat of an extremely fancy pair of lacy black panties, the seat pretty well see-through to show off the crease of her bottom.

'Very pretty,' Pippa remarked. 'I bet Dad loves these.'

Danielle let out a hiss of fury like an angry swan. I giggled as I began to stroke her bottom, just the way she'd done to mine when I was the helpless one. She was shapely, her cheeks bulging in the see-through panty seat, but quite soft, although definitely spankable.

'Very spankable,' I said, echoing my thoughts. 'Feel her, Pippa, she's got a lovely bum.'

'I think I'd better hold on,' Pippa replied, as Danielle gave another furious hiss and a violent lurch. 'You have fun.'

'I intend to,' I told her. 'Watch me, Summer. Watch me spank Mummy's naughty bottom! Yes, that's right Danielle, I'm going to spank you in front of Summer!'

She gave a violent lurch, but we had her helpless and I was laughing as I continued to feel her up, squeezing her cheeks through her panties as I carried on. 'I'm going to enjoy this so much, Danielle. Really, really enjoy this. And you do have a lovely bottom, you know, ripe and cheeky. Just right for spanking, and that is what you're going to get, Danielle. A good old-fashioned spanking. Just the sort you like to dish out. Only now it's you on the receiving end, isn't it. In front of your precious daughter. And of course it's got to be bare-bottom, hasn't it, Danielle? Because you know how it feels for a girl to be made to go bare-bottom, don't you, Danielle?'

She gave another lurch, so hard she nearly knocked me over, but Pippa tightened her grip until Danielle cried out in pain.

'It's silly to struggle,' I told her, enjoying every word as I took hold of the waistband of her panties. 'Because it's going to happen, so you might at least try to take it like a lady, and not the grubby, gold-digging little tart you are!'

'You wait, you little bitch!'

'Bitch, is it? Well, we all know that's a spanking offence, don't we? We'd better get you dealt with then. Right, on three your panties come down. Watch me, Summer, watch me take your Mummy's panties down.

One, two, three …'

Danielle let out another piercing shriek as I levered the fancy black knickers down over her bum, nice and slowly, to unveil her to her daughter and to Pippa and I; her lovely bottom now bulging naked behind her, with her smooth, pale cheeks just open enough to hint at a wisp of fur between, and the darkness of her anus, while the way we had her legs locked meant she was giving a good show of cunt from behind too.

'Such a pretty bottom!' I laughed, and gave her a pat, just hard enough to make her cheeks quiver. 'And such a pretty cunt. Don't you think Mummy has a pretty cunt, Summer?'

Summer didn't answer, but she looked as if she was about to wet herself and Danielle had begun to sob, provoking a sudden pang of guilt which I got rid of by laying in. It was so good to spank her, to watch that lovely round bottom bouncing to the smacks of my hand, to feel the softness and warmth of her flesh, to catch glimpses of the pitted brown star of her anus in its nest of fur. To see her sweetly turned cunt too, and to know her own daughter could see every rude detail. But best of all, I knew who it was over my knee: Danielle, who'd spanked me on my panties in my own front room; Danielle who'd pretended to be my mother while she punished me and masturbated me at her breast in front of a load of dirty old men; Danielle who'd been going to do me bare bottom in front of her daughter and was now getting the same treatment herself.

My anger was rising as I spanked her, and her bum was getting very red. But if her sobs had become more urgent and broken, then there was no denying the state of her sex. She was wet, sopping, the juice running so freely from her swollen cunt that as I turned my attention to the tuck of her cheeks it began to splash out over my hand and her thighs. I knew what was going to happen, or I hoped I did, because she'd stopped fighting and there was a note of panic in her voice as she began to beg me to stop. 'Please, Jemima, no! Not this. No!'

I began to laugh, indifferent to the sound of hysterics in my own voice as I began to spank harder still, aiming every smack at her sweet spot. There was juice splashing all over her bottom and into her panties, onto my hand and over the floor. Her pussy had started to squeeze as she gave a last, despairing cry and stuck her hips up to the smacks, showing off her winking bumhole and the open, ready hole of her cunt. She'd come, and we'd all seen, including Summer, and Morris Rathwell, who was standing in the open doorway.

'Have I arrived in the middle of a party?' he asked.

'No,' I told him. 'We're spanking her because she was going to spank me, and to get her back.'

'Fair enough, I suppose,' he remarked casually. 'Hello, Pippa, did you enjoy Australia? And you must be Danielle's daughter?'

He was addressing Summer, who still looked stunned. Danielle had been making odd little bubbling gasps and not paying much attention to anything, but finally reacted, twisting around with her face set not in the fury I'd expected, but panic. Pippa let go and Danielle jumped to her feet, speaking hurriedly as she struggled to get her panties back up over her bottom. 'We have to go, Summer, come on.'

She grabbed Summer's hand, pulling her from the house almost as brusquely as she'd come in. Summer went, throwing me a last astonished look over her shoulder before she'd been bundled into the car. Morris spoke as the engine started. 'Something tells me Danielle would rather I didn't get to know her toothsome little daughter. But she should know that I never approach a girl unless I know she's willing. Then again, perhaps that's the trouble?'

'It is,' I assured him. 'So what's up?'

I spoke cautiously, expecting him to come up with some impossibly perverted scheme, and given the casual way he was taking what we'd just done to Danielle I wouldn't have been surprised if it involved a combination of my entire family, the livestock of a small farm and several hundred foreign businessmen.

'You left some photos behind in your chalet,' he said, and tossed them down on the table.

It was the one thing I had not told Pippa, although I had meant to, and her mouth came open in an O of shock. 'Jemima!'

'Two of my gentlemen,' I explained hastily, gathering up the pictures.

'You're terrible!'

'It was rather nice, actually,' I said, trying to sound cool but betrayed by my blushes. 'He's the one who's coming round later.'

'You're a disgrace, Jem,' she said, but she was laughing. 'And I want to see those.'

I handed them over, blushing crimson, but strangely proud of myself because just for once I'd done something she hadn't.

'He's not coming round, as it happens,' Morris put in. 'Things have changed a little since you left the hotel.'

'Oh?'

'Yes,' he went on. 'Suffice to say that Danielle came to a party at my Hampstead place last night and ah ... reached an accommodation with Mr Morozov. She'll be living at his London flat, which is just as well considering silly Harmony accidentally sent the party invitation to Danielle's old work email. She'll have to be spanked.'

'Hang on,' I said, trying to clear the image of Harmony bottom up over his lap from my head and focus on what he was saying. 'Do you mean Dad caught her out and she's gone off with Mr Morozov?'

'Exactly. You, apparently, were too willing. He likes real shame, it seems.'

'Danielle, with Karay?' I demanded.

Morris shrugged. 'So it seems. They went upstairs. But yes, it seems safe to assume he had her.'

'Karay?' Pippa queried, holding out one of the most embarrassing of the pictures, with me in obvious ecstasy as I got my bottom humped.

'Yes,' I confirmed and turned back to Morris. 'And Dad?'

'Well, he's not best pleased, let's put it that way.'

I began to cry, calling Morris an evil, scheming bastard even as I took him in my arms and kissed him. His hands went straight to my bottom, but I let him grope, both cheeks, then one of them as Pippa cuddled into us and was given the same treatment. When we finally pulled apart he was beaming with satisfaction. A new and disturbing thought struck me.

'What about Summer?' I asked.

'She'll be living with her father, I believe. And now, as I've driven all the way from London to deliver your filthy pictures, how about a spot of lunch?'

I knew that wasn't all he was after, but it seemed only fair. He'd obviously set the whole thing up, and while he undoubtedly had his own interests at heart they coincided with mine, and with Pippa's. He was going to want us to say thank you too, which meant going nude in the pool with a sister and sister double blowjob to follow.

We were still splashing about when Penny came back, but once we'd explained the situation it wasn't difficult to persuade her to strip off and join us, or to go over Morris's knee for a quick spanking while Pippa and I posed for him with our wet bottoms stuck out for inspection. The three of us sucked him off together as he lay back on one of the sun loungers with a drink in one hand and a cigar in the other, taking turns with his cock in our mouths while the others licked at his balls or snogged to give him something extra to get off on. He came in my face, and all over his shirt, in Pippa's hair too, so the three of us went inside to clean up.

Penny stayed outside, towelling herself off before lying down on the sun lounger. She'd put her panties back on, but soon had them pulled aside, masturbating shamelessly in the warm sunlight. We'd been about to start getting lunch together, but stopped to watch, calling Morris to the window so that he could enjoy the view. Her eyes were closed in bliss, her thighs spread to show off her open cunt, her head no doubt full of dirty thoughts; of spanking and sucking cock and snogging with her nieces, so she never saw the slim, steel-haired woman who came into the garden, not until far too late. A single, sharp word reached us through the window.

'Penelope!'

Pippa and I began to retreat from the window, dragging Morris with us.

'Who's the old dragon?' he demanded.

'Great Aunt Geraldine!' I told him.

'Her mum,' Pippa added.

Epilogue

IT WASN'T THE FIRST time Mum had caught me in an embarrassing situation. There was the time she'd walked in on me while I was being spanked by Marjorie Burgess, and the incident with AJ on Paddington station, which had been even worse. Yet in both cases I'd had very little say in what was happening, so had been able to at least try to explain myself without admitting what I was into. Now it was different. Not only had I been masturbating, but I'd been whispering "spank me, spank me" as I thought of how it had felt to be done across Morris's knee with Pippa and Jemima watching.

I couldn't speak for embarrassment, my face burning with blushes as she looked down on me in shock, disapproval, disappointment; expressions I remembered so well from every time I'd failed to meet her standards. Her tone of voice when she spoke was equally familiar, showing that same touch of patient exasperation I could remember right back to the nursery, but what she said was far from familiar. 'I really rather think I'll have to, spank you, that is. Get up.'

She sat down on the other sun lounger, her face stern but unemotional as she patted her lap.

'Come across my knee, Penelope.'

I couldn't stop myself, but my heart was hammering in my chest and my face must have been crimson as I got down across her knee with my bottom lifted, in the same humiliating position I'd adopted a thousand times for a hundred people, but never like this, never across my own mother's lap with my cheeks bulging out my big white panties behind and not a stitch on besides, my little tits dangling down by her leg. My tears had come even before I was properly in position; big, oily drops rolling down my face to splash on the concrete beneath me; tears of shame and sorrow and self-pity, but also of relief. A vast, all embracing sense of relief for what was about to be done to me: smacked by my own mother.

She took down my knickers. That is so easy to say, but it meant so much, to have my bottom laid bare, without comment or fuss; my panties just pulled down for the sake of convenience. And after all, why should a daughter have any modesty in front of her mother? I needed it though, and maybe she knew, because instead of just turning them down to get me exposed and vulnerable, she took them right off, to leave me baby-bare naked across her lap; trying to be a big girl about it but crying softly as I waited for her to begin.

'I should have done this a very long time ago,' she said, and her hand had settled on my bottom.

'Yes,' I answered, the only word I'd spoken, and my spanking had begun.

She wasn't clever about it, let alone rude. There were none of the little tricks I was used to, and she didn't say a word. She just spanked me, and if my bottom was lifted and my anus and cunt on show to her, then that was as it should be, my rear view completely exposed as I was given what I deserved, and needed: a firm, purposeful spanking from a stern but tender mother to her naughty daughter.

I didn't know why she'd done it; whether she'd been

talking to Aunt Elaine, if she wanted to punish me for masturbating in the garden, or if she just felt it was about time I got it for a lifetime of being a dirty-minded, stuck-up little know-all. Maybe it was all three, but it didn't matter anyway. It was her right: to take down my panties and spank my bottom, whenever she liked and wherever she liked, because I was very sure that although it was the first time, it wouldn't be the last.

When she finally stopped I was hot behind, but not really in pain, and while I knew my bum would be very red there wouldn't be bruising. That was just right, not hurting me, but putting me very firmly in my place, at thirty-eight years old, exactly where I ought to be, lying nude and spanked across my mother's knee. I didn't want to get up either, but lay there, still crying, with my red bottom lifted for the world to see exactly what had been done to me, everything forgotten, until Morris Rathwell's voice brought me sharply back down to Earth.

'Mrs Birch, I believe? Er ... I wonder if I might interest Penny and yourself in a little proposition?'

Also from Xcite Books

Ultimate Spanking

Twenty tales of over-the-knee fun

Explore the sensual pleasures of spanking in tantalising detail in this brand new collection.

Featuring a diverse range of cheek-warming, eye-watering, and always arousing, scenarios, disciplinarians and brats reveal the thrills of shame and retribution. Be it over the knee, the desk, the chair, or on the bare, the desire to punish and be punished doesn't let up for a moment.

Serena discovers her date, Oliver, is a master of kink who wastes no time in introducing her to the joys of bending over and obeying ...

Outspoken, headstrong Tamara calls in a favour from a special uncle to aid and abet a shameful surrender that requires a humiliating correction by the firmest hand ...

Kat pays a painful price when she becomes the client of a specialist service provider ...

After hours in the office, when Scarlett sees a red hand print on Blake Cooper's bare behind, an erotic war of wills begins between two professional rivals ...

£7.99 ISBN 9781907016127

The Education of Victoria
A novel by Angela Meadows

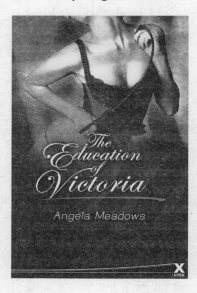

Lessons in love and a whole lot more are in store in this saucy romp set in a European finishing school for young ladies.

Packed off to a continental finishing school, 16-year-old Victoria thinks she will be taught how to be a dutiful wife for a gentleman. But she soon discovers that she has a lot to learn in the arts of pleasure at the Venus School for Young Ladies.

There she encounters the strictness of Principal Madame Thackeray and her team of tutors. Under their guidance she learns the finer arts of sexual pleasure and discovers that there are plenty of fellow students and staff willing to share carnal knowledge with this sweet young English rose.

On returning to England, she finds her father in financial difficulty and must turn her newfound education to good use to survive.

£7.99 ISBN 9781906373696

Sex in the City Range

Four fabulous city collections
edited by Maxim Jakubowski

Sex in the City – London
ISBN 9781907106226 £7.99

Sex in the City – New York
ISBN 9781907106240 £7.99

Sex in the City – Paris
ISBN 9781907106257 £7.99

Sex in the City – Dublin
ISBN 9781907106233 £7.99

Xcite Dating – turning fiction into reality!

Xcite Books offer fabulous fantasy-filled fiction. Our unique dating service helps you find that special person who'll turn your fantasies into reality!

You can register for FREE and search the site completely anonymously right away – and it's completely safe, secure and confidential.

Interested in spanking?

Spanking is our most popular theme so we have set up a unique spanking site where you can meet new friends and partners who share your interest.